I0668267

DRAMA CITY

by

Colie LevarLong

Published by

Midnight Express Books
POBox 69
Berryville, AR 72616

DRAMA CITY

by

Colie Levar Long

DRAMA CITY

Copyright 2013© by Colie Levar Long

ISBN 9780989874809

All rights reserved. No part of this book may be reproduced or transmitted in any form or by any means without written permission of the author.

Disclaimer: This is a work of fiction. All characters are totally from the imagination of the author and depict no persons, living or dead; any similarity is totally coincidental.

Published by

Midnight Express Books
POBox 69
Berryville, AR 72616

DRAMA CITY

by

Colie Levar Long

Published by

Midnight Express Books
POBox 69
Berryville, AR 72616

NOTE TO READER

The story in this composition of literary madness was based on actual events. All names of all individuals and locations in this story have been changed or purposely made up, to prevent anyone from being incriminated. Any resemblance a character in this story may have to an individual you may know (living or non-living) is unintentionally coincidental. (Except for you hot-ass, snitching-ass, back stabbing-ass, lying-ass rats! Let the world look upon you and see you for what you truly are.)

Sincerely, SHAKA
(The Last of a Dying Breed)

ii

Table of Contents

PROLOGUE

When I first laid eyes on the kid, I knew he was nothing but trouble. Youngblood was his name, but for short, everyone called him Little Blood. I heard a lot of things about this young brother named Blood when I was on the bricks (in society), and everything I heard summed up one conclusion; the boy was a complete mental case!

A lot of my comrades from my neighborhood knew Blood personally by being locked up in different juvenile detention facilities with him. They told me different stories about how Blood had stolen a cab and had driven it around the city picking up passengers, robbing them at gun point, putting them out, and driving off; and how by the age of 15, he had a small portion of Northeast D.C. riddled with bullet holes and utterly shaken up.

Well I'm quite sure you heard the old proverb; "hearing it a thousand times is never like seeing it once." And believe you me, the Blood I was looking at now, I would have never suspected that this was the same Blood I had heard about back then. I mean the kid looked like he was 15 years old. He kept to himself mostly, walked around the prison rec. yard with a mischievous smirk on his face like that of a precocious adolescent.

I have been incarcerated for almost ten years now, and at the invigorating age of 27, I came across my share of personalities, so it's safe to say that I can (in most cases) make a generalized assumption of people by looking into their eyes, or watching the way they walk and talk. But Blood was a different case all together. Although my first impression of him was that of a sneaky little pillager who would have known that fate would entangle us in her web and bring Blood and me to be the closest of friends.

Prison is more than an institution developed to house society's undesirables. Prison is in itself a society, a chaotic and savage world, of its own. It brings out the animalistic attributes of its occupants and forces them to submit to its social order: Survival of the fittest. Only the individuals that are mentally strong and physically apt can endure the burden of living in a monotonous cycle of unmitigated misery.

That's just what prison is: pure misery. Show me a person who says that they live better in captivity than some people do in third world counties, and I will show you an institutionalized drone; a fool.

Chapter 1

And they say how you survive
Weighing one sixty five
In the city where the skinny niggaz die
Tell mama don't cry
Cause even when they kill me
They could never take the game from a young 'G'...

-Tupac Shakur

Drama City

It was another hot and humid Saturday night. The neighborhood was like a ghost town, void of any signs of life. Even the continuously active and clamorous streets held an unearthly silence. Only the residual pile of rubbish and filth left over by crack heads, winos, dope fiends, hustlers, and hood rats served as a reminder of how life is in the inner city.

Seventeen minutes after two was the time, as Youngblood glanced admiringly at his new watch. It was an authentic Tag Hauger time piece that he had bought for only seven dime bags of crack cocaine from some geeked out pipe head. "Man... I come off like shit," Youngblood said to himself as he took another deep pull from the Backwood cigar, which he had previously rerolled and stuffed with marijuana. With every inhalation of smoke from the sticky green skunk weed, he felt the burning tingle in the back of his throat from the Remy Martin that he'd dipped the Backwood in earlier. This was a custom he had inherited from his partner Jay.

Reclining back in the passenger seat of the hooptie, Youngblood reached down for the side switch to readjust his position, so he could stretch out his legs. The hooptie was the type of car that he had always enjoyed riding in. It was an inconspicuous looking, tan colored '78 Caprice with dark tinted windows. It used to be a police squad car before Jay had bought it at the Goodwill Car Auction on South Dakota Avenue, so it had the acceleration capability and necessary speed to elude the cops, if the need arose to do so.

The thought of any type of police car chase was far from his mind, as he continued to puff on the Backwood. His thoughts were centered on one thing and one thing only; the hit. Youngblood was only 15 years old and had never shot another person with a real gun before, and the thought of him actually catching a body was a matter he had never really taken seriously before, either. After tonight, all that would soon be changed, because this night Youngblood was going to put some work in.

While parked in a dark alley, so many incoherent thoughts raced through his mind as he waited for what seemed like an eternity for Jay to come out of the house. To appease some of the anxiety he was feeling, Youngblood turned the car radio on, and popped his Diary tape in the cassette deck. In the thick haze of marijuana smoke, he nodded his head to Scarface's drama filled lyrics, while focusing on the inevitable event. "Life has no meaning, no meaning... we was all born to die, so no

4

screaming, and that's a muthafuckin' shame, you let a nigga come around and kill your ass just like Jesse James," Youngblood said, repeating the verses in unison with the tape.

"Man, I can't believe this bitch-ass nigga carried me like that," he said to himself, thinking back in retrospect on his situation. Taking another hit off the weed, Youngblood propped his legs against the dashboard as he scooted down in his seat. Allowing the memories of the previous day to foment his already growing agitation, he closed his eyes and replayed in his mind the entire incident which led to the reason why he was now parked in a dark alley, dressed in all black.

"What's up, Youngblood?" Jay said as he came out of Mama Son's convenience store. Still groggy from a hangover earlier, Jay stumbled up the sidewalk, shielding his eyes from the blazing rays of the early morning sun. "Ain't shit slim, just chillin' ya know? Trying to make a million," Youngblood said, grinning at his best friend's disheveled appearance.

"Goddamn champ, what the hell happen to you; lookin' all like a gay Snoop Dog, n' shit."

"Nigga fuck you." Jay said laughingly. "I just woke up around 'bout twenty minutes ago, and Tracy broke-ass ain't have shit in her refrigerator, so I rolled out to Mama Son's to get somethin' to eat."

"Ugh?" Youngblood mockingly screamed as he hopped off the corner mail box he was sitting on. "You mean to tell me that you spent the night over Tracy's house?"

"Look, don't even start the bullshit!"

"Ugh, you freaked out, nasty, dirty dick-ass nigga. How could you put the dick in Tracy? Man, that lil' broad look just like Danny Glover! Ugh, I bet y'all was all tongue kissing and making love, and all that other crazy shit, huh?"

Jay, who was now laughing uncontrollably, placed his arm around Youngblood's shoulder as they both started to walk across the street toward the corner phone booth. "Aye slim, I know I'm dead wrong for puttin' the dick in that monkey bitch," Jay said still laughing, "but I was out here on the graveyard shift last night by myself and all of a sudden, I started to get horny as a muthafucka. I smoked two blunts back to back; straight to the head, so I was high as shit. And slim, the old boy got so

5

hard, I had to say 'fuck hustling,' I need to get some pussy!

"Blood, I felt so freaky I was on the verge of finding me a big butt pipe head to trick wit' or get some head or something. And all of a sudden, out of the blue, I seen Tracy walking up the block toward me wit' a brown paper bag cradled in her arms. When she got to the corner, she stopped and posted up right beside me and started rapping me up on some ole 'she all alone' type shit. After a couple of minutes of listening to this hooker yap, I cut her off and asked her what the fuck was that in the brown bag.

"Next thing I know, she reached for the bag and pulled out a bottle of Absolute, a thing of orange juice, and some little plastic cups. Man, the broad asked me to drink wit' her, and you know by now I had caught a vicious case of the cotton mouth, so I said fuck it. I started to drink wit' the bitch. And slim, I think Tracy knew what the fuck she was doing, to be honest, because I was already high as a muthafucka, and the more I start to drink, the more she started to look like Halle Berry!

"Blood, I started kissing her right there on the block, and after that I just blacked out. The next thing I know, I wake up, it's seven twenty in the morning, I'm butt ass naked, and Tracy was balled up beside me."

"So what you saying, basically, is you can't remember fucking, huh?" Youngblood asked.

"Oh yeah, we had sex a'ight."

"But how do you know for sure, if you'd blacked out like you said you did?"

"Because Blood, when I woke up this morning and saw that big ole ass staring me in the face, I jump dead in that pussy. And slim, I know you might not believe it, but that ugly bitch got some bomb ass pussy." Jay said laughingly as he finished telling Youngblood about his late night creep.

At the phone booth, the two boys discussed among themselves varying street matters, such as who they would get to restock their supply of coke, to who owed them money and how much they owed. Money, power, and respect were their aim, as it was the ambitions of every other young thug and local hustler in the 'hood. Jay was unique compared to the other youngsters in the projects, and although he was only seventeen years old, he had the mentality of an old timer who'd been around the block a few times.

Instead of wasting his money on the typical street life frivolities like expensive tennis shoes, designer clothes, jewelry, go-go clubs, and fast women, Jay was economizing his drug money for future purposes. Things like legal assistance (in case he'd ever needed a criminal lawyer), college tuition, and for buying a house out in Maryland, so his mother and three sisters could have a decent and stable place to call home. Despite the fact that he was a teenage drug dealer, the majority of folks in the projects showed him much love, especially most of the senior citizens.

Jay had always respected the elders in the neighborhood. He would help them carry their groceries to their apartments, clean up the trash in front of the apartment buildings for them, and there were even certain occasions where he had given them money to help pay their bills. Most importantly, Jay had always made an effort to keep his illegal activities outside of the eyesight of the older folks, because he knew that they did not approve of the way he chose to make his living, but would tolerate his street dealing to a certain extent on account of the fact that most of the senior citizens witnessed the poverty which Jay was forced to live in. A few of them even fed and clothed him when his own mother was too busy out wandering the streets, looking for more crack to smoke. Subsequently, they turned their heads to his drug dealing.

While the boys were finishing their conversation, the streets were rapidly coming alive as the crack heads and dope fiends began to flood the street corners; all of them searching for that early morning hit of their drug of choice, and all willing to do just about anything to get it. All the hustlers in the 'hood called this the 'early morning rush,' and knew that this was the best time to sell their drugs in the quickest amount of time.

"Hey Youngblood, let me holler atcha' boo!" Linda yelled as she made her way out of the alley, walking toward the two boys.

"Aw shit, here come crazy Linda." Jay whispered to Youngblood as he began to search for the box of blunts he had placed on the top of the phone booth.

"Blood, what 'cha workin' 'wit?" Linda asked while reaching into her pants pockets, pulling out old crumbled up dollar bills.

"Whatever you need," said Youngblood, pulling a small sandwich bag of crack rocks out of the waistband of his sweatpants.

"I need five for forty."

"Oh hell naw! What the fuck you need is ten more dollars," Youngblood said as he put the bag of rocks back into his waistband.

"Come on boo, you know I'm good for it. All that muthafuckin' money I spent wit'cha the other day. How you gonna try to carry me like that?"

"Man, I ain't tryin' to hear that shit. The only thing you did for me was brought me a few sells, and every time you did I looked out for you. Plus you keep coming at me wit' short money, you be making my shit come up uneven."

"Well, just give me two for fifteen then, I know you can do that for me."

"Linda, I ain't fuckin' wit'cha right now. I'll do something wit'cha later on when I re-up."

"You know what Blood, that's real messed up. And you better remember that shit the next time you lookin' for a trick."

"Speaking of tricking, what the head hittin' on," Jay asked, jokingly grabbing his crotch area. Putting her money back into her pocket, Linda placed two fingers into her mouth and started simulating an oral sex act.

"They don't call me 'Linda long lips' for nothing," she said as she turned around and headed back up the alley.

"A slim, I ain't gonna lie, Linda got some crucial head," Youngblood whispered to Jay, leaning back against the phone booth.

"What! Nigga, you always screaming on me talkin' 'bout 'I need to stop trickin' pipe heads,' and now you over here talkin' 'bout somebody got some crucial head. Nigga, I'm hip to you now, you one of them ole young undercover freaks," Jay laughed out playfully hitting Youngblood in the ribs.

Suddenly the vibrator went off on Jay's pager. "Man, I hate when they be paging me, puttin' in 911, but when I call back they don't even be wanting shit."

"Who that on the box? Probably Tracy gruesome looking ass," Youngblood mumbled under his breath.

"Naw," Jay said putting the pager back into his windbreaker. "Aye Slim, I forgot, I supposed to give Mink some money today for her baby shower. How much money you got on you?"

"I got seventeen hundred put up in the glove compartment in the hooptie."

"I mean how much you got in your pockets?"

"Enough — how much you need?"

"About three would do."

"Goddamn," said Young Blood, thrusting his hand into his pants pocket and pulling out three crisp one-hundred dollar bills. Folding the money in half, he gave it to Jay.

"Man, I don't know how your sister let herself get pregnant by that nigga Vamp. I mean, she wrong as a muthafucka."

"Yeah, Mink snap like shit," Jay said, "but what can I do, she's a grown woman, ya dig?"

"I feel you slim," Youngblood said slightly unsettled, "but for real... If I was you,

I'd punish that dope fiend ass nigga."

"For what? Ain't like that'd change anything."

"Yeah okay, let that had been my sister, I'd a —"

"Yo' scared ass wouldn't a done shit," Jay said over exaggerating his smile. Unfolding the hundred dollar bills he held in his hand, Jay studied the money carefully.

"Blood, you gotta be careful keeping them large bills on you like that. Them joints could be marked or anything."

"You right slim," said Youngblood," I was 'bout to roll out anyway after I finish these last joints."

"Well check this out," Jay said, putting the money into his back pocket," I'm a go ahead and take this money over the house so Mink can stop paging me. Then I'ma come back and pick you up so we can go to II-10Ps and get something to eat."

"That's cool wit' me."

9

"Aight then, I'll holler at 'cha when I come back," said Jay as he extended his hand out to give Blood a quick embrace and a playful kiss on the cheek. Turning his head towards the alley, Jay crossed the street when he realized he'd forgotten his keys. "Blood, you got my car keys?" Jay asked.

"Oh yeah, my bad." Youngblood said with a laugh. Digging through his pockets he pulled out the keys and tossed them to Jay. "You know I got them blunts you'd left on top of the phone booth," he said. "Make sure you go ahead southwest to pick up some smoke."

"Aight, I got that," said Jay as he spun around and started to jog to the hooptie. Unlocking the front door, he hopped in and started the engine. Winding down the driver's side window, Jay stuck his head out and said: "Blood, won't 'cha hop in and ride over the house wit' me? I got a flicked up feeling something going down today," he yelled to Blood.

"Man, it's Saturday! Police ain't gon' jump out today."

"That ain't the point," Jay said. "I got a funny feeling something is going to happen today, so come on and ride wit' me."

"Man look, I'm out here 'til I finish these last joints, after that I'm gone! Just come back and pick me up at Mama Son's. I'll be finish 'bout time you get back."

"Aight then," Jay yelled back, slightly upset. Winding the car window back up, he placed the car in reverse and backed out of the alley. "That nigga hard headed as shit," he muttered to himself as he slowly drove up the street. Looking through his rear-view mirror, he shook his head and started laughing as he watched Youngblood climb on top of the mailbox and drop his sweatpants. "That's a wild young nigga there," he whispered to himself "A wild young nigga."

Bending over with his pants pulled down around his thighs, Youngblood mooned Jay until the hooptie rode out of sight.

"Young'un, you get off mailbox right now, and pull pants up!" yelled Mama'son, holding a push broom in her left hand, while making a tight little fist with the other, shaking it sternly at Youngblood. "You act like you have no good sense!"

Startled by the abrupt raspy voice of the old Vietnamese woman, Youngblood almost lost his balance. In one fluid motion he jumped off the mailbox while pulling up his sweat pants, and landing clumsily on his feet. Extending out his hands so he wouldn't fall on his face, he stumbled until he regained his balance. "Damn Mama-san! You almost made me break my neck," he said as he knelt down to pick up the bag of crack rocks he dropped.

"I break' a your neck if you show backside out here again," said the old woman with her thick Asian accent. "Youngan, you come help clean store today. You no pay for food yesterday, I no forget! You come sweep store now!"

"Aight Mama'son," he yelled, "goddamn, you just opened up so the store can't be that dirty. Just give me a couple of minutes; I'll be in there to clean up."

"Hmm," grunted the old Vietnamese, leaving the push broom leaning against the store front barred window. Stepping back into the store she closed the door and resumed her duties of tending to the store.

Meanwhile, standing on the street corner all by himself, Youngblood watched as the other local dealers made their routine drug transactions. Eight forty-seven in the morning, and already the neighborhood was bustling with addicts of all sorts. Usually, if no dead bodies were found, Saturday mornings were pretty much quiet in the projects.

The senior citizens would get their early morning walk on, the winos would still be asleep by their rusty drum barrels, and everyone else would just be recovering from their Friday night clubbing.

But on this particular morning, the 'hood was alive and pumping. It seemed like everybody was out and about trying to get their hustle on. The crack heads with their rags and buckets were all anxiously setting up shop to wash and wax cars for whoever would give them something to smoke. Even the pugnacious prostitutes were out and quarrelling with one another over territorial routes and potential customers.

The streets were extremely active. From across the block where Youngblood stood, he could look directly into the alley and see the dope fiends sitting on the back steps of the abandoned buildings, shooting heroin into their veins. They looked like zombies as they sat on the steps rocking mindlessly back and forth.

A few of them would walk around the block as if they were sleep walking, constantly scratching and rubbing themselves as if they were

11

trying to remove the skin from their bodies. While others would just sit on the curb of the sidewalk with their heads nodding like they were fighting to stay awake, occasionally vomiting every now and then as the heroin completely took over their bodily functions.

None of this was new to Youngblood, as he leaned against the mailbox, watching with silent antipathy. Two years ago he had lost his own mother to a heroin overdose and had been surviving on his own ever since. With the exception of Jay, he had no family to take care of him, and as long as he had Jay in his life, he felt that that was all the family he needed.

Taking his attention away from the junkies for a moment, Youngblood noticed the sound of a vehicle pulling up beside him. Turning his head to look over his right shoulder, he saw the black, tinted window Cadillac with the suicide doors coming to a stop and double parking in the middle of the street.

Instantly, he knew who it was.

Stepping out of the car dressed in army fatigues, the man walked across the street and made his way to the mailbox where Youngblood was standing. The man reached into his pants pocket with one hand, and pulled out a pack of Newports, while searching for his lighter with the other. Looking Youngblood up and down, the man constricted his lips into a mock smile as he asked him for a light.

"Naw, I ain't even got one," Youngblood said vapidly, still looking at the black Cadillac in the middle of the street.

Everybody in the neighborhood knew that that car had once belonged to a well-known street hustler named Adam, and that Adam had once been Vamp's partner in crime. Rumor had it, that when Vamp came home from doing a seven-year bid down at Lorton for attempted murder, Adam drove to Vamp's mother's house to pick him up and take him shopping. Everybody knew that the whole time Vamp was locked up, Adam had never once went to visit him, sent him any money orders, or even accepted his phone calls. So on the night when they were both last seen together, Vamp drove back to his mother's house, all alone in Adam's car the following morning. When people started questioning him about Adam's whereabouts, he just told them that he didn't know and that the last time he'd seen Adam was when he had dropped him off at his house.

Two weeks later, while walking through the projects on foot patrol, two police officers got a call on their walkie-talkies to investigate a strange odor in one of the areas they were patrolling. Arriving on the scene to investigate the area, the officers noticed that the extremely nauseating smell was coming from a trash dumpster on the side street of the area.

Covering their noses with a handkerchief, the officers walked towards the dumpster and lifted open the lid. There they found Adam's naked and decomposed body laying face down in a pile of garbage, with multiple gunshot wounds to the back of his head. Only two blocks away from his house, Adam's body laid in a dumpster putrefying, devoured by maggots and alley rats, and nobody knew a thing.

Suddenly Youngblood's attention was brought back to the man standing next to him, when he felt the man's hand trying to pick something out of his pants pocket.

Spinning off the mailbox towards his left, Youngblood quickly grabbed the small sandwich bag of crack rocks that was sticking half-way out of his right pocket. "What the fuck you doing, Vamp?!" He growled, almost stumbling on the uneven pavement, as he stepped back to put some distance between him and the man.

"Eh, look here shorty," said Vamp, taking the unlit cigarette out of his mouth. "I'm jive fucked up. I feel sick, I need my medicine, and my money jive short. I need some them stones so I can get what I like."

"I'm jive low myself," Youngblood said, opening up the bag of drugs. "But I'll hit 'cha off wit' a couple of joint, so you can do your thing."

"Eh, a couple of joints?!" He said agitated. "You got me fucked up! You must think you talkin' to one of these crack head niggaz around here. You little young-ass nigga, I was doing seven years down Lorton before you even started hustling. Nigga, yo' little ass couldn't even come on the block when I was out here. Now you think you a big nigga around here. Bitch, I'll take yo' shit!"

Suddenly, it felt like the whole neighborhood became quiet, watching with eager eyes, anticipating a vicious and bloody street war.

In the back of his mind, Youngblood knew that he could not do too much damage to the six-foot, two-hundred-and-ten pound grown man with just his bare hands alone. Though he was about five-feet-nine inches himself, he only weighed a hundred and forty-three pounds soaking wet. He was just too small. Plus, everybody knew that Vamp always carried a gun everywhere he went, never hesitating to use it.

Though taking all of that into consideration, Youngblood felt that he could not afford to lose face in the eyes of the other hustlers and gangstas, who were no watching intensely, waiting to see how this drama would unfold. Any signs of weakness you show, and they attack like hyenas. Youngblood was not having any of that.

Before he even realized what he was doing, Youngblood stuffed the bag of crack back into his pocket, walking towards Vamp, clutching his fists together. "You dope fiend ass nigga!" he said, throwing up his fist. "I don't give a fuck about..."

Before Youngblood could finish what he was saying, Vamp landed a mind jarring right hook against his jaw. The blow came with such velocity that he didn't even see it coming. Only through feeling his teeth loosening from the initial impact did he know that he had been struck. Feeling his knees buckle, he tried to regain his equilibrium to keep from falling on his back, but he was disoriented.

The first punch Vamp threw had proved to be extremely effective; Youngblood was on the verge of losing consciousness. Dropping to one knee, he didn't even feel the second blow smashing against the side of his head. Though the punch was less devastating than the first one, it served as consummation to Vamp's physical supremacy in the brief street fight.

Falling back on the ground, Youngblood slightly regained his consciousness, only to find that he was now sprawled out across the pavement, bleeding from the mouth. In the distant crowd, he could hear a woman's voice yelling "please don't kill 'em Vamp, please don't kill 'em." Opening his eyes, it took him a few seconds to blink away the blurriness to see Vamp standing over top of him with a .357 bulldog pointed at his head.

"Bitch nigga, you lucky I don't kill you!" said Vamp, uncocking the hammer of the powerful revolver. Putting the gun back into his waistband, he bent down over Youngblood and started going through his pants pockets. Taking the small bag of crack rocks and all of his drug money, Vamp stood up and stepped over Youngblood as he put the drugs and money in his pocket. "Next time shorty, he said while walking

14

Colie Levar Long

back to his car, "stay your young-ass from around here."

Chapter 2

Startled by the abrupt sound of someone knocking against the driver side window, Youngblood instantly snapped out of the trance he had fallen under, while thinking back on his previous encounter with the man called Vamp. Leaning forward to pluck the ashes off his blunt into the ash tray, he reached over with his left hand and pulled the knob to unlock and open the car door.

"Nigga, I don't know why you got the muthafuckin' door locked!" said Jay, climbing behind the steering wheel of the hooptie, "'cause if I'd wanted to kill you, all I had to do is shoot through the window." He laughed mostly to himself, closing the door behind him, as he turned the key that was already in the ignition. Starting up the car engine, he reached for the radio and turned the volume down.

"What 'cha do that for?" Youngblood asked lazily, taking a slow and meaningful gaze at the huge bulge protruding out of the front of Jay's black Versace jeans.

"Man, you had that radio up loud as shit," he said, adjusting the rearview so that he could see himself in the small mirror. "I mean soon as I came out of the house, I heard that shit coming out the alley, and then when I walk up to tha car, you in this joint slip-pin'! Suppose I was the nigga Vamp? I could'a easily crept up, put two in your head, and left you slump, and you would'a never seen it coming! I'm telling you Blood, this shit ain't no joke, slim. You 'bout to take the game to a whole 'nother level, man, you can't afford not to be on top of your shit."

"Yeah, you right slim," said Youngblood passing the blunt over to Jay. "I ain't mean to be slippin', but I was just sitting here thinking 'bout this

16

bitch-ass nigga."

"Man fuck that nigga, when we catch him we gonna bless 'em. Simple as that!" said Jay. Taking a slow drag from the weed filled cigar. Inhaling, exhaling, and blowing the thick pungent cloud of marijuana smoke out of his nose. He repositioned the rearview mirror so that he could see if anyone was behind them. Rolling his window half-way down to let some of the smoke float out of the car, he looked over at Youngblood and took notice of how his partner was staring at him as if he was in a daze. "Blood, what type of freak time you on? All staring at my crotch 'n all that..."

"Huh, what 'cha say?" he asked blankly. Turning his head to look out of the window, he slouched down in his seat, cupping his hands over his face.

"Aw shit, let me find out you trippin'" said Jay, shaking his head to himself. "See, I told you not to smoke nothing tonight, but naw, you wanna go 'head and do it anyway. Now you over there — ."

"Man, I ain't trippin'!" Youngblood said menacingly. "It's just so much shit going through my head right now. What if I get caught? Suppose this nigga see me coming first, pull out his pistol, and get to humpin' off? Man, anything can happen slim, I'm just trying to get myself ready for whatever."

Plucking the ashes off the blunt, which was now a roach, into the ash tray, Jay took one last quick hit before he threw it out of the window. Using his hand to fan the excess smoke out of the car, he rolled the window back up, and checked the rearview mirror again. No one was in sight. Stepping on the brake pedal, he brought the car into

gear and slowly drove out of the alley on to the dark and deserted streets. "Blood, the only thing that's gonna happen tonight... is this nigga gonna die," he said mostly to himself. "Simple as that!"

Driving up towards the stop sign on the infamous street corner of 18th and D, Jay finally turned his headlights on. It was a well known fact that it was not wise to make niggaz in the hood more paranoid than they already were; especially at night. The mere sight of any vehicle driving through with tinted windows and no headlights on is enough to turn the street into Vietnam, and particularly in the Northeast area of D.C. Niggaz ain't never had a problem with turning someone's car into Swiss cheese.

17

Veering to his left, Jay turned the corner and drove a few yards, until he reached the intersection of Constitution Avenue. Not bothering to stop at the stop sign this time, he turned on to the intersection, and slightly accelerated the speed of the hooptie. "You know what? He asked, "We should ride up the Carbarn, and see if this nigga is out there on the front or somewhere. What 'cha think?"

Not getting a response, he looked over at Youngblood and found him just staring out of the window. "Blood, you a'ight?" he asked, hitting him lightly on the arm. "I know you ain't over there having second thoughts 'n shit? Man, if that's the case, I'll put the work in myself."

"Man, I'm a'ight, damn!" he said as if just snapping out of a spell. "I'm just chillin' slim. I don't need you to put no work in for me. I got this! And matter of fact, let me ask you a question; that nigga Vamp is damn near your brother in law, you know Mink is pregnant by the dude, and 'bout to have his baby. Plus, she love the nigga at that! So how in the hell can you kill him?"

Pulling up to the curb in front of the rustic style apartment complex, the two boys looked through their windows on both sides of the street, desperately searching for the man they were after. It was pointless; they could look directly through the gaps of the wrought iron fence that surrounded the Carbarn, and clearly see that there was nobody out soliciting in front of the apartment building tonight.

Jay leaned back in his seat. He reached into his jacket pocket and retrieved a pack of Newports and opened it. Pulling out two cigarettes, he gave one to Youngblood while placing the other one between his lips. Lighting his cigarette with a book of matches, he thought about the question Youngblood has asked a couple of minutes ago, as he lit the cigarette for him.

"Blood, I don't care if the nigga was my mother's baby father," he said with a little shrug. "If I had been out there when y'all was fighting, I would'a smashed that nigga off in front of the whole neighborhood, for real. And far as for Mink... I mean, she's my sister 'n all, but fuck all that... You my heart!"

"Basically, you saying fuck that nigga, huh?" Youngblood asked.

"Pretty much."

18

"Ooh, that so sweet," Youngblood said theatrically. He reached over, extended his arms, and tried to embrace Jay. Laughing he said, "let me give my baby a hug," as he jumped out toward him.

Lifting his forearm to ward off Youngblood's clumsy attempts to grab a hold of him, Jay pushed him back into his seat. "Won't 'cha stop playin', before you burn me wit' that cigarette," he giggled. "You blowin' my high." For a brief moment he continued to playfully tussle with Youngblood, until he twisted his body slightly, feeling the sudden shift of the object that was concealed in the upper area of his jeans. "Ouch, damn!" he winced, "see, I told you stop playin'."

"Man, what's wrong wit' 'cha?" Youngblood asked.

"Nigga, you made me scratch my stomach wit' this joint."

"What the hell is that poking out the front of your jeans, anyway?"

Looking over at Youngblood, he smiled and lifted his jacket to display the huge metal handle of the chrome plated pistol that was wedged in the waist band of his jeans. Turning it around so that the handle was facing Youngblood, he handed him the weapon. Jay watched him as he held the gun with his fingers eagerly running down the length of the gun's triangular barrel, and grin like a kid with a new toy.

"Man, this joint mean," Youngblood said, trying to cock back the gun with his left hand, "but what type of joint is it, though?"

"Good god — can't you read the side of the joint? It's a Desert Eagle, .45 caliber handgun," he said, pointing to the tiny inscriptions on the side of the pistol, "but you don't have to worry about what type of gun it is, all you gotta do is make sure you ain't faking wit' it. And don't cock the joint back, 'cause it's already one in the chamber."

"Oh yeah... Well I'm straight then," said Youngblood with a quick nod of his head. "Slim, you ain't gotta worry 'bout me doing no faking, 'cause when I see that nigga, I'm a split his head to the white meat. Off the no bullshit!"

"Yeah, yeah, yeah..." Jay nodded his head, full of sarcasm and amusement. "Been there, heard that. You just make sure you don't choke, and get both of us hemmed up."

"Man, whatever," said Youngblood giving a little wave of his left hand.

Demonstrating his murder tactics, he raised the gun and pointed it directly at Jay's head. "Bang!" he said, pretending to fire the weapon. "One to the dome, and he's out of here. Simple as that."

"Nigga!" Jay cried, pushing the gun away from him. "You think Vamped beated your little ass, point that gun at me again, hear! Boy you done lost your mind, playin' wit' that. Matter of fact, won't 'cha put the joint up anyway, before you fuck around the shoot both of us in the head bullshittin'!"

"Aw, man, shut 'cha scared ass up! Nigga, you know I ain't gonna shoot 'cha. Well... Not intentionally anyway. And besides, I told 'cha I got this. All we gotta do is catch the dude slippin', and put him to sleep. Just like you said; simple as that."

Putting the pistol under his lap, Youngblood slouched back down in his seat, and leaned his head against the window. Closing his eyes, he heard the clicking sound of the car blinker, as Jay brought the car into gear and made a u-turn in the middle of the street. None of this really meant anything to him. The only thought that registered in his mind was the thought of death; the violent snatching of someone's soul.

Being only fifteen years old, Youngblood would not be the youngest person to kill someone in the 'hood. Jay was only fourteen when he had first caught his body, and it had been rumored that Vamp himself had been killing people since the age of twelve. Never has it been shown in the ghetto that just because a person is of a young age, that they are not a threat. In fact, the truth was that the younger the individual was, the more aggressive he or she appeared to be. The ghettos of D.C. were nothing more than the perennial stomping grounds for a myriad of young niggaz, all eager and ready to take another person's life away just to make a name for themselves.

None of this really meant anything to Youngblood. The only thing that mattered to him was that he gets his opportunity to pay back the man who had publicly humiliated him in front of the whole neighborhood. Vamp must die!

Intensified by the marijuana smoke the anxiety and paranoia of the inevitable moment of execution wreaked havoc upon Youngblood's mind. There had been plenty of times where he had gotten high while smoking blunts, and experienced the occasional trick playing of the mind, but never before had he ever felt the way that he was feeling at that particular moment. The sudden churning of his stomach constricting the entire length of his bowels, and the bombardment of 'what if' scenarios plaguing his thoughts were striking a silent fear into his heart. He even found himself fighting the incessant urge to go to sleep.

All of these sensations were foreign, as well as unpleasant to Youngblood as he tried to figure out what was causing him to feel this way. Yet none of these things were more disturbing than vivid images he held in his mind of his mother. Even with his eyes tightly closed, he could still see the distinct details of his mother's face as she lay across the bus stop bench with the syringe still lodged in her arm, and dead from an overdose of heroin.

The very thought of her drove spikes through his stomach. He relived the memories of her lying there on that old tattered wooden bench wearing nothing except an old sweatshirt, and a pair of jeans to protect her from the harsh winter winds. Her face laid in a puddle of thick white vomit, while urine soaked through her pants, streaming on the pavement. She was dead only a few hours before the police actually showed up. When he had arrived at the scene, they were just starting to check her for any identification. There was none.

Earlier that day, Youngblood had stolen her ID card to keep her from cashing her welfare check, so she couldn't buy any more drugs. They had had a terrible fight, and eventually he was chased out of the house. When he came back home a few hours later, he found that this mother had ransacked his room, taking anything she thought may have had some value.

Initially, Youngblood wasn't angry, and actually thought the whole situation to be somewhat humorous. Especially the way his things were all frantically scattered about, showing the palpable evidence of his mother's hopeless search for her ID card. He walked through his room and gathered up a few things that were lying on the floor, tossing them on his bed. Picturing in his mind how angry his mother had been, not being able to find her ID, he started to laugh, until suddenly he realized that his closet door was wide open.

There, he discovered that all of his clothes had been ripped from their hangers and thrown down to the floor. His brand new tennis shows pummeled out of their boxes, laid helter skelter in a pile directly on top of the heap of clothes, his sweat suits, jeans, t-shirts, and everything else were all slovenly littered across his closet floor. Except for his jacket! His band new Polo Sports pull over wind breaker, which cost him four hundred and eleven dollars, was missing. Youngblood went ballistic.

Running out of the house, he jumped on his Gary Fisher mountain bike, and rode to the nearest dope strip in that area. She wasn't there. He continued to ride through the neighborhood, asking anyone he came across if they had seen his mother that day. Everyone claimed that they hadn't seen her, until he came across a woman by the name of Joyce sitting on the front steps of her apartment building, smoking a cigarette.

Youngblood knew that Joyce and his mother would often shoot dope and get high together, and if there was anyone who might know his mother's whereabouts, she would be the perfect one to ask. He stopped his bike, looked down at the woman, and asked her where his mother was, but she gave no response. She sat there tacitly on the steps with her head bent down, and the cigarette slowly burning between her fingers. She appeared to be high herself.

Getting off of his bike, he walked over to the woman, and noticed how her hands were shaking. Suddenly, she lifted her head and Youngblood saw that her eyes were completely red with tears as she sat on the steps crying. Instantly he knew something was wrong. "It wasn't my fault," the woman pleaded, and tried to jump off of the steps, to sprint out of harm's way, but before she could move fast enough, Youngblood kicked her directly in the chest.

Falling backwards against he steps, the woman began to scream. She begged him not to hurt her as she curled up and tried to protect her face from any punches he might rain down upon her, but Youngblood didn't hit her. He grabbed her by the hair, stood over top of her, and demanded that she tell him what had happened to his mother, but the woman just continued to cry out: "it wasn't my fault..."

Youngblood became furious. He yanked the woman by her hair, and started slapping her in the face with his free hand until finally she yelled that his mother had gotten sick while shooting up some dope. After a few minutes of explaining the situation, she then told him where she had left his mother to try and find someone to help her. He knew that she was lying about trying to find help for his mother, because Joyce was too afraid that the police would lock her up for her repeated drug usage.

However, he couldn't afford to think about that at that particular moment. The only thoughts in his mind were of his mother, and that she needed his help.

Getting back on his bike, Youngblood pedaled fiercely up the busy streets of Benning Road, nearly getting hit three times, by three different cars. He showed no concern for his own safety. Dodging in and out of oncoming traffic, he rode his bike as if he were trying to outrun the inevitable, until suddenly, only a few blocks away, he heard the blaring sound of a police siren. Instinctively, he slammed on his brakes, bringing himself to a complete halt.

Quickly, he hopped off of the bike and ran the remaining blocks to where the sound was coming from. Once there, he stood in total shock as he watched the two officers stoop down over his mother, searching for her identification. Slowly, he moved across the street. He walked towards a crowd of people who had gathered around to see what was going on. He moved through the crowd to get a better view. Immediately, he noticed that she had his brand new jacket tied by the sleeves around her waist. He was decimated.

Standing amongst the crowd of on-lookers, Youngblood dropped his head. He felt the tears forming in the corners of his eyes, and he fought back the sudden impulse to run over to his mother, snatch the jacket from around her waist, and put it on her to shield her from the strong winds that were blowing. If he could just touch her one more time, he thought to himself, maybe he could bring her back to life. That was just wishful thinking, and Youngblood knew his mother was dead and there was no changing that. He took one final look before he dropped his head again, and turned away.

Heading back towards his bike, he whispered a short prayer to himself, as he walked through the crowd; "have mercy on her," he said, "until the day you come back, 'tit the day we meet again... Amen. I love you ma!"

Feeling a sudden jolt as the hoopty rolled over a pothole, Youngblood opened his eyes and rose back in his seat. It had been almost three years since his mother passed away, and not until that moment had he allowed himself to deluge his mind with those painful memories. "Man, I'm about to quit smoking," he mumbled to himself. "I'm over here trippin' 'n shit."

23

Wiping his face with his hands, he started massaging his eyes. He glanced at his watch, it was twenty minutes after three a.m. Raising both his arms, he began to yawn while stretching his back, when he felt the car come to a halt. He looked out f the window, and saw that they had stopped at a red light on the corner of 17th and Benning Road. The same street corner he had once stood on two years ago, and watched the officers search his mother, while she laid dead on the bench.

Youngblood turned his head and looked at Jay. "What we doing way over here?" he asked with genuine curiosity. "I mean, the dude don't hang around this way, do he?"

Jay grabbed the cigarette from his pocket, placed it in his mouth, and lit it. "Man, I've been driving all around Northeast while you were asleep," he said with the cigarette hanging loosely between his lips. "You know the dude got peoples that live over Trinidad, so I rode through there. Plus, I just went around Langston Terrace and 21st and I Street. Ain't shit happenin'. The nigga must be gone slim, so we might as well call it a night. Fuck it... We'll just crush 'em tomorrow. Ya dig?"

"I can dig that," said Youngblood, "but before we go in, let's get something to eat. I'm hungry and my mouth is dry as I don't know what."

"Blood, where we gonna get something to eat at this time of night?"

"Man, you know the Subway up Hechinger Mall stay open late on weekends," he said, pointing in the direction of the mini-mall. "Since we already here, we might as well get something to eat."

"A'ight then," said Jay. "But I ain't getting out the car dress like this, so you gonna have to get the food yourself."

"Dress like what? You got some Versace jeans on wit' an all black Coogi sweater, and some Dolce & Gabana show boots on. Nigga, we supposed to be wearing all black to kill this nigga Vamp, and you lookin' like you 'but to go to a goddamn Puff-Daddy concert!"

"Slim, you always on joke time," Jay laughed out as he flipped his turn signal with the light changing to green. He drove only a few feet before he noticed a figure sitting at the bus stop a couple of yards away. "What type of person would be sitting at a bus stop this late," he thought to himself. The closer he drove to the individual, the more familiar that person became. "What the hell…" he said, stopping the car.

Youngblood raised his head and looked through the windshield to see what it was that had grabbed Jay's attention. He couldn't believe it. He placed his left hand over his forehead and squinted his eyes to make sure that he was seeing what he thought he saw. It was him. The man who they were looking for all night was now sitting asleep at the bus stop, on the same bench his mother had died sitting on two years ago.

"Oh shit… That's that nigga Vamp right there!" said Jay. He quickly checked in the rearview mirror to see if anyone was driving behind them. The streets were deserted; not a car in sight. "Give me the joint…" he said while trying quickly to take off his jacket. Before he could finish what he was about to say, Youngblood was already out of the car.

Youngblood was only twelve feet away from the man, as he started walking towards him, clutching the heavy .45 caliber pistol in his hand. A whirlwind of thoughts ripped through his mind, as he slowly moved towards his victim. With every step he took, it felt like a drum was pounding between his ears, causing a slight dizziness. His throat became parched while his eyelids started to become heavy. He was feeling the same urge he had felt earlier to go to sleep. Maybe it was only his conscience telling him not to do it, or maybe it was just fear that was making him feel the way he was, but whatever the reason, it didn't matter to him. Vamp was going to die.

Finally approaching the man, Youngblood stood straight in front of him, and slowly raised the gun, holding it in both hands. In that brief moment, time felt like it was standing still. Everything seemed to be moving in slow motion.

He glanced at the man, gradually nodding his head back and forward, and noticed that he wasn't really asleep at all. He was high off of heroin. Instantly, tears welled up in Youngblood's eyes, as he immediately thought about his mother lying dead on that very same bench from a heroin overdose. "Fuck that shit!" he said to himself, thinking out loud. He aimed the pistol directly at the man's head, and started to gather his nerves to pull the trigger. He took a deep breath, tightening his grip as he held the .45 in both hands; he braced himself for the gun's powerful recoil.

Suddenly, Vamp raised his head, opened his eyes, and looked at him. In those few seconds, he stared at Youngblood in such a blank manner, that it had sent a chill down his spine. "Oh yeah?" Vamp said casually, appearing not to even take Youngblood serious, he leaned back against the glass of the bus stop booth, and started to smile. "Shorty, do you know who I am?" That was the last question he would ever ask.

Youngblood closed his eyes and tightly squeezed the trigger. Boom! The resonant sound of the hand-held cannon seemed to shake the buildings with thunder as the gun shot echoed through the streets. He opened his eyes and immediately saw that the bullet had gone through Vamp's head and shattered the glass that was behind him. Blood was everywhere.

Looking down at Vamp as he laid slump in the corner of the booth, Youngblood could clearly see the perforated wound on the side of the man's head. He walked towards him and pointed the gun. Boom... one shot. Boom... two shots.

Youngblood had shot Vamp in the head three times, making the man practically unrecognizable. Standing there watching the man as if he were in a daze, he heard the gurgling sound of the man's excretions rushing out of his bowels. Vamp was dead.

Hearing the sound of Jay honking the car horn, he turned around and ran towards the car. The door was already open. He jumped in and closed the door, as Jay slammed his foot down on the accelerator. Quickly leaving the scene, he checked the rearview. No cops in sight.

Jay looked over at Youngblood, and saw that he had bits and pieces of flesh and brains all over his shirt and pants. "Aw, hell naw," he said laughing. "We ain't going over my house like this. I ain't got time to be housing no murderers. We going to the hotel tonight buddy!"

Colie Levar Long

Chapter 3

> Murderer... Inside must be hollow —
> kill us today you gotta kill us tomorrow.
> Murderer... inside must be shallow —
> how does it feel to take a life of another?
>
> - Buju Banton

Two months had passed since the murder. Within the first few weeks following the killing of the old dope fiend, the neighborhood was in a buzz. Speculations on "who did it and why" were debated on the street corners. Rumors were exchanged in the laundry mats; local barber shops where most of the small time pushers, as well as a few heavy hitters, would meet up, were jumping with the latest gossip.

Vamp was found dead at a bus stop with multiple gunshot wounds to the face. Homicides were prevalent throughout most inner cities, to the point where unprovoked murders have become a malignant past time to escape the unrelenting misery of poverty within the ghetto. Everybody's eager to talk about the misfortunes of someone losing their life just so they don't have to think about the unfortunate conditions in which they live.

Vamp was no exception. For the most part, there was a general consensus that the neighborhood would be better off with him dead. Yet still, there were a few people who felt that his murder was not justified, and secretly desired for the day that his killers would be punished. Despite how many folks may have hated Vamp's guts, there were still a few people who had actually loved him... And Mink was one of them.

* * * * *

"Jameel, come on and get this food before it gets cold." Ray-Ray yelled out from the kitchen, scraping the last bit of scrambled eggs off of her skillet. It had been seven months since her release from the drug treatment facility for her crack habit that Racine Hinton settled back into the role of a loving mother and caregiver to her four children.

28

Racine truly lover her children, and enjoyed the experience of cooking, cleaning, and caring for them. In her eyes, the Good Lord above had given her another opportunity to be a mother to her kids; yet in her heart, she knew that that opportunity had been squandered in Jay's eyes.

Jay was a major factor to her recovery. At seventeen years old, her only son had proven to be the young man of the house. Although Mink was the oldest among her children, Jay was by far the most mature. Along with maintaining a B average in high school, he also made sure that his two younger sister, Rasheeda, and Nadia, had had all that they needed for their classes. Taking them to and from school every day, making grilled cheese sandwiches, and noodle soup for their dinner, checking their homework, and even making sure that they wash up for school the next day. He took responsibility for the daily task of caring for his siblings — while she was off in some dilapidated crack house smoking her life away.

For that selfish act of betrayal, Racine knew that Jay would never truly forgive her, yet he would always love her unconditionally, and that was enough to make her not ever want to get high again. Or so she thought.

"Mama, why you cooking breakfast so early in the morning for?" Jay asked as he slowly made his way into the kitchen. Walking over toward his mother, he leaned over her shoulder and gave her a kiss on her cheek, as he grabbed his plate off the stove counter.

"Boy, did you brush your teeth before you came in here?" Ray-Ray asked, brushing off the area where he had just kissed her.

"Naw, I ain't brush my teeth," said Jay. He pulled a chair from under the dining room table and sat down to eat his breakfast. "How can I brush my teeth, or do anything else, when Mink fat ass is always in the bathroom throwing up? Man, I ain't took a piss in three days 'cause she always got the damn door locked."

"Jameel, stop talking like that at the breakfast table! What's is wrong with you this morning?"

"Ain't nothing wrong with me, ma. I'm just still tired, that's all. My bad."

Jay stuffed a fork full of eggs into his mouth, while turning his head to face his mother. Suddenly, he saw the slight movement of someone toward his left side. He quickly spun around to see exactly who it was that had moved up on him, and caught the sight of a tiny little hand snatching a strip of turkey bacon off of his plate.

Knowing that she had been caught in the act, the little girl dropped the turkey meat on the table and tried to make a break for it, but before she could get two steps out of the kitchen, Jay had wrapped his long arms around her waist and picked her up in a playful bear hug.

Holding her tightly against his chest, Jay stated blowing his breath in the girl's face. "Mama! Tell him to stop... his breath stinks!" Nadia screamed out with laughter as Jay tickled her ribs.

"Jameel, put her down before you drop her on her head, please," said Ray-Ray, opening up the refrigerator and grabbing a bottle of orange juice.

"Ma, what time is it?" Jay asked, as he yawned. Still holding his little sister in his arms, he walked back to his chair and sat down, placing Nadia on his lap. Immediately she grabbed Jay's fork and started eating the rest of the eggs and turkey bacon on his plate.

Ray-Ray checked her watch as she placed two glasses of orange juice on the table. "It's twelve minutes after ten," she said as she sat down in a chair directly across from Jay and Nadia. She smiled as she watched them feed each other with their fingers. Nadia was seven years old — the youngest of the four, and the object of Jay's affection. Yet Ray-Ray could not help but feel a tinge of guilt and jealousy at their closeness. She was supposed to have been the parent in Nadia's life — not Jay.

"Mama, when am I going shopping for my school clothes?" Nadia asked, after gulping down the last of her orange juice. "I want some of them Mickey Mouse shirts like Jay got, and I want —"

"Girl, why you want to copy off of me?" Jay asked, plucking her softly behind her right ear.

"Ouch!" she said, holding her ear. "Leave me alone."

"Get off of my lap then."

"You two are crazy," said Ray-Ray. She stood up grabbing the plate and glasses, and walked over to the sink to clean the dishes. "Nadia, go get yourself cleaned up and bring me the brush when you finish, so I can straighten your hair up. We're going to the mall as soon as Rasheeda and Mink get they self together."

"But I don't want to go with y'all... I want to ride with Jay," she said, sliding off her brother's lap. "Rasheeda thinks because she's thirteen she's all like that, and going to try to leave me with you and Mink. Plus, I don't want to ride in Mink's car. It smells like some ass."

"Girl, if you don't watch your mouth..." Ray-Ray turned and glared at the little girl. "Just take your little foul mouthed self on up out of here and get ready!"

Nadia turned and looked at Jay for some type of help. He gave her one of his joker-face smiles and rose from his chair. Stretching his arms in the air as he faked like he was yawning, he tilted his head slightly forward so Ray-Ray couldn't see his face, and slipped Nadia a quick wink to put her on point. "Mama, I was thinking," he said while placing an arm around Nadia's slender should, "since y'all also got an appointment for the hair salon, I'll go ahead and take shorty to the mall and babysit her while y'all do y'all thing... You know how she can get when she gets restless."

"And you know damn well that it's a Saturday morning," said Ray-Ray, "you ain't gonna want to watch her for all that time while we're gone. And besides, school starts this Tuesday coming up, and she's going to have to get her hair done, too."

"Don't even trip." Jay grabbed a hand full of Nadia's long straight hair and yanked it back causing her to grimace a little from the pressure. "You know Samiko work up at the Hair Gallery now, so she'll give me a discount for doing Nadia's wig."

Ray-Ray focused her attention back to Nadia, and saw how she was beaming with excitement at the thought of hanging out with her big brother, and it broke her heart that her baby-girl would rather be with him than her own mother. Ray-Ray gave a sigh of resignation, and turned back to the sink pretending to wash the rest of her dishes. "As long as she has everything she needs for school and gets her hair taken care of, I don't care what y'all do," she said. When unexpectedly she felt Nadia's tiny arms wrap around her waist, while Jay hugged her from the side.

"We love you Mommy!" they said in unison, tickling her ribs.

Ray-Ray squirmed and laughed out loud, telling them to stop while allowing herself to be held in their embrace. Jay kissed her on the cheek again, and then lifted Nadia up so she could do the same thing. With a quick kiss, Nadia told her mother thank you.

Her heart melted as she looked into her daughter's hazel eyes. "Anything for you, squirt," said Ray-Ray. She kissed her and Jay on the lips and watched them walk out of the kitchen. A teardrop suddenly escaped from her eye as she became flushed with shame, thinking back on the years her crack habit had stolen from her. Now it appeared that Jay was stealing her baby away from her — and silently she resented him for that.

Mink lay curled up in her bed, rubbing her hand back and forth over her swollen stomach. She had had another vicious bout of morning sickness about a half hour ago, yet the nauseous feeling still lingered, threatening to make her throw-up the Chinese food she had just forced herself to eat.

Being pregnant was far from what she had expected it to be. The back pains, swollen ankles, weird food cravings, and the sicknesses were all phases of child bearing she could have done without. Although these physical discomforts coupled with her constant mood swings at times seemed too much for Mink to handle, they were all overshadowed by the grief she felt from losing her child's father.

Six months into her pregnancy, on a Sunday morning, a day after her baby shower, Mink was informed by a phone call from a detective from the Fifth District Police Precinct that Vincent Jefferies — also known as Vamp — was found shot to death at a bus stop on Benning Road. The news nearly caused her water to break as she went into a mild state of shock. Ray-Ray had to rush her to D.C. General Hospital where she was placed under sedation, and was kept for two days by the doctors for observation.

For days Mink had laid in her bed crying over the death of her baby's father. She knew Vamp was into all types of criminal activities from armed robbery and extortion to kidnapping and murder, yet she loved him nonetheless.

She'd overlooked his heroin addiction which he constantly abused himself with. As far as she was concerned, as long as he didn't start to abuse her, it didn't matter what he did, because just as Vamp was stuck on his dope habit, Mink had found herself sprung off the dope-dick. She was only seventeen when she first held the multi-orgasmic experience of having sex with a twenty-seven year old man who couldn't come for hours at a time. Now, two years later, her lust for wild sex had left her in love with, and pregnant by, a straight dope fiend.

Mink heard the knock on her bedroom door, and rolled on her back with a groan. She reached for a pillow to prop underneath her neck, when she saw Jay stick his head through her doorway. "I ain't tell you to open my door," she said, pulling at the bottom of her t-shirt.

"Man, shut the fuck up," said Jay, walking into her room. He was half-dressed with an all black wife beater on, and a pair of Gucci safari shorts hanging loosely around his waist. "How much money you need for Rasheeda's school shit?"

Mink forced herself to sit up as Jay came and sat beside her on the edge of the bed. "I don't know," she said. "It depends on what she wants. Fro real-for real, mama and I basically got everything she and Nadia needs already. We probably just gonna get them some shoes and their hair done. That's about it."

"Don't worry about Nadia, I got her, but what you and mama need?"

"Give me about thirteen hundred."

"Thirteen hundred?! Man, what the hell you gon' buy with all that?"

"Shit, nigga, we still gotta stop by what's-it-name to pick up some stuff for the baby."

"What tha fuck is a what's-it-name, and what kind of stuff you gotta get for the baby, 'cause I thought me and Blood got everything last month?"

"I mean, y'all jive got everything... but I still need some more pampers and Infameal, just to be safe."

"You lying ass hussy." Jay stuck his hand into his sports briefs and pulled out a wad of dollar bills.

"You's a nasty black ass..." she said, watching him count out the money. Mink placed her hand on Jay's thigh and stood up, using him to support her balance. She walked over toward her bureau, looking into the mirror, and started brushing her hair into a ponytail. "I'm ready to get this damn baby up out me!" she lifted her t-shirt to reveal the stretch marks covering her protruding belly.

Jay looked up from the stack of bills he held in his hands to see his sister in her underwear, exposing her pregnancy. Amina Hinton was a beautiful nineteen year old woman. Their father had given her the nickname Mink because of her long silk-like hair when she was a little girl, but that was a long time ago. For, since her coming of age, her name has been accredited to her high fashion status as a ghetto queen, more than anything else, which often placed a small dent in Jay's pocket.

He walked over and tossed the money on top of her dresser drawer. "Man, your titties got big as shit," said Jay, poking his finger at Mink's breast. "You made us buy all those cans of milk, and you already got that shit up in you... that's crazy."

"Boy, get the fuck out my room," she said, snatching the money off her dresser. Counting through the bills, she frowned when she noticed he had shorted her a few hundred. "Hold up nigga." She grabbed the back of Jay's shorts as he turned to walk out of the door. "This ain't nothing but ten-fifty! You said you was gonna give me thirteen, why you gon' renege like that?"

Jay spun around, softly smacked her hands, and said, "Man, get up off me. That's all I got." He took a step backwards to keep her at arm's length in case she tried to grab hold of him again. Jay couldn't keep himself from smiling, seeing the scowl across his sister's beautiful face. "Aight, here's what we gon' do. I'm gonna call Youngblood and tell him to bring the car over so we can take Nadia to the mall. I know slim will have a little extra bread on him, so I'll ask him to look out for you."

"Why you just can't give me the money?" Mink asked, folding her arms across her chest. "You acting all stingy and shit — let me find out that bitch Samiko got your nose open like that. And that nigga Youngblood ain't been around the house in God knows when. Every since the funeral, that boy been acting like he's on some secret squirrel type shit. What's up with that nigga, anyway?"

"Girl, you tripping. Ain't nothing up with Blood — he's just doing him right now, that's all. And Samiko ain't got shit open!"

"Well, I sure can't tell, because you've been acting real funny since you started fuckin' with that hooker. And I know that bitch pussy ain't popping like that."

'She must be going through one of her mood swings,' Jay thought to himself. He pulled his shorts up snugly around his waist, brushed some lint off his tank top, and said, "What difference does it make to you who I'm fucking with or who's pussy is popping?"

Mink was about to respond, but Jay cut her off "For your nosy ass information, I owe Mojo eighteen thousand for that brick he fronted me, so I'm jive fucked up 'til I grind that off But I told you, Youngblood'a look out for you when he come over — what tha fuck you always pouting for when you don't get your punk ass way?"

Mink made a loud smacking sound with her lips and rolled her eyes at Jay. "You niggaz make me sick!" was all she said as she stormed past him, leaving the room and heading toward the bathroom.

"Man, I ain't even use the bathroom yet!" said Jay as Mink slammed the door shut. He walked over to the bathroom, banged on the door with his first, and said "I know you hear me talking to you." He heard the loud flushing of the toilet, and what sounded like Mink laughing in the background. "Don't be fucked up when I start shitting on the floor around this muthafucka."

Jay left the door, walking to his room in the basement. He patted his pocket, feeling the knot of folded up hundred dollar bills. "Seven thousand more..." he said to himself, thinking on how much better he would feel getting out of debt with Mojo. Jay hated owing debts, but eighteen thousand for a kilo of crack during a drought season was a deal any hustler would love too much to pass up.

Chapter 4

Rasheeda sat at the edge of Jay's bed, frantically thumbing the buttons on the control pad of the Super Nintendo. She was so engrossed in the video game that Jay's cell phone had rung four times already before she realized it was ringing. She reluctantly paused the game, and reached underneath a fold in the down comforter to retrieve it.

"Hello," she answered the phone, irritated by the interruption of her game. Rasheeda heard the familiar sound of Youngblood's voice speaking to someone in the background. She had had a crush on her brother's best friend for as long as she could remember. Since they were little children, Youngblood had always seemed to give her the attention she so desperately wanted from her mother and two older siblings. Even now, as her body began its development into womanly form, he continued to shower her with the sought after attention she craved. Except lately Rasheeda's intentions were focused on getting Youngblood to notice her as a little woman, instead of his partner's little sister.

Feeling butterflies in her stomach crawl their way up her chest, Rasheeda cleared her throat and repeated her hello in a tone of voice which she felt made her sound older and sexy.

"Man, who tha hell is this?" Youngblood asked.

"Boy, stop playing with me! You already know who this is."

"Rasheeda?"

"What!"

"Man, stop playing and put Jay on the phone. It's important."

"Jay's upstairs eating breakfast," said Rasheeda, feeling slightly disappointed that Youngblood didn't call to speak to her. "But I can go and get him for you, if you want me to."

"Naw, that's a'ight. Just let him know I'll be around there in like thirty minutes. I got scales in the joint with me, so I gotta drop him off before I head over there, ya dig?"

"I can dig it," said Rasheeda. Thinking to herself, Youngblood swears he's an old timer. She sucked in her cheeks and bit down to avoid laughing into the phone. She didn't want to hear how giddy he made her feel. There was a brief pause of silence on the line, until when she was about to speak, she heard Youngblood asking her what she wanted from the mall. Blushing as she jumped off the bed, Rasheeda propped her hands on her hips and said, "I want that Louis Vuitton book bag they had on display in Georgetown."

"You got that," he said, also promising Rasheeda a brand new pair of Nike Air Maxes if she would promise to give him another rematch in their John Madden football video game. They exchanged threats of who would conquer who, before finally setting on a date for their rematch. Rasheeda was up seven games to his two, and in their last match she had beaten him 41 to 17. Shit was getting serious.

They shortly said their goodbyes to each other, when Youngblood clicked his cell phone off and refocused on his current predicament. Up ahead he saw the traffic slow down as the cars in front of him began stopping at an intersection where the police were directing traffic because of a three car accident a few blocks away.

Youngblood turned and glanced at Scales, who was slouched down in the passenger seat with his head tilted against the window. As Youngblood brought the car to a complete stop, he drew his window down an inch to let some fresh air into the ride. The fumes from the gas canister in the back were starting to make him feel somewhat lightheaded. He turned the volume down on the stereo, and scanned the streets for a possible escape route. If worst came to worst and the cops tried to pull him over, he would just have to shoot it out with them. Surrender was not an option.

Four cars were left in front of Youngblood as they slowly made their way across the intersection. He counted at least twelve policemen around the area, all with a crew of firemen and EMTs. Youngblood reached under his seat and grabbed the Mac-11, placing it on his lap. Thirty-two 9 millimeter caliber bullets were in the clip, and one was already locked in the chamber. 'The first cop who tries to pull me over,' Youngblood thought to himself, 'is going to be the first one to die. Simple as that.'

The car Youngblood was riding in was a champagne colored Acura Legend. In the summer of 1994, Legends were pretty much going out of style — the hustlers' new cars of choice were the Infinity Q45 and the Lexis SC300, but in Youngblood's mind, he could have cared less about the car for two reasons:

1) It was stolen, and 2) he was going to set it on fire.

Earlier that Saturday morning, Youngblood was sitting on the steps of his apartment building smoking a blunt. He had just waked an hour ago, before he started geeking for some weed. He would have preferred to blaze up in the comfort of his own room, but since his grandmother was off from work on the weekends, and she would have raised all sorts of hell if she found out that he had brought any type of drugs, home, let alone smoke some in her place. He decided that it would be in his best interest to take it outside.

Youngblood checked his watch, taking a deep drag from his blunt; it was 8:53 AM. He raised his head and looked off to his right, seeing a car coming down 17th Street in his direction. Since Youngblood's only intention was to chill out front and smoke, he was simply dressed, in a white t-shirt, a pair of Joe Boxers, and some Nike Aqua shoes he wore as bedroom slippers.

It was a common practice for niggaz in the 'hood to wear a tight pair of briefs underneath their boxer shorts so that in the event of the jump-outs hitting the block, niggaz would have a quick stash spot when trying to make a run for it. In Youngblood's case, he wore his because the tight elastic waistband kept his pistol from falling out.

With his right hand, Youngblood pulled his gun out from his underwear, and held it firmly underneath his t-shirt. It was a Smith & Wesson 10mm Still sitting down, he slid over towards the metal handrail lining the steps. Youngblood inhaled another deep lung full of smoke, and plucked the ashes while inspecting the approaching vehicle.

He noticed it was a champagne gold Legend — a kind of luxury sedan niggaz don't use for drive-bys. With the car windows darkened by the limousine tint, it was virtually impossible to see who was driving, and Youngblood wasn't taking any chances. He stood up, placing the pistol behind his back. If needed, Youngblood would simply hop over the handrail, and get to busting off if some shit was to go down. With all of the beefs going on with certain niggaz in his hood, Youngblood couldn't tell who it was who would've wanted to bring him a move, but he would have to worry about that later on.

Youngblood's grip tightened around the 10mm as the car pulled up and stopped in front of Youngblood's building. The driver's front window came down, revealing the driver and another occupant in the passenger seat. It was Mojo and Scales. Youngblood relaxed a little, but decided to keep his pistol in his hand and at the ready. Even though Mojo and Scales were some official niggaz from the hood, it was widely known that Mojo was one of the most vicious snakes around 18th and D. The type of nigga you never knew what he was up to.

"Aye shorty, what the fuck you tripping off? Out here in your drawers and shit," said Mojo, leaning out the car window. He turned around speaking back to Scales who was smoking a cigarette bobbing his head to the music from the stereo. Mojo opened the car door, stepped out and walked over towards Youngblood.

Mojo was in his early twenties, though he looked way younger than what he was. He was six feet even, dark skinned with jet black curly hair, and had a very lean and muscular physique. Mojo looked like one of those dudes from India, and stayed on some pretty boy shit, so when Youngblood saw how he was dressed in a dingy old Dickie's Workman's jumpsuit, his antennas immediately went up.

"What 'cha think you's on Gilligan's Island or something?" said Mojo, smiling, with his tooth pick sticking out of the side of his mouth. He made it up three steps before stopping, when noticing Youngblood's hand behind his back. He knew the boy had a gun on him. "Damn blood, you on some we come strap shit, huh?"

"Naw, slim, it ain't like that," said Youngblood while exhaling a cloud of smoke out of his nose. "But you know how shit is around this muthafucka. I can't afford to let a nigga slip up and catch me slipping, ya dig?"

"I feel you shorty; I feel you... but check this out." Mojo walked up the remaining steps and stood beside Youngblood. He pulled a pack of Juicy Fruit from his chest pocket, popped a stick of gum in his mouth and said, "I got a move for you, if you trying to make a come up."

Youngblood pondered the thought of hitting a lick with Mojo, knowing fully well the type of nigga he would be dealing with. He wished Jay was there with him, so he could get his opinion on whether he should go or

40

not. Since he wasn't, Youngblood went with the first thought that was on his mind — more money. "What kind of move you talking 'bout?"

"Aye shorty, I got a sho'nuff sweet ass lick for you, if you down." Mojo paused, looked over his shoulder, then back to Youngblood. "But I can't say shit unless I know you're in or not."

"Why you hollering at me about this, anyway? We ain't never fuck wit' each other on this type of level before."

"Because I need an extra hand and you the only nigga out here on the block right now. For real-for real, I think you'll see that you was in the right spot at the right time, if you jump on this opportunity."

"Aight, I'm in. What 'cha need me to do?"

Mojo smiled, reaching for Youngblood's blunt. He turned, looking over at his car again, then back at Youngblood, who was now holding his pistol down at his side. Mojo took two pulls from the weed, held the smoke in his lungs for a few seconds, exhaled and said, "I need you to kill that nigga Scales over there."

"You need me to do what?!" Youngblood thought he was tripping, and hearing shit twisted.

"Nigga, you heard me — I need you to slump that nigga for me."

"But I thought Scales was your partner?"

"'was' is the operative word here... Besides, I found out this nigga Scales has been working wit' tha fedz for the past couple of months now. That bitch-ass nigga is a rat, he ain't my partner, so fuck that nigga."

"So if I put the work in, how much you gonna give me?"

"See, that's the sweet part." Mojo said, giving the blunt back to Youngblood. "I just took this nigga on a caper with me last night. We hit some New York niggaz uptown for like thirty-some thousand and a few bricks. So once you take care of this for me, I'ma give you Scales' share of the breakdown."

"And how much is that gonna be?"

"Fifteen G's and a key of hard rock."

"Oh, yeeeah?" Youngblood said, not believing his luck. Just by sitting out front doing nothing, he had stumbled up a hell of a move. He guessed he really was just at the right spot at the right time. "Shit, for fifteen G's, I'll kill that nigga two times for you."

Mojo laughed, spitting the toothpick out of his mouth. "Just once will do." He looked down at the huge pistol in Youngblood's hand and asked, "You want to trade that 10mm for a Mac-11?"

"Hell yeah," he said, taking the clip out of the pistol. He cocked it back to eject the bullet that was lodged in the chamber, and gave the gun to Mojo. He then thumbed the rest of the bullets out of the clip and gave them to him as well.

"I see yo' young ass on point, huh?" said Mojo, inspecting the gun, then tucking it inside his jumpsuit. "The Mac is under the driver's seat. There's also an old Ruger up in the cushion of the driver's seat. That Joint got like four bodies on it, and that's the one I want you to use on slim. Once you handle your business, I want you to take the car to the parking lot behind Spingarn and set it on fire. That car is stolen, so don't let the fedz pull you over, you feel me?"

"I got that," said Youngblood, throwing the blunt, which was now a roach, to the ground. He looked at his watch; it was Eleven minutes after nine. "So where you want me to shoot him at?"

"Do it in the car, but make sure you set him on fire with the car, too. There's a can of gasoline in the trunk. I slipped some sleeping pills in that nigga's beer this morning when we was drinking. He should be real woozy by now."

Youngblood bent over and grabbed Jay's car keys from off the steps, tossing them to Mojo. "Meet me around Maryland Avenue in like forty minutes, and have my shit with you, please."

"Don't even worry 'bout that Blood. I gotcha," Mojo said as he watched Youngblood walk towards the car. "Ain't you gonna put some clothes on shorty?" he asked, wondering if the boy was too high for this move.

"In a minute, I'ma be able to buy some new ones, ya dig?" Youngblood hollered back, winking as he jumped in the car and pulled off. He drove through the upper half of Northeast for at least ten minutes, before Scales somewhat woke up to see Youngblood driving him around. By that time the boy already had the Ruger pointed at his head.

"What tha fuck is you doing, Blood? And where tha hell is Mojo at?"

Scales tried to shake his drowsiness, and clear his mind. He couldn't figure out why he was so tired, anyway.

"Youngblood pulled up at a red light on Montello Avenue. Checking his rearview mirror, and seeing no cars, he said, "cut the radio up and roll your window down."

"Aye blood, please don't shoot me, slim. I got money, coke, weed — fuck, whatever you want you can have. Just please... Don't kill me!"

"Dawg, I'm gonna tell you one more time — cut the radio up, and roll your window down. Don't make me slob yo' ass off in here for bullshitting."

"Okay, okay, okay... you got it! Just please don't kill me." Scales begged as tears began falling from his eyes. He slowly leaned forward to turn the volume up to its maximum capacity, and couldn't believe his luck was that bad — the radio station was WPGC 95, and it was playing I Never Seen a Man Cry, 'Till I Seen a Man Die by Scarface. 'I swear I ain't never gonna listen to another rap song ever again. I'm turning my life over to Jesus.' Scales thought to himself as he rolled the passenger window down.

The traffic light had just turned green when he heard Youngblood's voice saying, "Get 'cha bitch-ass out tha car, now." Scales was about to turn and tell the boy thank you for sparing his life, but quickly decided the sooner he was out of the car, the safer he would be. Scales grabbed the handle on the side of his door, knowing it was already unlocked, but before he even got a chance to pull it open, he heard the loud discharge a second after the bullet tore a chunk out of the back of his skull. Darkness spread like fog; memories faded instantly. 'I always thought I'd be a living legend...' Scales thought to himself — 'it's fucked up I had to die in one...' That was his final thought as his soul journeyed into outer space.

Youngblood shot Scales in the head two more times before rolling the passenger window back up. He then continued to drive around the city, sightseeing in mid-morning with a dead body slumped over next to him. Youngblood had made a stop at a public restroom at an Exxon gas station on his way to Springarn Senior High School. He wiped the passenger side of the car down with an old rag he had found in the trunk, along with the raggedy old sweatshirt he was now wearing, and the gas canister which he threw on the floor in the back of the car.

Now, as Youngblood finally pulled up to the intersection, his paranoia kicked in full throttle. It seemed like it was a million cops on the outside, all looking at the car. Youngblood's palms began to sweat, holding the Mac-11 in his right hand, and the steering wheel in the other. Twenty minutes had passed since he had shot Scales, who was now slouched down in the passenger seat, leaning against the door.

Lucky for Youngblood, the policeman who was directing traffic was too preoccupied with the commotion from the accident. He could barely see the silhouette of the two occupants in the Legend through the dark tinted windows. Normally, the officer would have pulled the driver over to inspect the car — he was hip to the "drug dealers' type of cars, but with the accident, the officer didn't have time, so he just waved the car on.

Youngblood slowly drove off from the intersection, relaxing a little as he leaned back in his seat. He was five minutes away from Spingarn's parking lot, where he would set the Legend on fire with Scales inside it. 'Why would Mojo want to burn up a car behind a high school?' Youngblood thought to himself, though it really didn't make a difference anyway.

He pulled into the parking lot and started pouring the gasoline all around the back seats and on top of Scales. Youngblood stepped out of the car holding the Mac-11 while tossing the Ruger on top of Scales' lap. He struck a match and tossed it into the car — flames ignited instantly. He closed the door, concealing the Mac-11 underneath the old sweatshirt he was wearing and walked the four blocks towards Maryland Avenue, where Mojo was waiting for him in Jay's car. Youngblood hopped in the passenger seat as Mojo pulled off. He looked on the back seat and saw the brown Macy's bag with the money and cocaine wrapped in some clear plastic.

"I bet that's the sweetest move you ever had," said Mojo, heading back towards Youngblood's apartment. "I only pulled you in 'cause I figured you the type of young nigga who could hold his own, and don't be running his mouth and shit."

"You ain't got to worry about that — its death before dishonor with me."

"Oh yeah, death before dishonor, huh?"

"To tha muthafuckin' fullest!"

44

"I see now," Mojo said with a fox-like smile on his face. "You the type of young nigga I can fuck wit — all the way live."

Drama City

Chapter 5

... And I fear that what I'm saying won't be heard until I'm gone
But it's all good 'cause I really didn't expect to live long
So if it take for me to suffer, for my brother to see the light?
Give me pain 'til I die!
But please Lord treat him right

-DMX

At this present moment, I am locked down in my cell, looking in a mirror. It's not really a mirror, just a polished strip of stainless steel welded to my wall. Nonetheless, it has become sort of a ritual that I devoutly stand in front of this thing, as a self-made man admonishing his creator.

To be honest, I can't really explain why I seem to just stare into this mirror the way that I do. Sometimes I guess I do it out of vanity, taking my shirt off and flexing my muscles, imitating Ronnie Coleman posing in a flex magazine. Or maybe it's out of sheer boredom, but once in a while, there are times where I find myself staring in the mirror just to see if I still recognize the person looking back.

Physically, with the exception of a few facial hairs, I practically look the same way I did ten years ago: I still have all of my teeth — which compliments my handsome smile; I don't have any distinguishable scars from acne or injuries on my face; and most noticeably, I definitely do not have a receding hair line. So outwardly, I still might be able to pass for a seventeen year old young man. Yet it is on the inside where I carry the weight of an unrecognizable tethered old soul.

I guess that's one of the numerous adverse effects of being incarcerated — feeling a thousand years older than what you are. I mean, just surviving in here could make you feel like you've lived a thousand lifetimes. Lord knows, if you're condemned to a sentence of life imprisonment without the possibility of parole... it feels like each day you wake up living just to die.

At this present moment, I am locked down in my cell, looking in a mirror. It's not really a mirror, just a polished strip of stainless steel welded to my wall. Nonetheless, it has become sort of a ritual that I devoutly stand in front of this thing, as a self-made man admonishing his creator.

To be honest, I can't really explain why I seem to just stare into this mirror the way that I do. Sometimes I guess I do it out of vanity, taking my shirt off and flexing my muscles, imitating Ronnie Coleman posing in a flex magazine. Or maybe it's out of sheer boredom, but once in a while, there are times where I find myself staring in the mirror just to see if I still recognize the person looking back.

Physically, with the exception of a few facial hairs, I practically look the same way I did ten years ago: I still have all of my teeth — which compliments my handsome smile; I don't have any distinguishable scars from acne or injuries on my face; and most noticeably, I definitely do not have a receding hair line. So outwardly, I still might be able to pass for a seventeen year old young man. Yet it is on the inside where I carry the weight of an unrecognizable tethered old soul.

I guess that's one of the numerous adverse effects of being incarcerated — feeling a thousand years older than what you are. I mean, just surviving in here could make you feel like you've lived a thousand lifetimes. Lord knows, if you're condemned to a sentence of life imprisonment without the possibility of parole... it feels like each day you wake up living just to die.

Throughout my incarceration I have witnessed the effects of the afflicted men slowly dying from a life sentence. Time... which was once the creator of countless opportunities; now becoming the destroyer of young men's' dreams. I struggle to show some compassion, seeing these desperate men cling on to the false hope — praying for some relief on their appeals, but let's be real; I can't be focusing my thoughts and energies on another brother's problems. That's a waste of time — and I have all the time in the world, but no time to waste.

Frankly, I got my own damn issues I have to deal with. I mean, don't get me wrong, I feel for my beloved comrades, as we all suffer the same fate, but what can I do for them? It pains me deeply to be in such a helpless position. It's similar to watching your brother drowning while standing at the water's edge, not knowing how to swim.

I don't make these fake-ass laws — hell, I don't even know all the laws we're supposed to be breaking. All I know is that these so-called "law makers" (congress) and their socially depraved flunkies (the judges), got a vicious hustle going on. And we (blacks) are the ones getting hustled. The average brother in here seems to be more concerned about escaping reality than making a real escape.

Every day I wake up in here, I think about escaping; escaping from the confines of my surroundings; the ignorance; the self-hatred; the weakness. It's almost to the point where every time I go out to the recreation yard, I imagine myself making a run for it and hopping the fence to regain my freedom, but a quick glance at the redneck prison guard holding the AR-15 in the watch tower is all it takes to change my course of thinking.

I swear I never hated anything so much in my life, like the way I hate prison. I hate this place (and everything about it) with a pure and unadulterated hatred, a righteous hatred. An absolute hatred! It sickens me to the core of my inner-most self to see these brother run around in here like they have an Energizer battery stuck up their hind-parts, just having themselves a good ole time (serving time).

In my opinion, we (blacks in America) have completely fallen from grace; imitating the customs of the prevailing culture. We have become a weak race of people due to our ignorance and dependencies on life-diminishing vices. Every day I walk through the compound to see the countless faces of our young black brothers being marshaled to some institutional job by some big fat tobacco-chewing, coward-ass, racist, hillbilly guard whose greatest achievement is landing a job where he can legally torture and torment blacks and get paid for it!

The whole prison scene period, reminds me of those antebellum years where slavery was a common and socially accepted practice to obtain a source of income. It's as if we can't see that the founding fathers of this stolen land drafted a serious blueprint for today's "capitalist devils" to further and continue the exploitation of the black race for cheap labor. The Unicor factories, state owned prisons leasing out inmates to private corporations, and local jails charging inmates who are housed in its facilities... Man, this country is making a killing on our dumb-asses being locked up.

Try explaining this to the majority of these brothers in here and see what happens. Try to take them to the law library to show them a copy of the U.S. Constitution, where it legalizes the servitude (slavery) of a person convicted of a felony. I'm telling you from first-hand experience, a lot of our brothers just don't care — and to be honest, those are the main ones who need to be executed!

You see, I'm not psychopathic or anything like that, and yes, I truly do love my black people, yet it's only out of love that I feel that someone should administer euthanasia to the stagnated portion of our dwindling population to prevent the further contamination of the impressive minds of our young babes with erroneous ideologies. I mean, let's face reality; our black babies are like precious acorns when we plant the seeds of knowledge into their young and fertile minds, but before they can even get a chance to grow into powerful oak trees, the weeds (stagnated negroes) always seem to stunt their growth by choking away their hopes and dreams.

I swear these are some dark times we are living in, as our society is reaching an unprecedented stage of depravity. It seems everybody's on some cut throat type of time — almost to the point where having sympathy and compassion for your fellow brother can be a lethal liability.

Just take a look at the people still living in the ghettos and housing projects in our inner cities. Once upon a time, there was a sense of solidarity amongst our people, as we all were pulled together buy the strings of poverty. "The harder the times, the tighter the bond..." that was the universal mentality of the people living the inner city struggle. As a child, all my friends' mothers were my mother, as my mother was theirs. Everybody was everybody's play brother, sister, or cousin. To sum it all up in a nutshell: even though the way we were living wasn't all the way right, and times were almost always rough, shit was always real!

Nowadays though, it's a completely different story. Everywhere you turn you see the majority of these niggaz today are on some "new wave" shit — that's way beyond me! Sometimes I sit back and wonder who it was who founded this "get-down first" mentality, which is running rampant throughout the projects and prison system. Me personally, if I had to blame someone for this widespread phenomenon that is plaguing my city, it would have to be that hot-ass nigga Rayful Edmond.

I know snitching has been going on since the beginning of time, and Rayful, no matter how much of a rat he is, didn't create this snitching craze. However, he did contribute to that abhorrent cause, which makes him even guiltier than the cowardly punks who follow his filthy footsteps. And to set the record straight, I am not advocating my opinion against snitches, nor do I hate snitches just because some rats snitched on me before. No, I hate snitches with a passion because they (in their selfish attempts to save their own asses) have single handedly destroyed the cohesive structure which once held our beautiful communities intact.

I remember a time when neighborhoods were so close, that when some drama popped off, and the cops came in looking to lock somebody up, you could always run up in somebody else's house and hide until the cops rolled out, especially in the early 80's when I was growing up. Back then, if someone killed a person in your family or a friend, you didn't go and get the police involved. Even if the cops came to you first to question you, because they knew that you knew who did the crime — you never under any circumstances cooperated with the fedz! No, if someone violated to the point where they had to be dealt with, then you took it upon yourself to deal with that individual. That was the law of the land. That was our system of "checks and balances," which maintained the orderly running of our communities. We didn't settle any beefs in the court of law... We held court in the street!

Now what's really mind boggling, is that snitching has become so prevalent these days, that weakness is now permeated throughout the prison system. Niggaz who are known rats are no afforded the luxury of living in prison without the fear of anyone doing anything to their "hot-asses." It's unbelievable! These "new wave" niggaz (young and old alike) in prison and society are accepting these rats in their circles.

For whatever the reason may be: because the rat has a lot of money; or the rat is a cold blooded killer (on some Sammy the Bull type shit), "new wave" niggaz embrace these rats with open arms, but then have the nerve to act like they didn't see it coming when the rats set their ass up.

I tell you, I tell you, I... tell... you! These are some wicked niggaz we're forced to deal with, and things ain't getting any better. I know there's a divergence of opinion when it comes to pinpointing the direct source of this plague, which has all but eroded the central fibers of our once prominent society. Most are quick to blame the crack epidemic as the cause of our fall, others say the younger generation, with their violent music, guns, and drugs.

Me personally, I say the snitches are responsible for the deterioration of our neighborhoods. Just think about it, the majority of the niggaz who told (and in some cases lied) on us, are the same niggaz who grew up with us; Niggaz who used to sleep in the beds with us as kids; Niggaz who were so close to us that if they were to cut their finger, we would start bleeding. These were the niggaz we once loved as brothers. These are the niggaz who get us every time...

Snitching turned crews against crews, hoods against hoods, and family members against one another. Niggaz are literally telling on their own mothers. So you know what they'll do to a brother like you and I. To top that off, these "new wave" niggaz won't even scream on, let along slob one of them hot niggaz off for telling on their men. I swear, these suckers got us real men outnumbered twelve to one. And this whole situation always seems to take me back to one of the many "rules to tha game" my old timers instilled in me.

They always taught me that a gangster always got to keep his foot on a suckers neck because when a sucker gets the upper hand, a real man don't stand a chance! I swear that's true bill.

What's really scary is that these snitches nowadays are so good at blending in, that a rat could be reading my book right now, acting like a straight man. Nodding his head, talking about "I feel what this nigga sayin' — this some real shit." All the while his "hot-ass" is just trying to keep the cheat up off of him. These hot niggaz are vicious.

So if you're a straight man, who came through the ranks of tha game, and know all about the heartaches of betrayal; then the gangster in you will recognize the real. Also, if there's a nigga in your circle who you think is "suspect" — let that nigga read this chapter. If he all of a sudden gets quiet and starts looking funny, then nine times out of ten, that nigga is a rat. If you can get away with it, bust his hot-ass as soon as you get a chance! You just might be saving your own life, wasting his...

Chapter 6

Jay pulled out an old shoe box from underneath his bed when the Channel 7 news reporter appeared on his television. "Breaking news," flashed at the bottom of the screen in bold, bright red letters. Jay was on his knees, kneeling over the shoe box, which was filled with dollar bills bound with rubber bands in 5 thousand dollar stacks.

"We now join Susan Whitfield, who has live coverage of a gruesome discovery." Jay heard the news anchorman say, as the camera switched to the footage of a reporter standing in front of an area sectioned off with yellow tape. Jay got up and worked the TV's remote control to increase the volume. He stared at the image of the reporter, who was an attractive middle-aged black woman, sporting one of those short Toni Braxton haircuts.

"Damn, I need some pussy," said Jay to the television while looking at the reporter, who was now pointing at the remains of some burnt up car. Some young niggaz probably just got tired of joy-riding in a stolen car; Jay thought to himself as he watched the reporter hold a microphone in front of a detective who was standing at her side.

"Detective Bell," the reporter said, "Can you please tell us what happened when you arrived on the scene."

Why yes, ma'am." The detective cleared his throat. "We responded to a call from residents who claimed to have heard an explosion. When we arrived on the scene, we noticed a vehicle was set on fire, so local firemen were dispatched to extinguish the blaze. Once the fire was contained, officers observed what appeared to be the charred remains of a human body in the front passenger seat. The body was burnt beyond recognition, so crime scene investigators will have to compare dental records to identify the victim. An investigation is currently being conducted to apprehend the culprit of this heinous crime. Anyone with information concerning a person or people involved should immediately contact their local authorities or dial (202) 555-TELL. I repeat, (202) 555-TELL. Your cooper-"

Jay cut off the television and sat back down on his bed. "Where the fuck is this nigga blood at?" he thought to himself, checking his watch. Youngblood was supposed to have been at the house twenty minutes ago, so they could go to the mall and finish shopping. Ray-Ray and Rasheeda were still upstairs waiting on Mink, who refused to step one foot out of the house until Youngblood came by and gave her the extra two-fifty Jay had promised her earlier. Shit was getting tense, and it was time for him to get the hell up out of there.

Jay reached in his shorts pocket and pulled out a wad of folded up dollar bills. It was mostly twenties in the small bank roll, as he counted out $1,500, dropping the rest of the money into the shoebox. He closed it, slid it back underneath his bed, and started searching for his cell phone. Jay was checking inside the compartments of his miniature bureau beside his bed, and everywhere else, wondering where he had misplaced it.

Two minutes after he gave up his search, he heard Rasheeda's footsteps as she ran down the basement steps into his room. "Jay, Samiko's on the phone for you," she said, barging through his door with her arm stretched out, extending the cell phone towards him. "And Youngblood just pulled up in front of the house, too."

"What I tell you 'bout taking my phone out my room?!" Jay said as he snatched the phone out of her hand. Rasheeda quickly turned around and bolted back up the steps to avoid one of her brother's vicious tongue lashings. Jay picked up one of his Timberlands boots and launched it at her back. The boot missed her by a few inches, but he still heard Rasheeda scream, "you make me sick — you black-ass dog!"

Jay laughed, placing the phone to his ear. "What's up, Bubble butt?" He said as he put back on his boot.

"Boy, what 'cha doing to that girl over there?" Samiko asked, sounding sexy as ever.

"Man, that lil brat keep coming in here taking shit. She had me looking for my phone, and all that time she had it. She gon' make me suplex her lil' ass fo' real."

"Jameel, leave that little girl alone, you always being a bully," said Samiko, letting out a soft seductive laugh. "Anyway, I just called 'cause I was thinking 'bout 'cha and I wanted to know if I was gonna see you tonight at the Metro Club?"

"What's poppin' at the 'Met' tonight?"

"You know Back Yard throwin' a back to school jam tonight. Everybody's gon' be there. Me, Shawnie, Pepper, and a rack'a other bitches going up there early, 'cause ladies get in free before 11."

"Yeah, I guess me and slim will drop through then... And probably slut out some hoes while we up there."

"Nigga — whatever!" Samiko said, smacking her lips together. "The only hoe you sluttin' out is me. Boy, I can't wait to catch you so I can fuck tha shit out 'cha."

Instantly Jay felt his manhood grow stiff. He had met and ran through a lot of women during the course of his young life, and in his opinion, all pussy was good pussy, but when it came down to Samiko; she shut out every single broad he knew — 'cause she had tha bomb-ass pussy! Samiko was the only young broad he knew who could actually control her vagina muscles to the point where it felt like a tiny fist milking his penis when she got on top and rode him. She was like his personal freak.

Jay had to regain his train of thought, remembering Youngblood was out front waiting on him. It was a little passed 11:00 AM, as he checked his watch again. He grabbed his t-shirt and house keys, making sure everything was straight before leaving. "Aye 'miko, I need you to do me a favor," said Jay as he walked up the basement steps.

"Anything for you, boo. What's up?"

"I need you to do Nadia's hair for school 'n shit."

"Boy, you know that ain't no problem. Just bring her back up here around two something; I'll hook her up on my lunch break."

"Good lookin' out, girl. You a life saver. Oh, by the way, you want something from the mall?"

"Naw, I'm straight boo. Thanks though. Just stop by Ben's Chili Bowl and get me some chili cheese fries and a strawberry milkshake for lunch, when you come by."

"You got that. Well, I gotta go. I'm a holler at 'cha later."

"I love you, boo." Samiko said, making kissing noises into the phone.

"I love you too," said Jay, clicking off the cell phone.

When Jay walked on to his front porch, he saw Youngblood sitting in the passenger seat, playing with Nadia who was already in the back seat wildin' out. Mink was going through another one of her mood swings, and was mad that Youngblood took so long to get there, and was just pulling off Ray-Ray yelled out the window for Jay to make sure he got Nadia taken care of Rasheeda was just looking at him, rolling her big almond shaped eyes.

Jay headed towards his car, thinking to himself that it was time to get a new ride.

The Caprice was cool and all, but niggaz was jive steppin' their shit up. A Benz Station Wagon would be cool right about now, he thought as he opened the door and hopped in. "Nigga, where tha fuck you been at?" was the first thing Jay said, as he readjusted the driver's seat to accommodate his long legs.

"Aye slim, you won't believe what type of shit fell into my lap this morning!" said

Youngblood, still animated from his early morning escapade. He watched Jay put the car into gear; as he began giving his partner a play-by-play account of the events that lead him to being fifteen thousand dollars richer. They were damn near over the 14th street bridge by the time Youngblood finally finished telling him about the lick, but he kept getting mixed signals, as he tried to study Jay's reaction to see if he was flicked up at him for not calling and putting him on point first.

For the most part, Jay seemed rather preoccupied, constantly checking the rearview mirror to see whether or not Nadia was paying too close of attention to their conversation. When they finally passed over the 14th Street Bridge, crossing into Arlington, Virginia, Jay started speaking his mind. "So, you mean to tell me, that shit wit' the burning car and the nigga inside it was your work?"

"All the way live."

"And that nigga Mojo gave you fifteen thousand to hit Scales because he was supposed to be hot, huh?"

"In that order."

"Well, you know I seen that shit on the news already," Jay said, shaking his head as he leaned back into his seat. "The feds said they got a description of a light brown skin young man with short wavy hair leaving the scene that morning."

"Stop bullshittin' slim!" said Youngblood, now sitting straight up in his seat. He searched Jay's face to see if he was just playing and all that — but Jay looked dead serious. "You fo' real, dawg?" Youngblood asked, scratching the side of his neck, which had become a habit of his every time he got nervous.

Jay sensed he jive spooked Youngblood and immediately started laughing. "You scared-ass nigga!" He punched Youngblood in the side of his ribs. "Let me find out your lil ass can't think under pressure."

"Shiiiit, you got me fucked up!" said Youngblood, even though he really felt like kicking himself in the ass for biting into Jay's mind games. "Remember you said pressure may bust pipes, but it also makes diamonds... That's where I'm at. Fuck tha police, I ain't stuntin' they bitch ass."

"Yeah, yeah, yeah," said Jay, placing emphasis on his sarcasm, and waving Youngblood off with his hand. "I feel you champ." Jay made a left turn into the underground parking lot of the Pentagon City Mall, and found a space to park not too far from the mall's front entrance. He placed his T-shirt on, smoothing out the wrinkles, while looking over at Youngblood. He said, "But for real though, next time you pull a move like that, let a nigga know first so I can be on point. Anything could've happened to you, and I wouldn't have known shit 'cause I'm in the blind, ya dig?"

"I can dig it, slim," said Youngblood, knowing Jay was genuinely concerned about his well being. "Next time, no matter how sweet a lick comes my way, I'm going to check wit' cha first. That's my word, but in the mean time, this for you." Youngblood reached underneath his seat, and pulled out a small brown paper, tossing it to Jay.

Jay opened up the bag and looked into it. There was a rack of fifty dollar bills. "What's this for?" he asked, counting seven thousand in the bag.

"I'm just hitting you off Joe, 'cause you's my man," said Youngblood, smiling from ear to ear. "But check this out; you know that eighteen thousand you owe slim for that brick?"

"Yeah, what about it?"

"Why I got that nigga to squash your bill."

"Nigga, stop faking," was all Jay could say as he opened his door and got out. Nadia had already jumped out of the car, and was pacing back and forth, waiting for them to come on. "You serious?" Jay asked Youngblood, while grabbing Nadia's hand and heading towards the mall.

"That's on my mother, slim," said Youngblood, as the three of them walked into Pentagon City Mall.

It took a little over an hour for them to get everything they wanted. Mostly all the bags that were in the back seat with Nadia were Nadia's stuff. Jay brought himself a couple of Hugo Boss outfits, as well as a few pairs of blue jeans and sweatshirts from the Banana Republic and the Gap. He also bought a Coogi sweater for Samiko, even though she said she didn't want anything from the mall. Jay knew Samiko was just running game, acting like she didn't really want anything, and that as soon as he showed up at the hair salon empty handed, he knew she would have copped a vicious attitude. That would have caused a fake-ass argument, which would have lead to her faking on the pussy later on. It was a vicious cycle indeed, when dealing with broads from the 'hood. So to alleviate all unnecessary headaches, he just went ahead and bought her a gift anyway.

Since the noon time traffic was light on their way back from the mall, it only took them twenty-three minutes to get 'uptown,' as they cruised along Georgia Avenue in Northwest D.C. Nadia was climbing all over the backseat, singing her "I love you — you love me" Barney song, which was driving Jay crazy. Youngblood was doing him as usual, leaning out his window hollering at all the young college broads who were attending Howard University.

Jay pulled up to the curb on Georgia and Princeton, and saw Samiko standing in front of the Hair Gallery, talking to one of her girlfriends by the name of Dorey. Youngblood was the first one out of the car, carrying the small bag containing the food they had picked up from Ben's Chili Bowl. Jay picked up Nadia, who was holding the box with the Coogi sweater inside, and carried her to catch up with Youngblood — already trying to shoot his game at Dorey.

Samiko greeted Jay with a kiss on the lips, while scooping Nadia out of his arm, she held the little girl on the hips, and thanks them both for her little gift. She waited until they were all inside the salon, well within the eyesight of every female that was up in there to put on her Oscar-winning performance of exaggerated appreciation. "Oooh, thank you boo!" said Samiko, kissing Jay again. "You ain't have to get me nothing from the mall today," she said, over emphasizing every word, while placing the sweater box on display in the middle of her styling counter.

Jay hated when Samiko would tamma-out' in public like that putting him on the spot, but in this case, he played into her games, letting her shine in her little glory. He knew that by Samiko making a scene, she was also inadvertently making the other broads in the salon jealous, which in turn, made it much easier for him to get some booty from one of her friends, if he ever decided to make a creep move. "Anything for you, boo," said Jay, watching Samiko switch her hips, as she showed Nadia off to the other hair stylists.

Samiko was a 19 year old red bone, with the body of a goddess. She was 5'4, with deep dimples in her cheeks when she smiled. She also had those "cat eyes" that sometimes change colors, with long black hair that always looked wet, which she mostly kept in a pony tail. Samiko was a suburban hood rat from Largo, Maryland who started hanging in D.C. when she was a little girl. She made a name for herself at a young age as being a conservative gold digger who only dealt with major players in tha game. Until, unexpectedly, Jay came into her life stealing her heart, as she found herself actually in love for the first time.

Jay looked around the Hair Gallery, which was actually a medium sized house converted into a salon, and found a group of waiting chairs and took a seat. He was about to flip through a collection of Ebony magazines when he noticed three dudes walking down the staircase off towards his left. Jay recognized one of the dudes as they walked over by the receptionist's desk, where Youngblood was still sitting rapping to Dorey.

"Aye Ned, man, what's up Joe?" Jay stood up so that Ned could see him across the lobby. It had been over three years since the last time he seen Ned up Oak Hill Juvenile Detention Center. Jay was 14 at the time, awaiting trial for a murder case he caught back then. Ned was 17 and was awaiting trial for a body, too. During the early '90's there was a vicious beef between young niggaz from Northwest and Southeast. Basically, the juveniles from Southeast were trying to crush anything that wasn't from the Southside, and by Jay being so little and from Northeast, he would have pretty much got fucked around if Ned didn't look out for him the way he did back then.

Ned walked over to where Jay stood and gave him some dap. "Gotdamn Joe, a nigga ain't seen you in some years!" he said, looking Jay up and down. "I see you jive gettin' it too, huh?"

"Naw slim, I'm just fair for a square, ya dig?" said Jay grinning. He leaned back checking Ned out, who was dressed in a silk Versace shirt, and a pair of crush linen slacks, with some quarter length Gator boots he had imported from Italy on his feet. "But I can see you jive got yourself in the mix."

They sat down and kicked it for a few minutes, reminiscing on their old Oak Hill days, gradually making their way up to their recent accomplishments in tha game. They shared an occasional laugh as they traded a few war stories, and talked about the broads they slutted out. Their conversation went that way for a moment until Ned changed the subject to more serious issues. "Aye slim..." Ned took a quick glance around him to see if anybody was paying attention to their conversation. "Are you hip to a favor for a favor?"

Jay had to think deeply before answering that question. Of course he knew what a "favor for a favor" was, but he also knew what type of nigga Ned was. Ned was one of them First Street Niggaz — and those niggaz was like the mob; putting in work throughout the Northwest area of the city. Jay knew that if he committed himself to a deal with Ned, it was either all or nothing — blood in — blood out. "Yeah, I'm hip to it," said Jay studying Ned's face.

"Cool, 'cause I got a situation that needs to be addressed over there by your end of town."

"On my end of town?" Jay asked, somewhat confused.

"Yeah, 21st and Vietnam."

"Who's tha nigga?"

"Some homosexual-ass nigga named Tracy," said Ned in whisper like tone. "The nigga did some foul ass shit on my man Black, plus he got tha nigga Steve locked up for a triple body on your end."

"As a matter of fact... I know just who you talkin' 'bout." Jay tilted forward resting his elbows on his knees. He was already setting up a move for smashing Tracy in his mind, when he turned and looked at Ned, and said, "a favor for a favor, huh?"

"You take care of this for me, and next time I'll take care of whoever you need me to take care of." Ned stood up and extended his hand. "Is it a deal?"

Jay got up and shook his hand. "When you get tha Washington Post next week, make sure you check tha obituaries in the Metro section."

They walked back to the receptionist's desk where Youngblood and Ned's two homies, Wayne and Stink, were kicking it. Senia, who was a Cuban dime piece came and joined them, as she strolled her way over to Ned, wrapping her arms around his waist. "Aye papi, you ready to go?" said Senia, with her thick Cuban accent.

Ned just grabbed Senia on her ass and headed for the exit. Right before they made it out of the door, Ned turned back to Jay and asked, "Aye slim, y'all try'n a go to tha Will Downing Concert with us tonight?"

"Naw, we partying wit' tha 'BYB' up tha 'Met' tonight,' said Jay, giving Ned the thumbs up.

"Aight slim, but I'm telling you... you keep fucking with them Go-Gos, and you gon' wind up crushing one of them wild-ass young niggaz up in there," said Ned, as he and Senia walked out the door together, followed by Stink and Wayne.

Jay and Youngblood made their way into the lobby to discuss Jay's plans on killing Tracy. Murder really wasn't Jay's thing for real, as he was a pure money getter at heart, but sometimes you just got to accept the fact that, more often than not, in order for a nigga to make a killing, he got to commit one first.

Drama City

Chapter 7

Mink waddled down the basement steps into Jay's room carrying a Nostrom & Taylor shopping bag. She had bought Jay a Nautica outfit and Youngblood a Polo sweatshirt while she did her shopping at the White Flint Mal out in Maryland. It was the least she could do, since it was Jay's money she was spending anyway. Mink tossed the bag on the bed as she walked over to Jay's closet, searching through his stock pile of designer clothes.

Mink knew Jay would have had a fit if he knew that she was in his room ransacking through his stuff, but she had a reasonable alibi — pretending to be just dropping off her gift. Mink's real intentions though, were on borrowing Jay's Donna Karen sweater, as she searched through the closet for it. By Mink being only 5 feet tall, she had a difficult time trying to reach the top shelf where Jay had his sweaters neatly folded. She grabbed an empty hanger, standing on her tip-toes trying to snag the sweater with the hanger's hook.

She almost fell forward, losing her balance, knocking down some shoe boxes that were stacked in the corner. All hell's going to break loose, she thought to herself, when Jay finds out she messed his closet up. She quickly bent over to straighten things up, Mink was working on her third shoe box, placing them all back in order, when she noticed that the one she was holding was particularly heavy, and whatever it was that was inside of it, made the sound of metal rolling and clinking into metal when she shook the box.

Her curiosity got the best of her. She stood straight, removing the top off of the shoe box. A puzzled expression came across her face, looking down at the contents of the shoe box. She saw it was a pistol — a chrome-plated .45 Desert Eagle. There was also a small box of hollow point slugs beside the gun, with a few loose bullets scattered around inside. Mink picked up one of the bullets and closely examined it, seeing the tiny inscription on the back of it saying "Winchester .45 cartridge."

Mink dropped the bullet back into the shoe box and closed the top.

"These crazy-ass niggaz with these big ass guns," she said to herself as she placed the box back into the corner. She picked the hanger off the floor and reached for the sweater again, finally snatching it off the shelf. She stepped out of the closet and checked to make sure everything was neat as possible. Mink closed the door and made her escape back up the basement steps. She didn't give any second thoughts to the gun she found, because she knew all about the bullshit that came along with tha game. What she didn't know, was what that gun was used for two months ago... and who used it.

Jay and Youngblood pulled up into the alley around 18th & D, smoking a Back-wood. They had bought some 'Hydro' weed from around 10th & W on their way back from the hair salon. Youngblood was geeking to smoke as usual, but had to wait until they first dropped Nadia and their stuff off at the house. It was worth the wait though, Youngblood thought, feeling the burning sensation in his throat. Only after a couple of hits off the Backwood he was blitzed already, as he passed the joint to Jay and got out of the car.

They walked out of the alley into the dying rays of the mid-evening sun, and were greeted by a smorgasbord of niggaz on the block. It was 7:37, and the 'hood was live and pumping! Crack heads were everywhere and niggaz were just doing their thing, getting their hustle on. Jay and Youngblood crossed the street and walked over to Mamasan's Economy Market, where Lil' Pat, Fat Derrick, and tha Twinz, Lil' Derrick and Darryl, were standing smoking a blunt.

"What's up Joe?" said Lil' Derrick, as he smiled and blew a heavy stream of smoke out of his nose.

"Ain't shit slim," said Youngblood, cocking his head, giving the Twin that curious look. Youngblood was high as all outdoors himself, but he wasn't so high that he couldn't tell the smell of the shit they were smoking. "I thought you said you wasn't gon' smoke no more Love-Boat? After the last time you lunched out and shot that nigga in the face 'cause you thought his dreadlocks was trying to eat you."

"Aye slim," said Lil Derrick stretching his eyes open wide as they could go, "that nigga dreads turned into snakes fo' real that day!"

"Nigga, you trippin'" said Jay laughing. He passed the Backwood to Lil' Pat who wasn't high off the PCP yet. "Here shorty, you don't need to be

64

fucking wit' that shit they got." Lil' Pat who was the young gun of the crew took the joint and was about to say something, but Fat Derrick cut him off

"Man, fuck that shit — we tryin'a see Elvis!"

"Nigga, your fat-ass gon' fuck around and get one of them young niggaz stuck up Saint Elizabeth," said Jay shaking his head.

"Yo' Mutha!" Fat Derrick shot back, throwing up his hands in a boxing stance. That was all it took for him and Jay to get into their regular slap boxing bouts.

Youngblood, Lil' Pat, and the Twinz all started laughing as they walked off, heading over to Dumb Wayne's apartment, which was the first building on the 1800 block of D-Street. They were all posted up on the front steps, when Lil' Pat buzzed the intercom to Dumb Wayne's place. It took like 3 minutes for somebody to answer, when they finally heard the voice of Dumb Wayne's sister, Sherry, asking, "Who is it?"

"It's me, open up," said Lil' Pat in between coughs, choking on the hydro.

Sherry buzzed open the building's front door and they all walked into the hallway. Dumb Wayne's apartment was on the first floor, so as soon as they entered the building, Wayne's door was right there to their right. Sherry was already standing in the doorway wearing a long t-shirt, with nothing but a pair of panties on underneath, when they all made it to the door. She just stood there blocking their entrance into the apartment, looking at them all, shaking their head.

"Ya'll don't make no muthafuckin' sense," said Sherry as she put her hands on her hips. "You niggaz always be coming up here when I got company."

"Who up in there?" Darryl asked in his usual aggressive tone.

"Ebony and them from up Langston Terrace."

"Oh yeeah!" said Youngblood, as he tried to make his way into the apartment, but Sherry wouldn't budge. "Man, what tha fuck is up wit' cha?"

"I'm tryn'a hit that joint y'all smoking on first," she said, reaching for the Back-wood that was in the corner of Lil' Pat's mouth.

"Man, move your geekin' ass out the way!" Lil Pat yelled, pushing Youngblood past Sherry, as the boys all bum rushed the door. Once inside they saw Ebony, Tameka,

Pooh, Leia, and Kim; all sitting on the couch drinking Moet, grooving to the sounds of Rare Essence pumping out of the stereo. The girls were a part of the Hechinger Mall Honeys, which was a clique of broads from various parts of the Northeast area. The Hechinger Mall Honeys were ghetto celebrities on the Go-Go Scene, and were well known throughout the city, especially for being some vicious set-up artists.

Tameka saw Youngblood walking towards her, so she got up and met him half way. She walked straight up to Youngblood and started kissing him on the mouth. With no hesitation, he kissed her back, tasting the sticky sweetness of the Moet on her tongue.

"Boy, I was waitin' over here for a minute for you to show up," said Tameka, taking him by the hand and leading him into the bathroom.

"What 'cha waitin' on me fo'?" asked Youngblood.

"I'm a show you in a minute," she said, pulling him into the bathroom and closing the door. Tameka's hands went straight for Youngblood's belt buckle, pushing herself up against him. "You know I seen you get out that car earlier this morning up Springarn."

Immediately Youngblood's antennas went up. "What 'cha talkin' 'bout 'Meka?" he asked, pushing her backwards a little.

"Blood, I seen you get out that legend this morning. I was standing on the hill of 21st Street, walking my pitbull when I saw you set the joint on fire. And I know that bitch-ass nigga Scales was the one burnt up in it, 'cause I seen it on the news later on where they identified the body... but fuck that nigga!"

This bitch seen too much, Youngblood thought to himself, and started plotting on ways he could kill her and get away with it. "So who you told about this?" he asked.

"Come on now," Tameka folded her arms across her chest. "You know I know how to mind my own business, so I ain't gon' say shit to nobody, but the reason I came over here is because I wanted to know if you still got the gun you shot'em wit?"

66

"If I got what?!" shouted Youngblood. "Bitch, what tha fuck is you wired or something?"

"No, no, just listen," Tameka quickly explained. "When I was a little girl, that nigga Scales raped me and took my virginity. I hated that nigga ever since, and prayed he get killed on a long ass time ago. So when the news people said that Scales was shot to death and then burnt up, I knew you did it, and I wanted to see if you still had the gun you used."

"What' cha worried about the gun fo'?"

"Because I want to buy it and use it for my personal dildo."

"You wanna do what?" Youngblood said, not believing what he just heard.

"Nigga, you heard me," said Tameka, with a dead serious look in her eyes. "I wanna get flicked wit tha gun you used to kill Scales with."

"Hold up fo' a minute." Youngblood bolted out the door and ran straight for Dumb Wayne's room. He was excited by the fact that he was going to get some booty from Tameka, but also saw himself more turned on by her crazy-ass freak fantasy. Youngblood busted into Wayne's room, where he found Dumb Wayne masturbating off a Black Tail magazine.

Startled by the sudden intrusion, Wayne jumped off the bed and covered himself with a sheet. "Gotdamn Joe! You bust up in here like the muthafuckin' bodines n'shit!" said Wayne, as he put on a t-shirt.

"Nigga what tha fuck yo' dumb ass doing?" asked Youngblood, walking over to

Dumb Wayne's dresser, checking the drawers for a gun. "You got a house full of hoes in tha living room and you in here jerkin' off. What tha fuck you think you down Lorton or something?"

Niggaz in the hood nicknamed Wayne "Dumb Wayne" because he was the type of dude who had all the wrong answers for every situation. Always coming up with some type of philosophy for why he did what he does. Today was no exception. "Naw nigga!" he said, sitting back on the bed, flipping through the freak magazine. "I'm 'bout to get some pussy from Pooh in a minute, but first I wanted to bust a quick nut now, so that when I do start fuckin' her, it'll take me longer to skeet next time, ya dig?"

Youngblood stopped in the middle of his search, and turned and looked at Wayne, "you really is dumb as shit, huh?"

"Man, ya'll niggaz keep sleepin' on me Joe, but why you think the hoes keep sweatin' a nigga." Dumb Wayne smiled, feeling proud of himself for coming up with another bright idea. The whole time he was watching Youngblood rummage through his stuff, but just now noticing what he was doing. "Gotdamn Joe, what tha fuck you lookin' for?"

"I need a joint."

"What's up nigga, you aight?"

"Yeah I'm aight, I just need to borrow a joint real quick."

"Here." Dumb Wayne reached underneath his pillow and pulled out a Glock .40. He tossed it over to Youngblood, who caught it with both hands.

"Thanks slim, I'll bring it back in a minute." Youngblood headed back towards the bathroom, thinking about the Ruger which was the real gun he used to kill Scales with. She'll never know, he thought to himself, laughing at how crazy the whole situation was. Youngblood opened the door and found Tameka butt-ass naked, sitting on the edge of the sink.

"Is that it?" asked Tameka, looking at the Glock in his hand.

"Yeah, that's it, so what's up?" Youngblood stepped into the bathroom and closed the door.

Tameka placed her left hand against the wall and stretched her right leg out, placing her foot on the edge of the bathtub. She scooted her ass forward and leaned her back against the medicine cabinet. "I want 'cha to fuck me wit' it," said Tameka, positioning her vagina to where he would have full access to it.

With his left hand, Youngblood spread Tameka's vulva (pussy lips) apart and saw the pink tender flesh of her insides. She let out a deep moan, as he slid the barrel of the gun into her vagina with his right hand. Youngblood eased the gun in and out of Tameka's vagina, not trying to get too worked up. Since the Glock didn't have a safety switch, he didn't want to get too excited, and wind up shooting her before he could actually hit the booty.

68

But it was beyond his power to control himself, as Tameka started going crazy, climaxing from the rigid motion of the gun barrel's penetration. Her orgasm was deep and powerful, causing her vaginal juices to overflow down the shaft of the gun. Tameka was like a woman possessed by a sex crazed demon, as she grabbed Youngblood's hand, pulling the gun out of her vagina and putting it into her mouth. She began sucking on the Glock as if it were a big black plastic dildo, enjoying the taste of her own sex juices in her mouth.

That was too much for Youngblood to take. He immediately snatched down his pants and underwear in one quick motion. His manhood was so hard; it felt like a bar of black steel, as he slammed all eight inches into her tight, wet pussy. Tameka wrapped her legs around Youngblood's waist, while he frantically pumped his love muscle into her piping hot vagina. With each powerful thrust he went deeper inside Tameka, forcing her to cry out in ecstasy, digging her nails deep into his back. If it wasn't for the loud Go-Go music coming from the stereo in Dumb Wayne's living room, everyone in the whole house would've heard Tameka moaning like a wild animal.

Youngblood could tell she was about to have her second orgasm, because her vaginal muscles constricted around his penis. He couldn't hold off much longer himself, as he felt his testicles tightening, preparing him to shoot his load. Youngblood started machine-gun fucking Tameka, grabbing her by the hips and slamming into her with brute force. The overwhelming sensation of his climax was just too much It caused his knees to slightly buckle, as he busted his nut inside her.

Instantly, Tameka felt the waves of her orgasm flush through her body, sinking into the delirium of erotic please. She held onto Youngblood with her hand around the back of his neck, while grasping the Glock .40 in the other. Tameka was so into her climactic episode that she didn't even pay attention to the fact that she was holding the gun with her finger wrapped around its deadly trigger. She accidently squeezed it, causing the Glock to go off, knocking a huge chunk of plaster out of the bathroom wall.

Youngblood jumped back, damn near tripping over his pants that were still around his ankles. He bent over, cupping his hands over his ears, as the gun's loud discharged had his ears ringing something terrible. Dumb Wayne busted into the bathroom suddenly, holding a Mossberg 10 gauge pump action shotgun. "What tha fuck y' all doing in here?!" he yelled, pointing the shotgun at Tameka's head.

Youngblood stood straight, pulled his pants back up to his waist and said, "This crazy-ass bitch done flicked around and shot a hole in the wall." He quickly snatched the Glock .40 out of her hand, knowing how mad broads got when a nigga called them a bitch to their face.

"I ain't mean to shoot that joint in here," said Tameka, jumping off the sink, getting into Youngblood's face. "But don't be calling me no bitch, either!"

"Bitch, shut up," he said, kissing her in the mouth. "You know I love you."

Tameka scooped her clothes off the floor, and looked up at Youngblood. "I want 'cha to be my boyfriend, then."

"You for real?"

"Yeah, I'm for real!"

"Aight then, so from now on, you my girl... I'm cool wit' that," said Youngblood, placing his arm around her shoulders. "But first, I need to talk to you about faggy Tracy up 20 Street."

"What about him?"

"We'll talk about it in a minute," said Youngblood, walking Tameka out of the bathroom, and heading towards Dumb Wayne's bedroom.

Dumb Wayne was still standing in the bathroom holding the 10 gauge, trying to figure out what the hell just transpired before his eyes. He looked at the big ass hole in his bathroom wall, and then looked back at Youngblood and Tameka walking into his room. "I know one muthafuckin' thing," he said, coming up with another one of his bright ideas, "somebody gon' give me some pussy fo' this bullshit here. That's fair exchange!"

Chapter 8

> Open yo' muthafuckin' eyes
> You see a nigga standin' over yo' bed, bitch surprise.
> It's time to pay yo fuckin' tithes
> And him being the bitch that he is, he cries
> It ain't no muthafuckin' mercy
> It's over fool
> You gots to die you muthafucka
> You broke the rule
> And that's the reason I've been sent here
> So now you feel the presence of death
> Because I'm in here...
>
> -Scarface

J&W was a small convenience store right off the corner of D Street. Ms. Julie Ann had first opened the store up back in the early 70's for the neighborhood kids, so they could have a safe place to hang out and kick it. It was sort of a ghetto sanctuary for the children trapped in the violent and heartless streets — a type of safe haven where kids could go and just be kids, but nowadays, two decades later, J&W had become the local hangout sport for the neighborhood dope dealers, peddling their heroin in the alley beside the store.

Preacher-man stepped outside the store and stood on the front, holding a 22 oz. can of Red Bull in a brown paper bag. The beer, a pack of Kools, and the Slim Jims were all he had to his name since he spent the last five dollars he bummed from a fellow dope fiend. The past few months were rough on old Preacher-Man, being 42 years old, he wasn't really an old man yet, but the hard life of being a heroin addict added a few extra years to his haggard appearance. His body was still in good shape though, muscular and cut-up from all those years of working out behind "The Wall" (Lorton Maximum Security Facility). Yet mentally, the stress of living in the "free world" was beginning to take its toll.

71

Drama City

Down at Lorton, Preacher-Man had everything a convict could want. Prison guards would bring him in street food, he kept cartons of cigarettes, and had a vicious fat girl named Andrea who smuggled in 20 balloons of dope for him every visiting day, but now, since his release from prison, shit just ain't been going his way. He had been on the "bricks" for five months after doing 14 years straight in Lorton's prison system. Preacher-Man was supposed to have been released from prison 11 years ago, since he was originally serving a 1 to 3 year sentence for a simple assault, back in 1980, but he ended up stabbing a dude to death on "the hill," and took a "cop" to man slaughter out in Alexandria, Virginia.

By him maxing out on his prison sentence, Preacher-Man was off "papers" and didn't have to go through the hassles of seeing a parole officer. This basically meant that he had a free pass to get high as the sky without the fear of catching a violation. Preacher-Man started walking up the street where he saw Jay standing on the block talking on the payphone. Everybody in the 'hood had their own personal cell phones they used to conduct their daily activities, but the D Street pay phone was used for the homies that were locked up down at Lorton and over at D.C. Jail, so they could call on the block and holler at whoever they wanted to speak to.

Jay was talking to his man Ernest on the payphone when he saw Preacher-Man walking his way, but he was too wrapped up in his conversation to pay him any mind. Ernest, who was an official "head buster" from D Street, was telling Jay how he and his partner "Tre" had punished some bammas for fakin' behind "The Wall." Ernest then told him about the rumors he had been hearing that were floating around Lorton. The word on the prison yard was that some niggaz from 18th and D had robbed and killed New York Steve up at 14th and W Northwest, and came off with a hundred thousand in cash, and twenty seven "bricks."

Since that was the first time Jay heard about that, he simply dismissed it as being just a rumor, and told Ernest that he didn't know anything about that. They talked for a little while longer before Jay ended the conversation, by promising to send Ernest a $500 Money Order and some naked flicks of some stripper broads from the Zulu Cave. Jay hung the phone up and was about to walk off, until he noticed the tall lanky shadow of a person off to his right side. He stopped and looked over his shoulder, seeing the disheveled appearance of a man dressed in old army fatigues.

It took a few seconds for Jay to recognize Preacher-Man, being that it had been 14 years since he had last seen him, but when his memory finally kicked in, Jay stood in shocked disbelief — he was standing face to face with Youngblood's father. Jay immediately thought back to the childhood stories he heard about Preacher-Man being a cold blooded killer back in the day. During the '70's, in the era when niggaz ran the streets in gangs, and dominated one another with their fists, Preacher-Man was a one man killing machine, ruling the hood with his .38 revolver.

"Gotdamn slim, when tha fuck you get out?" Jay said smiling. He gave Preacher a hug, and then took a step back, looking him up and down. "Man, Youngblood gon' trip out when he find out you home."

Preacher-Man looked at Jay with a dejected expression on his face, knowing the embarrassment his son would feel seeing him the way that he was. "I swear time flies... I remember when your lil butt was in pampers. Now you a grown man. Uhh, uhh, uhh... I swear time flies."

"How long you been out?"

"About five months."

"Gotdamn Preacher, you should'a been came around and holered at a nigga! 'Specially Youngblood, you know slim would want to see you."

"I know shorty," Preacher Man shrugged his shoulders and took a swig from his beer. "Lord knows I do. But I can't let my boy see me like this. Just look at me! I'm a muthafuckin' dope fiend... But I got too much pride to be actin' like one, ya dig? I was just creepin' thru tha neighborhood tryin'a catch a glimpse of my son, I wasn't gon' show myself. Not until I get myself straight first, ya dig'?"

"I feel you slim," said Jay, genuinely understanding where Preacher Man was coming from. By his own climb through the ranks, Jay saw many prominent street personalities fall to the wayside, while still trying to hold on to their former titles. One deep look into Preacher Man's dark eyes told Jay that he wasn't the average "has been." Jay reached into his pockets, and pulled out a thick wad of folded up dollar bills. He peeled

73

off $500 and put it into his pocket, while giving the rest of the bank roll to Preacher Man. "If you love Youngblood like a father supposed to love a son, then you'll get yourself together. But now since you took this money, you can never say you wasn't given an opportunity to do my partner right."

Preacher Man took the money, which was a little over seven thousand, and put it in his pocket. He was kind of flicked up, thinking back on the time when he used to be the one giving Jay little dollar bills when he was a kid, but times have changed, and by the look of things, it was definitely Jay's time to shine. Preacher Man pulled Jay to him and gave him a firm embrace. When he finally let Jay go, he looked him in the eyes and said, "I need you to do me one more favor."

"What's that Preach?"

"Promise me you won't tell Blood you seen me today."

"Come on Preacher Man... You know I can't do that shit."

"Look shorty; just do this for me, please."

"Man, aight," Jay puffed up cheeks blowing out a sigh of resignation. "I gotcha slim."

"Good lookin' out baby" said Preacher Man, as he turned around, heading back down D Street. He just barely made it into the alley when Youngblood pulled up to the corner in an Eddie Bauer edition Bronco. Jay was still at the phone booth lost in thought, so Youngblood had to honk the horn to get his attention. Jay snapped out of his trance, seeing his man waiting for him, and he ran up to the truck and jumped in.

Sitting in the driver's seat, Youngblood looked way too young to be driving the huge truck. Luckily for them, the Bronco's windows were tinted, so the cops wouldn't be able to tell who was driving in the event that they got pulled over. Jay had bought the Bronco a year ago from one of the dudes around the 'hood named Kevin Ray. The Eddie Bauer edition was a rare truck in the city, and there weren't too many niggaz hip to them. Those were the main reasons why Jay bought it, but all in all, he didn't really care for trucks and was going to give it to Youngblood for his birthday next month.

They rode through the neighborhood while Youngblood told Jay all about him getting some booty from Tameka, and about how she shot a hole in Dumb Wayne's wall. He also informed Jay about how he set up a move where Tameka would bring Faggy Tracy up the Metro Club tonight. They went over a few more details on how the hit was to be carried out, and though Jay gave Youngblood credit for coming up with a decent plan to kill Tracy, he made sure that he himself, and not Youngblood, was the one to be doing the killing.

Youngblood started tinkering with the buttons on the CD player trying to switch to the McEight We Come Strap CD, when all of a sudden Jay just blurted out, "you know I seen yo' father back around the way before you pulled up." Jay knew he promised Preacher Man that he wouldn't tell Youngblood, but he just couldn't keep any secrets like that from his partner.

Youngblood casually looked over at Jay as if he didn't hear a word he had just said, and asked "you tryn'a pick up some smoke before we stop by Black's joint?"

"Yeah, we could get a couple of bag around Trinidad."

"In that order." Youngblood pressed the play button on the CD player, listening to the first track to the We Come Strap disc. He turned the volume up and started nodding his head to the violent melody of Niggaz That Kill; setting the stage for the upcoming event.

Down in Black's basement, Jay and Youngblood had changed their clothes and were chilling on the couch with Joyce, Samantha, and Bernadette. They were all smoking the weed they had bought, while just tripping off one another, enjoying their high. Black Andre, Levar, Lil' Pat, and Lil' Freddy were all scattered about doing what they do best — arguing over who was getting the most pussy out of the crew.

It was 12:47 a.m. when they heard a car honking its horn in front of the house. Black checked out the basement window and saw a mob full of niggaz sitting in two cars double parked in the middle of the street. Dressed in all black, Jay and Youngblood were the first ones out of the house, heading over to where the two cars were parked. Shank was driving a money green Delta 88, and had Ugly, DJ, Fat Derrick, and the Twinz all riding with him. While Jug Head was parked in front of them with Skip, D. Brown, KD, and Petty Rob all inside a white LTD.

They were all official niggaz from the 'hood, ready to represent their block in the club as party and bullshit was the theme of the night.

Everybody said their "what's up Joes" and kicked it for a minute before Jay and Youngblood hopped into the Bronco, along with Black, Lil' Pat, Levar, and Lil' Freddy all jumping in the back seat. Jay put the truck into gear and drove off, following Shank, and Jughead back around the strip. They all stopped in front of Dumb Wayne's building where Fat Larry, Mojo, and Big Ben were sitting on the front steps sipping on some Remy XO.

Levar rolled down the Bronc's side window and yelled at his cousin Fat Larry; "what's up nigga, you partyin' or what?"

"Nigga, once in tha yard... always in the yard!" said Larry throwing up his middle finger.

"Well, bring yo' fat ass on then," said Youngblood, jumping out of the truck and running across the street. He quickly ran into the alley to where Jay's Caprice was parked, and popped the back of the trunk open. Inside, underneath the spare tire were two pistols wrapped in an old blanket. Youngblood grabbed the AP-9 and .357 Bulldog, tucking them both into the front of his jeans while shutting the trunk with his elbow. He ran back to the Bronco and jumped in, while noticing that Mojo was the only one still sitting on the front steps. "What's up slim, you ain't partyin' up the Met' tonight?"

"Shorty, you know I don't fuck wit' that bamma ass Go-Go shit," said Mojo, taking another sip from his drink. "I'll just see y'all niggaz in the morning or something."

"Cool, I'll holler at 'cha." Youngblood closed his door as Jay pulled off, catching up with the cars in front of them. Ten minutes later, Fat Larry pulled up behind them in a cream colored Lexis LS 400, while they were waiting at a traffic light on Bladensburgh Road. Big Ben, Lonnie, Lil' Al, and Tay were all riding with Larry, smoking on a Back-wood jamming to the sounds of McRen's *In the Alley*, pumping from the car stereo. About the time that they made it up Bladensbugh's hill, the boys from 18th & D were a four car entourage, ready to party with the stars.

Arriving at the Metro Club, everybody could see the small crowd still waiting to get in as Jay found a parking space directly across the street from the joint. They all got out of the truck except for Jay and Youngblood, who were pretending to be stashing their drugs underneath their seats. As soon as the rest of the boys were away from the truck,

Youngblood passed Jay the .357 and stepped out of the car. He took a quick look around him to make sure there was nobody watching him, and bent down and stuck the AP-9 inside the Bronco's front fender placing the gun on top of the tire.

Youngblood knew all about how some young niggaz would ride around the clubs and wait until everybody was inside, then start breaking into niggaz cars searching for guns, and he didn't trip — he just left his door unlocked so a nigga wouldn't have to bust a window out to get inside the truck just in case they wanted to check it out for guns or what not. Shit like that just came along with the whole club scene, Youngblood thought to himself, thinking back on when he used to do the same thing when he was like 12 or 13 himself.

Youngblood checked out the Bronco one more time to make sure everything was straight before running over to where Jay was standing in the midst of a mob full of thugged out looking females. As Youngblood made his way beside his partner, he saw Jay pass the .357 off to Francine 'Tha Disco Queen,' who had come out to party with the Fairmont Street Honeys. By the .357 being a small, compact, snub-nosed revolver, Francine easily hid the gun inside the crotch area of her panties, concealing the guns imprint through her spandex tights with the bottom of her long black t-shirt.

Jay stood behind Francine with his arms wrapped around her waist, occasionally rubbing his hands up her stomach and copping a feel on her big firm titties. She was talking to him about how he needed to stop faking and take her out on a date, while pressing her ass cheeks hard against his manhood, being the sex tease that she was known to be. When they finally approached the front entrance of the Metro Club, Jay took a step back and watched Francine work her magic on the security staff posted up by the door.

She stepped into the club and paid the $20 admission fee, seeing Re-Run, who was the head bouncer, licking his lips in anticipation waiting to pat her down. She walked over to Re-Run, placing her hands on her hips and said, "you got one or two choices — you can either pat me down now and forget about ever taking me out... or you can let me go straight in and pat me down later at your place."

Re-Run looked like a contestant on Jeopardy, trying to figure out if she was being for real or not. "Don't be bullshittin' me Francine," he said with a fat faced cheesy smile, letting her walk right past him untouched. Jay and Youngblood were right behind her after being searched by some other bouncers in the lobby. They made it through as usual without any hassle, although Youngblood was jive mad he had to pay an extra $20 for being under aged and having no ID.

They stepped into the dance hall where Francine was waiting for them, swaying to the rhythm of the Back Yard Band's Socket Beat. She was already feeling the sexually charged energies coursing through the club as she started freaking on Jay while slipping him the .357. Jay leaned his head forward placing his nose to the gun, smelling the pungent odor of her womanhood. "Boy, you nasty!" said Francine with a laugh, and giving him a kiss on the cheek before walking off to join the rest of her girlfriends from Fairmont Street.

Jay and Youngblood walked over to the bar, surveying who and what neighborhoods were up in the joint, knowing that certain niggaz from D Street had little beefs with other niggaz from different 'hoods, but for the most part, niggaz from all over the city were partying tonight, and they intended on doing the same. Youngblood spotted Roy, Dat and J.R. from Langston Terrace and got them to order him a Zombie, since the bartender was faking on not serving him any alcoholic beverages.

Youngblood gulped down his drink as he strolled over to where Fat Derrick and the Twinz were at, kicking it with some broads from Montana Avenue. He said "what's up" to everybody and was about to start rapping with a few of the girls himself, but he saw how Derrick and the Twinz were still lunching off the PCP, he decided that it would be wise to just get the hell away from them crazy ass niggaz. Youngblood grooved his way through the crowed, sneaking a feel on every girl's ass as he walked by. The club was so packed that they couldn't tell who was grabbing their asses, but most of them didn't care anyway, since everybody was just freaking everybody.

The ladies were out in full force tonight, as Youngblood saw the different crews of females all scattered about in the joint. The Ice Cream Honeys, Bubble Gum Honeys, Hechinger Mall Honeys, and 1st & Kennedy Street broads were all doing their thing, but Youngblood had his eyes set on dancing with Porsche, who was a real dark skinned beauty, representing a crew of females that called themselves Tha Good Pussy Hoes. He was about to make his move, when he suddenly felt someone grabbing at his shoulders. Youngblood turned and saw his man A.B. from 7th & Taylor dancing with a broad.

"What's up moe," said A.B., shouting over the loud Go-Go music. "You partying or what?"

"What it look like?!" Youngblood laughed, giving A.B. some dap. "I'm 'bout to holler at that broad over there in a minute, ya dig?" he said, pointing over to Porsche. "That bitch phaaat as shit Joe, and you know—"

The girl who was dancing with A.B. cut Youngblood off, "Boy, you'll be wasting yo' time wit' that bitch over there!" she said, rocking to the music and pointing her finger to herself, "You need to be fuckin' wit' us if you tryn'a party fo' real."

"Who the hell is us?" asked Youngblood, looking her up and down. The girl automatically stopped in the middle of her dance and turned around, bending over, revealing the letters N.B.A. Honeys that were written across the bottom of her Parasugo jeans. Taking a good look at the girl's big, round, pear shaped derriere; he waited until she faced him again and then asked, "What the fuck is N.B.A. Honeys?"

"N.B.A. stands for Nothing But Ass Honeys!" the girl said, rolling her sexy eyes at him. "Nigga, you better get hip."

"Aight shorty, you got that," said Youngblood giving A.B. the thumbs up. "I'ma catch back up wit' y' all after I hit the bar again." Youngblood was working on his second Zombie when he caught sight of Tameka talking to Trina-boo from the Simple City Honeys. He quickly squeezed his way through the crowd, sliding over to where Tameka was standing, and pulled her to the side.

"Boy, I was lookin' all over for you!" said Tameka, wrapping her arms around his shoulder in a tight hug. "You know the nigga Tracy is out front wit' Faggy William. They in a U-Haul truck looking for a parkin' space right now."

"Oh yeeeah, good lookin' out Joe." Youngblood handed Tameka the rest of his drink, giving her a quick kiss on the lips before leaving to search for Jay. Feeling the alcohol from the Zombies kicking in, it took Youngblood a minute to find Jay, who was in a corner spot of the club, freaking on Samiko. Back Yard's lead rapper, Big "G" had just started hitting "Put tha Spotlight on the Butt Cheeks," when Youngblood walked up behind them both. Samiko was letting it all hang out, pulling down her tights, showing off the Victoria's Secret thong she was wearing while freaking Jay as if she was really having sex.

Seeing how Samiko and all the rest of the broads were going hard on the dance floor, Youngblood almost forgot about Tracy being outside until he saw the imprint of the .357 tucked in the back of Jay's pants. That snapped him back to his original train of thought. "Aye slim, the nigga outside right now!" said Youngblood, pulling Jay by the arm, interrupting him and Samiko's little freak session.

Jay immediately stopped dancing, understanding exactly who Youngblood was referring to. "I'm' a go check out the scene, ya dig?" he whispered into Youngblood's ear. "If everything's cool, I'ma' take care of hoe outside. But if shit ain't right, I'm just gon' lay on 'em till after the joint let out. Either way, y'all niggaz gon' have to ride back around tha way in Samiko's joint, ya dig."

"Shit, I ain't trippin' off that, but Tameka told me the nigga is in a U-Haul wit' faggy William, so you might need me to roll wit' 'cha slim."

"Naw, I'm straight... just make sure shorty get home alright, aight." Jay said, looking over at Samiko. He pulled her close to him, telling her how he had to roll out and take care of some urgent business. Samiko got upset like she always do, pouting her lips in that little girl fashion, but Jay promised to take her out to dinner at Planet Hollywood, so she quickly got over her little attitude.

Jay slid his way through the crowd, focusing his thoughts on how he could trick Tracy into a death rendering situation. Once he made it out of the dance hall, Jay saw Faggy William in the lobby room doing his gay-ass faggy-dance while waiting on Faggy Tracy to come into the club. Jay walked over to William, smiling his million dollar smile, and said "how many licks does it take to get to the creamy center of a Tootsie Roll pop?"

Being a typical homosexual, William looked down at Jay's crotch area, seeing the print of his manhood, then back up to his face. "I guess the world would never know, huh?" said William, blushing like a little school girl.

"I'm just messin' wit' cha boo, but f real though... don't 'cha be around

21st Street?"

"Yeah, I be around there sometimes wit' my girlfriends, but where you be at? 'Cause you look familiar too."

"I be around 18th and D."

"Oh fo' reeal. Me and my girlfriend Tracy be going through there to sell clothes to Fat Rico all time."

"Oh yeah, so you know Tracy too, huh?" said Jay, sounding genuinely surprised.

"Know her! Oh child, please; that's my sister. And as a matter of fact..." William checked his watch, "that bitch needs to hurry up and get her ass up in here. Out there smoking that nasty ass weed n'shit."

"You know what... since I'm 'bout to roll out, I'll holler at Tracy for you and tell him you waitin' on 'em."

"Why you leaving so early for?" asked William, looking slightly disappointed. "Shit, them bitches faking up in there fo' real fo' real, so I figured I'll go find somebody to party wit' on my own."

"Hell, I'll go out wit' 'cha if you tryn'a party sho' nuff."

"Cool wit' me," said Jay, opening the exit door, and holding it there for William to walk out first.

"Ooh, you such a gentleman," said William, switching out the door. Jay felt sick to his stomach just looking at the freak of nature, let alone acting nice to him, but that was the only way to kill two gay birds with one stone. They walked two blocks down to where the U-Haul was parked, and saw Tracy smoking the last of his blunt. Jay took quick side glances to his left and right, noticing how the streets were practically empty, which was definitely a good sign since they were still kind of out in the open.

Tracy gave Jay a curious look, then turned to William and asked, "who do we have here, young lady?"

"Oh girl, this is my friend, urn..." William looked over at Jay. "Boy, you ain't even give me your name, silly."

"My name's Jay," he said, shaking Tracy's hand, looking him in his eyes. "But you should already know who I am, as much as you come through

D- Street."

"Oh now I remember you!" said Tracy, lying, not wanting to feel left out. "I thought you looked familiar, but what's up though... what 'cha really try'na do?"

"I wanted to holler at'cha 'bout buying some clothes," said Jay, knowing fully well what the faggy was insinuating.

"What type of coins you workin' wit'?"

"I got $1500 on me now."

Tracy looked Jay over and smiled, liking what he saw. "Ms. Wilma, can you please open the back of tha truck for our handsome young guest?" William slid the rear door up and they all jumped into the back of the storage cab of the U-Haul. There was a leather couch to the left of the cab, with bags and bags of clothes on it. Jay walked over and examined the clothes, hearing the sound of Tracy pulling the sliding door down.

The next thing he knew, Tracy was right there beside him with the gump's hand on his shoulders. Jay immediately felt his skin crawl, hating the fact that the punk was touching him, but he played it off as cool as he could. "How much you want for them Versace sweat suits?" he asked.

"They worth $700 a piece," said Tracy, sitting his gay-ass down on the couch," but we can work out a deal, if you know what I mean."

"What kind of deal you talkin' 'bout?

"Well... I'll take $100 off for every inch of your dick you let me swallow," said Tracy, smiling like the devil he was.

Shit was getting way out of hand, Jay thought to himself, listening to the homosexual's abominable suggestions. "You know what... that's a bet! I ain't never really do no shit like this before, but fuck it, you only live once," Jay said, reaching his hand behind his back, while stepping directly in front of Tracy. "But first, see if you can deep throat this." Jay whipped the .357 out and shot Tracy in the mouth at point blank range. The impact of the high caliber bullet was so powerful that it tore the punk's jaw off his face, but Jay could see that Tracy wasn't quite dead yet, as he rolled off the couch, crawling on the cab's floor.

All the bitch really came out of William, as he started screaming like that black broad on Michael Jackson's Thriller video. He tried to make a break for the sliding door, but Jay shot him twice in the back, causing him to collapse in the corner of the truck. Jay pressed the gun's short barrel to the front of William's head and squeezed the trigger, knocking a fist-sized hole out of the back of it.

Jay then walked back over to Tracy and kicked him in the stomach, while grabbing two bags of clothes off the couch with his free hand. He dropped one of the bags, seeing as Tracy's blood had splattered all inside it. "You stupid bitch, you got shit all on the Versace." Jay said to Tracy, shooting him in the side of the head with his final bullet, making sure that Tracy was dead as humanly possible.

Sliding the U-Haul's door open, Jay jumped out of the storage cab and tossed the .357 inside the clothes bag he was carrying. Jay pulled the door closed, locked it, and started walking towards his Bronco when he noticed some niggaz were parked by the sidewalk a few cars down. Jay made it to the truck and bent down, grabbing the AP-9. He hopped in and pulled off, slowly driving past the Silver Lincoln where the two dudes were inside. Jay looked in as he drove by and saw it was June and Dink from Simple City. He didn't think anything of it though, as his main concern was just getting the hell away from the scene. Jay pressed play on the CD player and the dreary voice of Scarface filled the truck speakers — "There be no witness to this homicide, no re-enactment on the late night news to be re-dramatized..."

Drama City

Chapter 9

It was 2:30 on a cloudy Thursday afternoon. The autumn winds were creeping through the city, chasing away the last traces of a once glorious summer. Classes were just letting out at St. Augustine's Catholic School, while the man watched the young ones scatter to the awaiting yellow buses laughing and playing with one another and saying their goodbyes. It was the third week into the new school year as he started thinking back on how he used to be at that vulnerable age, remembering the stolen years of his childhood.

The man was parked in a brand new black 850 CSI BMW, fully equipped with an all black leather interior. The 80 thousand dollar car was a grand testament to his major come up in the game, but still, he wasn't quite satisfied with his position within the inner-city crime circuit. The man took another drag from his Newport before snubbing it out in the ashtray, when he saw the approach of a sky blue MPV with New York license plates turning off of 14'" Street. He casually threw on his black leather jacket, leaving it unzipped and exposing the long sleeved t-shirt he was wearing, with the photo-copy of another man's face on it, saying "We Will Always Miss You Scales."

The man reached into his pocket, pulling out a stick of Juicy Fruit gum and popped it into his mouth, as he stepped out of the car. He leaned his back against the car door, watching the MPV park directly across the street from him. All of a sudden, the mini-vans side door slid open, revealing four niggaz with sub-machine guns posted up at the ready while some big fat Rastafarian looking nigga named C-god got out of the passenger side and motioned for him to come over.

The man crossed the street to where C-god stood and together they both walked up the cement steps leading to Malcolm X Park. They found a little wooden bench a couple of yards away, and took a seat, checking their surroundings before discussing their order of business. "Yo son, I appreciate tha phone call god," C-God said in a thick Brooklyn accent. "You know it's been hard fo' my families, 'specially my old Earth... so pardon me god, if I get a bit irrational."

Since the robbery and murder of New York Steve, the news spread throughout the city that Steve's older brother C-god was offering 50 thousand dollars for the murder of whoever was responsible for Steve's death. Luckily for him, the man found out through some broads from up Le Droit Park that word had gotten back to C-god that two niggaz from 18th and D had killed New York Steve. That led to the man calling C-god himself and setting up their little meeting.

"I understand yo' pain slim," said the man, shaking his head as if he were experiencing true sorrow. "We both lost some people we cared about. That's why I'm here now, but truth be told, just as much as I would like to smash them niggaz who killed my partner — I would like that 50 thousand even better."

"Word to life, I feel what 'cha sayin' god, but money can't replace my lil' brother's soul, but anyway, who's the clown-ass niggaz who did Steve in."

"These two bitch-ass niggaz from my hood named Jay and Youngblood."

C-god looked at the man with bloodshot eyes, scrutinizing him with blatant suspicion. He had been in D.C. long enough to know all about the cruddy and back-stabbing ways of money hungry niggaz from tha Chocolate city, and was cautious, not taking the information at face value. "So how you know these cowards who did this? I mean, don't misread me son, I ain't doubting yo' word or nothing — but a nigga needs some type of certainty before I can seek closure in this matter, ya feel me?"

"I can dig where you coming from slim," the man said, nodding his head in agreement. "But I seen them niggaz the day after that shit happen wit' Scales. Youngblood wasn't gettin' no money like that before around D Street. But yet, soon as

yo' brother get hit up, tha nigga pop up around tha way in a gold Acura Legend wit' tinted windows and —"

"A gold Legend wit' tinted windows!" C-god jumped up and started frantically pacing in a small circle. "By almighty God Allah, yo' son, that was the car I bought Steve for his birthday, yo."

"I knew that shit!" the man said, standing up, snapping his fingers like he just figured out a missing piece to a puzzle. "I'm telling you Joe, them bitch ass niggaz did that shit slim. It ain't no muthafuckin' doubt them niggaz ain't kill yo' brother and my partner Scales."

C-god stepped straight to the man, looking him dead in the eyes. "Here's tha deal god, I'll give you 25 thousand now and the other 25 after you hand me the obituaries of them niggaz, word?"

"Hell yeah, that's cool wit' me, but just give me a couple of days, so I can get both of them niggaz and get away wit' it, ya dig?"

"You got two weeks. That's should be enough time for you to handle yo' business."

"That's more than enough," the man said, shaking C-god's hand. They talked about a few more business proposals as they made their way back down the steps, leaving the park. C-god's bodyguards were all posted up around the MPV, concealing their weapon underneath their jackets, when they made it back to the mini-van. The man couldn't help but to feel a little nervous, being outgunned four to one. But C-god seemed to be an honest crook the man thought to himself, as he got into his BMW, which took a lot of stress off of the whole situation.

Two minutes later, while he waited in the car, one of C-god's men knocked against his window carrying a small brown shopping bag with the 25 G's in it. The man rolled down the window, taking the bag and placing it in his lap. He looked inside seeing a bundle of dollar bills bound in thousand dollar stacks. Closing the bag, he placed it on the passenger seat, and drove off smiling to himself. In a few more days, after he got the other 25 thousand, he'll be a 150 thousand dollars richer than he was before, and that's not including the 27 bricks he got stashed up Langston terrace.

Ray-Ray walked into D.C. General Hospital's Maternity Ward, carrying a dozen blue helium filled balloons. She checked in with the nurse at the receptionist station to make sure she had the right room number, and then strolled down the hall to room 307 where a small name plate with Amina Hinton on it was glued to the side of the wall. Ray-Ray opened the door and was greeted by the sight of a room full of family members standing by her daughter's bedside fussing over whose turn it was to hold the baby.

Stepping beside the bed, Ray-Ray leaned over and kissed Mink on the forehead, seeing the 8 pound baby boy cradled in her arms. Arriving at the hospital late, Ray-Ray was highly disappointed that she had missed the actual birth of her first grandchild, but now, as she stood there marveling over the little bundle of joy, her heart became filled with motherly pride. "Ooooh baby, let me see my grandson!" said Ray-Ray, handing off her purse and balloons to Jay, who was standing at her side. She gently lifted the baby out of Mink's arm, soothing the infant with a rocking motion.

"So what did you finally decide to name him?" asked Ray-Ray, looking down at Mink.

"I named him after his father and his big head uncle." Mink weakly smiled, still feeling tired from the child birth. "Vincent Jameel Hinton... that sound okay, don't it?"

"Baby that sounds lovely," Ray-Ray said, kissing all over baby Vincent. She was enjoying the feeling of being a brand new grandmother, with her thoughts centered on how much she was going to spoil the little baby when several flashes from a Polaroid camera caught her attention, causing her to look up. "Demetrius Young, if you don't stop taking my picture wit' me all lookin' a mess..." Ray-Ray said, laughing.

Youngblood hated it when Ray-Ray called him by his whole name, even though he never remembered her ever calling him by his nickname either. "You know you too beautiful to be lookin' a mess," said Youngblood, winking his eye at Ray-Ray. "Besides, wait 'till you see the joints I took of Mink pushin' that hi' monster up outta her, like that scene from Aliens and —"

Mink threw one of the brown Teddy Bears Jay had bought her at Youngblood, catching him square in the face. "Boy stop lyin', 'cause you wasn't even in tha delivery room!" she said, flipping him the middle finger. "And don't be calling my baby no damn monster either."

Youngblood started laughing, taking a seat in one of the little wooden chairs in the room. "Oops, my bad," he said, reclining back in his seat, folding his hands behind his back. When unexpectedly, Rasheeda walked over and sat down on his lap. Being as there were no empty chairs left, Youngblood didn't really trip or think too much about her sitting there, He did, however, peep how soft her ass felt as she moved every now and then, talking to the rest of her aunts, uncles, and cousins.

Jay noticed how fresh Rasheeda had been acting lately, especially every time Youngblood's around. Her little coochie starting to get hot was the basic thought that came to his head, as he watched the two of them whispering back and forth to each other. Jay knew in his heart that he would not like the idea of his partner screwing around with his little sister. Youngblood was too much like a little brother to him, but if he and Rasheeda chose to get involved in a relationship, Jay would never try to skunk tha move. Matters of the heart are best left to those in love - unless you're one of those people who loves heartaches.

Ray-Ray came over to Jay, holding baby Vincent up to him, comparing the facial features of the two. "I don't care what nobody says," she said, "this baby looks just like you when you were born."

"That's my lil' man, ya dig," said Jay, wrapping his arm around his mother's waist.

"All he gon' do is cry all night, leaving stanky-ass diapers all over the place!" Little Nadia said, busting on the scene, already feeling jealous of the little baby for stealing the spotlight.

"Oh girl, hush yo' mouth," said Ray-Ray, shooing her youngest daughter to the side. She then looked over at Jay, placing the baby into his arms. "Jameel, how long you and Demetrius been up here wit' Mink?"

"Since last night. I tried to call your cell phone, but I couldn't get through. So I just left a couple of messages on the answer machine at home."

"I was so mad when I got home and found out y'all was already gone to the hospital. Something told me to take off from work last night."

"Don't trip off it," said Jay, smiling over his newborn nephew. "You should've known I was gon' make sure my lir man got to the hospital on time. The only hard part I had to go through was wrestling wit' Nadia's lil' crazy-ass in the waiting room."

Ray-Ray started laughing, leaning forward to kiss Jay on the cheek. "I swear I don't know what I would do without you. Baby, you've really been my rock, my sword, and my shield during my times of weakness. Jameel, honey... I'm so sorry for not being there for you and your sisters when I was an addict. I could never repay you for —"

Seeing the tears well up in his mother's eyes, Jay stopped her in mid sentence with a reassuring hug. "Ma, go head wit' all that sentimental stuff — you 'bout to make a nigga cry n'shit."

"Boy, watch your mouth around the baby," said Ray-Ray, playfully smacking Jay behind the head. "You ain't gon' get my grandson like you got Nadia, growin' up cussin' like a sailor."

"Mama, you too late fo' all that," he said as they both stood over by Mink's bedside. "'cause when the doctor tried to smack him, he smacked him back; his first words were 'thug 4 life' and 'Uncle Jay pass tha mac.'

"You fake Tupac wanna-be ass nigga," said Mink, smiling in between sips from a cup of apple juice. "My baby don't need to be hearing all that thug life rap shit. It's bad enough he's gonna have to see it growin' up all through the city."

"Man, shut cha dumb ass up fo' me and shorty jump you up in here," said Jay as he laughed and tickled the baby's little belly, making him giggle.

"Both of y'all two knuckle heads are too thugged out for my taste," Ray-Ray said, laughing. "Let me go holler at the rest of the family before they start thinking I'm tyn'a show off 'cause of the baby. I'll be back over here in a few."

Jay handed the baby back over to Ray-Ray and watched her walk off, proudly showing the baby off to a few of his cousins. He then turned his attention back to Mink, who seemed like she was lost in deep thought. "What's up wit'cha champ?" he asked, sensing something was wrong with her. "You supposed to be glowin' n'shit — not looking like you at some damn funeral."

"I know, I know... but it's just not fair my son has to grow up wit' out a father, like we did..." Mink quickly wiped the tears away from her eyes, not trying to show the pain of her sorrow. "I mean, Vamp had his problems and all that... but fo' real, he was a good man. Plus, he had just made a promise to me two nights before he was killed that he was gon' get his self together and marry me soon after the baby was born."

Trying to choose his words carefully, Jay thought for a minute, placing his hand on top of hers and said, "Mink, Vamp was a straight dope fiend and had too many niggaz that wanted to see him dead. I mean, you my older sister and I love you more than anything, but I can't tell you who to give your heart to. What I can tell you though, is that main-man was a cold junkie — and that ain't the type of nigga you needed taking care of you or the baby."

"But he was all I had, Jay!" Mink had to fight to control herself from screaming. The tears running full force down her cheeks. "Yeah, I know Vincent was a dope addict and all that other bullshit, but he was all I had. And now my son don't have nobody to call daddy or nothing."

"How can you say 'Vamp was all you had?' Ever since I started getting' a lil' change, I always made sure you, mama, and everybody else didn't have to want fo' nothing. So even though I ain't the one that got 'cha pregnant — that ain't gon' stop me from being a father, as well as an uncle to lit' Vincent, giving him everything he could possibly want."

Mink just laid there in the bed, not saying anything for a brief moment. Then turning her head in an owl-like motion, she looked at Jay with the saddest eyes he ever saw and said, "you just don't understand, Jay... it's just not the same."

Jay wanted to end the conversation as soon as possible, so he simply nodded his head in agreement and said, "You right," and squeezed the top of her hand. "I didn't mean to make you upset. I just wanted you to know that I love you, and to make sure you understand that I'm gon' look out for the baby wit' everything I got."

"I understand you, boo."

"Good," Jay leaned over, kissing Mink on the top of her forehead. "Now make sure yo' gold diggin'-ass get some rest, so you can get tha fuck up out this hospital."

Youngblood walked over and joined the two, catching the tail-end of their conversation. He knew that Mink was still tripping off of Vamp, mourning his death and whatnot, but he also knew that she would eventually get over it. Youngblood, personally, felt no remorse for the dead dope-fiend. He placed one hand on top of Mink's head, and starting massaging her scalp with his fingers. "I was just thinkin' that it's flicked up you ain't give the baby a part of my name n'shit, Mink," said Youngblood. "Especially after all tha shit we been through."

"Boy, get tha hell away from me — I don't know you."

"Aight, remember that shit next time yo' fat ass want some money got dammit." "Siiike!" Mink said, smiling up at Youngblood. "You know I really do love you **boy**."

"Yeah, yeah yeah, don't try to be my friend now — 'cause I'm broke as a muthafucka."

"You ain't got no money fo' real?"

"Nope," said Youngblood as he shrugged his shoulders in a helpless manner. "A nigga on his last leg out this joint." He reached into his pocket and pulled out $1,700, giving her the money. "But here's a lil' something for you and tha lil' man, ya-dig."

"I thought yo' lying ass ain't have no money," said Mink, snatching the money out of Youngblood's hand. "You make me sick," she said, counting through the money, then looking back up at Youngblood rolling her eyes. "You black-ass dog."

Standing in front of the sink, Mojo pulled the condom off of his manhood and flushed it down the toilet. Checking himself out in the mirror on the outside of the medicine cabinet, he went into his pretty-boy routine, searching for any bumps or blemishes on his handsome sable toned face. He opened his mouth, stretching his lips so he could see his teeth before hitting them off with a string of dental floss. He then brushed the thick hairs of his eyebrows, making sure every strand was in place, while once again, adoring the features of his damn-near flawless baby face.

Still smelling the scent of the woman's vagina on his fingertip, Mojo decided to hop in the shower and rinse the sticky sweat from the sexual workout he had earlier from his body. Handling his hygiene in the shower, Mojo grabbed a towel off the rack, not caring who it belonged to, and started drying his body with it. He then wrapped the towel around his waist, looking down at his rock-hard abdominal muscles, while stepping out of the bathroom with his huge cocky smile painted across his face.

Strolling into the bedroom, Mojo saw the girl still laying on top of the bed, ass naked, with the black satin sheets all tangled between her legs. There was also 70 thousand dollars all scattered across the bed. The same money he just used earlier to fuck the girl on top of, reenacting his favorite sex scene from the movie "Indecent Proposal." Just looking at the girl opening and closing her firm, shapely legs, to tease his eyes with the warm, pink, tender flesh between her legs made Mojo's manhood start to stiffen again. Unfortunately sex wasn't an option at that time due to the time constraints he was under.

Mojo sat at the front of the bed and started putting on his clothes, thinking about his plans for the following day. Slowly but surely, within the next couple of weeks he would be able to flood the block with coke, gaining supreme clientele over all the major dealers in tha game. First things first though; Mojo had to tie up a few loose ends while covering his own ass in the process.

Sliding on his blue jeans, Mojo was about to stand when he felt the weight of the girl's arm curling around his neck. She leaned her chest against him, pressing her hard nipples into his back, and started kissing the side of his face. Mojo wanted to give in to the sensations of the girls' thick lips caressing his skin, but his 'money over bitches' mentality kept his thoughts on the moves he needed to make. "Damn baby," said Mojo, as the girl worked her arm around the front of his jeans, "a nigga just banged yo' box out for like seven hours straight, and you still actin' like you ain't had enough. What the fuck, you got a white liver or something?"

"You got the good dick boy, you ain't know?" The girl started laughing, falling back against the bed. She rolled her body over top of the money, causing dollar bills to stick to her sweaty skin, and then she got off the bed and slipped on a silk nightgown. "Why you gotta leave already, anyway? 'Cause you said you was gon' be wit' me the whole night."

"I know baby girl, I got shit to take care of. You know how shit goes."

"Yeah, whatever. You niggaz always got shit to take care of — but what you need to be doing is taking care of me," she said, standing in front of Mojo with her hands on her hips.

Mojo stood up and grabbed her by the shoulders, forcing the girl to turn around. He then flipped the back of her nightgown up, and started pulling off the $50 and $100 bills that were stuck to her body. "Bitch, why you gotta get all low class n'shit?" said Mojo, slapping the girl on the back of the ass. The sting from the blow caused the girl to jump forward. She spun around and looked at him like he was crazy. "I know yo' cruddy ass gon' steal from me at any given opportunity," Mojo said, shaking his head, "but don't try to cuff shit in my muthafuckin' face."

"I ain't tryn'a cuff nothing from you daddy," the girl purred in her little baby voice. "Don't be mad at me, boo — but you know a girl needs shit for herself too."

Mojo looked at the girl with a raised eyebrow, laughing to himself at her weak con game. "You know what?" he said, slipping his feet into his Polo boots. "I can't be mad at cha' fo' real. 'Cause I'm a snake-ass nigga, you's a sheisty-ass bitch... fuck it. We can't go wrong 'cause we made fo' each other, huh?"

"Nigga, you crazy," the girl laughed, stepping in front of Mojo, kissing him on the mouth. She then dropped her hand to the zipper of his pants, massaging his manhood through his jeans, while whispering in his ear, "let me give you some head before you roll out."

"As much as I would love to, I must unfortunately decline. Besides, you swallowed enough babies fo' one night — you need to go and let that shit digest, ya dig."

Mojo walked over to the girl's closet and grabbed his Abercrombie & Fitch windbreaker, then crossed the other side of the room, and reached into a clothes hamper to pull out the Smith & Wesson .10 mm and a Glock 17 with a 35 shot extended clip. Mojo tucked the .10mm in the waist of his jeans while moving towards the girl with the Glock in his other hand. He stepped straight in front of her, placing the barrel of the gun directly underneath her chin. "Now, we both know there's 70 thousand on that bed over there, so don't fuck around and get fucked around, ya dig?"

"What 'cha talkin' 'bout, boy?!" the girl said, feeling the pressure of the gun as she took a swallow.

"If one dollar even comes up short when I pick that money up tomorrow, they gon' find yo' moms in the Potomac river, yo' sister in the Anacostia river, and god knows where yo' pretty ass gon' wind up, ya feel me?"

"Mojo, why is you trippin'? You know I ain't gon' fuck wit' yo' money baby." "Just making sure, that's all," said Mojo, still pressing the Glock under the girl's chin a while longer, before kissing her on the mouth. "Damn you got some soft ass lips."

Walking towards the door, Mojo opened it and was about to make his exit, when all of a sudden he remembered something he wanted to say.

"Eh, don't forget me and you gotta take care of them niggaz tomorrow," he said to the girl. "I already got the spot laid out for 'em, so you just make sure you get shorty up around 9:00PM — then I'll smash his man later on the next day."

"Don't worry about that shit," the girl said, with a mischievous smirk on her face, "I got that young nigga so pussy whipped, he basically eating out the palm of my hand. So setting him up won't be shit to do, but remember I got an appointment for the beauty salon at 6... So I guess I'll just have this nigga pick me up from there around 8:00, and keep him wit' me 'till it's time to bring 'em over to you."

"Take that money off the bed and put it in the duffle bag over there in that chair." Mojo motioned with his chin. "I'm a give you 10 thousand for setting them niggaz up for me, and after that, me and you going on a cruise to the Virgin Islands, ya feel me?"

"You damn right," the girl said smiling, anticipating the experience of leaving the city and going on an exotic vacation. "It's about time you finally decided on taking me out some place."

Mojo just smiled, winking his eye at the girl, and made his way out of the apartment's front door. Thinking on the plans he had for the girl after everything else was taken care of, Mojo mumbled to himself as he walked down the hallway, "cruddy-ass bitch, I'm a take you out alright..." The echoes of his laughter followed him down the hall.

Chapter 10

I'm sitting in the prison's chow hall, just watching the other inmates enjoy themselves with their trays filled with garbage. Today, the prison administration claims to be honoring a so-called Black holiday, by serving a somewhat edible lunchtime meal, but once again, to me it looks like the prison staff has found yet another opportunity to ridicule and make a mockery of the Black inmate population at this institution. It's a sad state of affairs, me being the only Black face in a sea of Black faces not smacking big greasy lips over some half-cooked chicken bone. Maybe that's just me... Maybe I'm just a miserable ole' brother with nothing else better to do than sit around and point at the faults of others.

I guess at times I can be a bit hypocritical here and there, wasting my precious energy on the frivolities of others. Yet in all honesty, this whole situation brings to mind a poem I once read entitled "Hot Sauce." Check this out:

Today is Dr. Martin Luther King Jr. Day. I'm in a Federal Penitentiary in Indiana. "Chow time," announced the prison guard. Inmates rush to the Chow Hall. I sit in my cell. One minute later, an inmate runs back to his cell. "Gotta get tha Hot Sauce!" he yells ecstatically. I walk into the corridor. Prison guards are debating whether today is a legitimate holiday. I enter the Chow Hall. Fried chicken, black eyed peas, pecan pie, and Kool-Aid! Brothers are in jubilation with their trays filled with mockery. I think it's ironic... I feel disgusted. I turn around to leave this degrading festival for the frivolous. The last thing I heard before I left; "Nigga, pass tha Hot Sauce!"

When I first read this poem, I thought it was rather humorous, as well as a thought provoking piece of another man's opinion, but now as I sit in this crowded dining hall, witnessing this modern day minstrel show first-hand, I now realize that the poem was a literary depiction of the psychological make-up of the majority of our people. In other words, showing how fucked up we are as a race.

Man, just think about this here for a minute; now, in this wealthy and powerful bastard country we call the United States of America, the Black man barely makes up 17% of its national population, but if you check the census of this country's prison population (state, federal, and local), Blacks are damn near 80%! Now, if that's not disproportionate, I don't know what the hell is.

I wish somebody would take the time to show me what type of games these people (the government) are running on us, or why we continue to fall for the ole' okey doke, pretending that justice in this country is justice for all. I tell you, for the life of me, I still can't figure out why we (meaning your black ass) act like we can't see that all the so-called war on drugs, war on terrorism, crime control bills, CC's, and RICO acts, Title 16 for juveniles, and domestic abuse prevention laws are all political fronts, designed to entrap the Black man, and force him back into the bonds of servitude.

I think it's so embarrassing, as I think back on the history books that I've read, showing how our Black ancestors drafted the blue-print for modern civilization. Yet, when you compare the stature of our people back then to the status of us negroes today, we are the ones portrayed as the uncultured savage, but what's even more humiliating, is that I can't find one reason why any other race should view us any other way. Almost every day, we add credence to the stereotypes they have for our kind.

I know it may appear at first glance that I am being too harsh and not giving our people the credit they deserve, however if you believe that I'm exaggerating about how messed up we are as a race, and how bad other races view use as a people, then all you have to do is take a trip to the nearest Federal Penitentiary, visit the Chow Hall during "main line." You'll see nigga mentality live and direct.

There are various ethnic groups incarcerated throughout all Federal Prisons, yet the social norm is to eat with your own kind. No other race that I have observed has a problem with sharing a table with a person of the same race, but when it comes to the Black man, more often than not, you can't even sit and eat at a table (and feel welcome) with your own brother, unless you're from the same gang or geographical area. Man, I swear it's crazy how we are the majority in prison, and the most divided! Try explaining this to the average Black man in here, and either one of two things will happen: 1) He'll listen to you and agree to everything you say, but still won't try to do better for himself, or 2) just be straight up with you and tell you they ain't trying to hear that Black brother shit.

Basically, I can talk about the negative traits my people have until I'm blue in the face, and I definitely ain't said anything that hasn't been said before. All the books I read, all the speeches I've listened to, and all the lessons the old timers broke down to me... They all sum up to this: We Blacks, as a whole, are a fucked up bunch of people. And no, I am not excluding myself — I'm fucked up too! But awareness is the first step to change... And a change is what must happen, if we truly want to better our conditions.

In all actuality, not only do we have to make a change in the way we live and think; we also have to learn how and what to change. The time has come where we can't afford to keep on going the way that we're going. Everybody's getting over on us; the whites, Asians, Hispanics, etc. while we continue to be the national laughing stock of America! Just look at how much this country doesn't take us seriously — America gives the Jews millions of dollars every year for the holocaust, and the Native American people get to own small reservations with tax-free casinos, along with millions of dollars for the massacre that this country inflicted upon them, but the Black race, who were stolen from their native land, forced into slavery to build this bastard country, and were issued out a wholesale slaughter by the hands of "the powers that be" can't even get a funky red penny for reparations for the atrocities we endured!

That's why, in general, I don't fault my people for doing or saying certain things. I know we suffer from a cultural amnesia... I know all about the effects of having been stripped of everything you once owned, and be forced to latch onto anything that you can get. This is one of the main reasons why, when we come to prison, most of us get caught up in the "penal politics," and start trying to govern the institution's telephones, televisions, chairs, and a whole bunch of other stuff that doesn't belong to us. That's the reason I made reference to how drugs, homosexuals, television, and the telephone in the previous chapter could easily get a man killed in prison, especially the whole drug situation.

I have seen firsthand where some dudes would get word about another dude (who they consider to be a sucker) who is coming off with the "pack," and started extorting the dude, his people on the street, and whoever else is involved with smuggling the narcotics up into the joint. I mean when drugs come into play in prison... shit can get heavy quick!

Take for instance, the time I was down the "Quack" (Lorton's high-medium correctional facility), in 6 Dorm (Tha Animal House), kicking it with a few comrades of mine, when all of a sudden I felt the urge to go take a leak. By the lavatory being in the front of the dormitory, adjacent to the recreational day room, it's not uncommon to see a bunch of brothers all posted up by the bathroom, doing their thing.

But on this particular day, I walk over to the urinal stalls, completely oblivious to the funny looks the dudes on the outside of the bathroom are giving me, as if I'm walking right into a lion's den. When right before my eyes, I see two niggaz holding a man to the ground, while another nigga had the man's legs spread open, with his hand inside the man's rectum, pulling out tiny balloons of heroin.

Now I'm acting like I don't see all this crazy shit that's going on behind me, while I calmly take a piss, but in the back of my mind, I'm thinking, "how in the hell can a man stick his hand into another man's asshole, just because he's chasing his habit!" Yet needless to say, I quickly handled my business at the urinal and got the fuck up out of there. Hear no evil, see no evil, say no evil... what the hell. I admit that that situation was ugly, but it wasn't any of my concern either. It's hard for me to feel sympathy for another man's stupidity. Because time and time again, one of the main rules in prison has always been the easiest one to remember — "you never get what you can't govern."

Albeit, I still ask myself what's the purpose of trying to govern something that's meant to keep you locked up (mentally as well as physically). When it comes to narcotics in the joint, maybe it's just a dope fiend thing... I'll never know. To each his own, I guess. But not matter how much I try to rationalize why we do a lot of the things that we do, I just can't (and I'm glad I don't) understand how a man in prison could proudly call himself a "jail-house pimp," and try to govern the action of a gotdamn homosexual!

Now I swear that demonstration right there is way beyond me. For example, there was an incident that occurred in a dining hall at a Federal Penitentiary I was once held captive in where there was an open homosexual sitting at a dining table, along with three other dudes. I just so happen to be sitting in an area close by, when I heard the loud laughter of the dudes behind me, so I turned around to see what all the commotion was about.

It was breakfast time at the moment, and all the inmates were feasting on a wide variety of fruits and cereal, but why this gay-ass gump was sitting at a table behind me, demonstrating his dick sucking capabilities by deep throating a big ole, long, peeled banana for the other dudes that were sitting at the same table — I have no idea. I was just about to turn back around to my own table, thinking to myself that things couldn't get no sicker than that, when all of a sudden the gump's lover/pimp came on the scene out of nowhere, having a fit, jealous that his piece of ass was out flirting with some other niggaz.

Well, to make a long story short, all hell broke loose as the lover's quarrel escalated into a full scale knife fight between the gump's lover and the other three dudes.

When it was all said and done, and the prison guards finally took control of the situation, the gump's lover was stretched out on the dining hall floor with over forty something stab wounds, and leaking like a faucet. While the homosexual just stood there in false disbelief, acting like his punk ass ain't know why the whole situation happened in the first place.

So now, three dudes end up on death row for killing one dude who thought he could control and govern the actions of some disease-carrying homosexual, while subsequently, the gump just slid right into the arms of another mentally challenged gay lover, not giving a damn about the lives of the four men he helped destroy.

No, I tell you it hurts my heart to see (and be a part of) the lunacy which these prison walls have inflicted upon my people. Every day that I wake up and take a look at my surroundings, I am reminded of the living death sentence of my brothers trapped in the belly of the beast. Existing only through the existence of others, I have no choice but to witness the madness of miseducated brothers with their misguided hatred; gauging the hearts of man with an all or nothing mentality, while viewing all men as potential enemies.

But I guess sorrow must be felt by those who must be real with themselves, and deal with life on life's terms. I know living in prison is far from living under ordinary circumstances, but I am a firm believer that conflict doesn't create character, it exhibits character. My people are no stranger to hard times; from the slave ships in the 1700's to being in

101

solitary confinement in some prison's disciplinary segregation unit (the hole), we have been blessed with the ability to improvise, adapt, and conquer all our unfavorable situations.

I just pray that Allah (most high) continues to have mercy and patience on me and my kind, because I'll be the first to admit that even though I am well aware of the plight which affects the masses, I am an integral part of the poison within the Black community. Maybe in due time I'll find the missing link, and become a whole person with my humanity still intact (Inshallah), but right now, I'm on some '87 type of time, where I feel like breaking a lot of these niggaz' backs just for breathing!

And that's fucked up, ain't man?

My Old Hands

The Original 18th-N-D St. Crew 1 (except for Alpo…Yeah, I know)

Lil' Pat & K.D.
Flesh of my flesh…
Oakhill Youth Correction Facility

Derrick   Daryll

18th-N-D St. The Twinz
North East Finest
Leavenworth, Federal Penitentiary

Fat Derrick
AKA
Fat Meat
USP Terre Haute 1

My old head Perry Woodall
AKA
Preacher Man
R.I.P.
USP Hazelton

**My Big Homie
Davin Hart-Bey
An 18th-N-Dst
Original Gangsta**

**My Cousin, Simeko (in the white)
and Big "G"
from the Back Yard Brand**

**My Favorite Cousin in the world
My Booga-Butt!
Muffy
AKA
Rochita Jordan**

**My Homie Vincent Smith
AKA
Roscoe
R.I.P.**

**My Brother Eyone Williams
Doing It Big 4 – the Home Team**

**My Partner in Crime
Karim AKA Twin**

Chapter 11

Stepping out of his '87 Cadillac Coup Deville, Preacher Man tucked the Sig Sauer 9mm into the waist of his Burberry London dress slacks, and walked up the front steps to Mae White's apartment building. Standing in front of the thick bullet-proof door, casually dressed in a gray Perry Ellis cardigan sweater, Preacher Man contemplated on the unspoken thoughts which ran amok inside the chambers of his mind. He had been anticipating a possible confrontation between Mae and himself ever since his release from the joint, but just like death, facing Mae's scorn was inevitable, so he might as well just go ahead and get the shit over with, Preacher Man thought as he buzzed her apartment.

It seemed like an eternity before Preacher Man finally heard the soft elderly voice speaking through the intercom asking, "Who is it?" "It's me, Mark," Preacher Man spoke into the voice box, identifying himself.

"Mark?" said Mae, not hiding the irritation she was feeling in her voice. "Who is you, and what do you want?!"

"It's me... Mark Davis, Ms. White. You know who it is, it's Preacher." There was a brief pause before Mae decided to buzz the door open and let him into the building. Preacher Man stepped in and walked up the two flights of stairs that lead to Mae's place. Reaching her door, he knocked four times and waited for whatever hell fire she was going to throw his way.

It took Mae about half a minute to come and open the door. She was dressed in a multi-colored house robe, tightly drawn around her slender waist, and with her silver-gray hair in plastic rollers, wrapped underneath a silk head-scarf. Even though Mae was in her late sixties, she had that young girl spirit which made it hard for the average person to guess her age correctly. The only tell-tale signs of her aging were the tiny lines at the corners of her eyes, but other than that, very few people would have thought that she was the grandmother of a dangerous and out of control 15 year-old man-child.

Mae stood in the doorway looking Preacher Man up and down,

inspecting him as if he were a piece of human garbage that she just couldn't get rid of. Every time Mae looked at him, she was reminded of the heroin addiction which killed her one and only child. Though she couldn't prove it, Mae truly believed that Preacher Man was responsible for turning her daughter into a junky, causing her death by overdosing from a bad batch of dope on a filthy bench at a lonely bus stop.

It had been nearly three years since her daughter's death, and though it had been over 14 years since she last saw Preacher Man in the "free world," seeing him in the hallway outside her door at the moment, brought back the memory of her daughter, as if she just died only yesterday. Mae had to fight her emotions, as every ounce of her being wanted to once and for all tell Preacher Man to get away and stay the hell out of her and Youngblood's life, but she knew that it wasn't her place to keep a father away from his son.

Leaning against the door post, Mae folded her arms across her chest, and said, "so, they finally fucked up and let you out, huh?"

"If that's how you want to look at it," said Preacher Man, knowing the source of Mae's resentment while trying to be patient with her attitude. "Ms. White, I know you don't particularly care for me and all, and I can understand and respect that, but I came over here this morning 'cause I have to speak with my son. I ain't seen my lit man in over 14 years, and I think it's about time for me and shorty to get together. A nigga missed too many years out his life already, you dig?"

"Jeeez, I wonder who fault that is," said Mae, slapping him in the face with her sarcastic remark. She couldn't stand the sight of Preacher Man any further, so she thought it would be best to end their little play of words before she really ended up slapping him in the face with a quick right hand. "Demetrius, somebody's here to see you!" Mae called out to her grandson, while keeping both eyes firmly glued to Preacher Man, watching him as if he were going to steal the hallway he was standing in.

It was 7:03 a.m. when Youngblood checked the digital clock on his dresser. He was already awake, thinking about what excuse he was going to give his grandmother for the reason he couldn't go to school that morning when he heard her calling out his name. Youngblood got out of his bed and slid on some Sobiato sweat pants, stepping his feet into his Timberland boots. Wondering who it could be that was paying him this early morning visit, Youngblood walked into the living room and saw his father standing in the hallway, while his grandmother stood in the doorway blocking his entrance into the apartment.

Youngblood started smiling, seeing how Grandma Mae looked just like one of those English Guards, posted up at the door. "What's up, granny?" he asked, already knowing how much she didn't like his father. "I thought you would be gone to work by now."

"Naw, I'm off today baby," said Mae, reluctantly moving to the side, letting Preacher Man into her place. "And it's a good thing, too," Mae said, cutting her eye at the man as she walked into the kitchen, and staying well within earshot of anything that was going to be said in her living room.

Youngblood walked over to the couch and sat down as Preacher Man joined him, taking his seat right next to his son. Preacher Man leaned forward not knowing where to start the conversation, and began speaking the words which he had kept locked away in his heart for over 14 years. "Blood, you know this shit it awkward as a muthafucka for me, shorty," Preacher Man said, looking down at his ashy knuckles as he rubbed his hands together. "What can I say? I flicked up. You know I made a lot of calls in life... did a rack of stupid shit, and fucked around and got locked up, causing me to miss all those precious years out your young life. I know you probably don't respect me as your father and — "

"Man look, what are you tryn'a say?" Youngblood cut Preacher Man off, while flipping through a TV Guide magazine, pretending like he was really reading the weather channel section. "'Cause I got shit to do, like get ready for school and shit, ya dig?"

Preacher Man looked over at Youngblood and snatched the TV Guide out of his hand, tossing it onto the carpet covered floor. Youngblood was startled and caught off guard by his father's reaction. All he could do was sit and stare at him in total disbelief while fighting back the urge to steal the gotdamn shit out of him. Seeing that he now had Youngblood's undivided attention, Preacher Man decided to speak his mind to his son, and give him the game in the raw. "Shorty, do you really think I'm washed up?" he asked, rolling up the sleeves of his sweater.

"You know what... you right," said Youngblood, standing and walking off towards his bedroom. As soon as he reached his bed, Youngblood pulled out an eight shot German Luger from underneath his top mattress. He really didn't have intentions on shooting his father; maybe pistol whip him a little bit, but overall, Youngblood just wanted to let him know that he wasn't a little boy any more, and wasn't going to be disrespected by anyone! Before he could even make it back into the living room, Youngblood turned around to find Preacher Man standing right in front of him with his Sig Sauer already in hand.

As the two men squared off, locked in the deathly silence, staring each other down like they were in an old western move, Preacher Man was the first to speak. As he clicked the safety off his gun, he said, "Blood, I don't know what you planned on doing with that there gun in your hand, but when it comes to the murder game... I'm like Parker Brothers."

"Dad, what the fuck you want from me man," said Youngblood, realizing that his father was just as crazy as him, or maybe even a little more. "I ain't seen you since I was a baby, and now you come to me with this fake ass 'I wanna be a father to my son' bullshit! Nigga, I don't know you..."

"Young nigga, that's why I came over here! So we can get to know each other. Blood, do you know for the first time in my life, I can actually say that I've found something that I care more about than myself... And it's you shorty. It's been three weeks since I gotten high. Blood, I said fuck that shit and went cold turkey. The first four days almost killed me, but it was worth it slim. I'm willing to do just about anything to have you in my life as a son."

Youngblood looked at Preacher Man and saw the sincerity in his eyes as he dissected every word his father said in his mind. Youngblood moved toward Preacher Man and wrapped his arms around him, giving his father a strong and affectionate hug. "Dad, I was fucked up at you, but I ain't never stop having love for you Joe," he said as he felt Preacher Man hugging him back.

Lost in her own private thoughts, Mae was still in the kitchen preparing Youngblood' breakfast when she notice how quiet it was in the living room. She stepped out of the kitchen and saw that no one was in sight, so she walked into Youngblood's room, and found the father and son embracing one another, while still holding pistols in their hands. "Lord Jesus," Mae whispered to herself, placing her hand over her bosom. "Please don't let the devil snatch my baby away from me."

Sitting at the breakfast table eating a bowl of Fruity Pebbles, Jay had already had it set in his mind that he was going to skip school that day. He was a senior at H.D. Woodson High School, and was an all around good student for the most part. Since this was his last school year, and since he had a secret agreement with one of his Assistant Principals for two thousand dollars to make sure he received a diploma, Jay had the luxury of going to school whenever he felt like it.

Feeling groggy from another night of sleepless rest, Jay looked at his distorted reflection on the back of his cereal spoon, and saw the dark rings of weariness around his eyes. It had been close to a week now since the baby came home from the hospital, and since then, sleep had been a rare commodity. Jay couldn't deny that he loved having a little nephew around to care for, but all that gotdamn crying late at night was definitely something he could do without.

Skimming through the colorful flakes of his cereal, Jay looked up from his bowl and saw Nadia come into the kitchen, grab an empty bowl, and sit down in a chair beside him. "Let me get some," she said, reaching over him, grabbing the box of cereal. "These my favorite joints Joe. I could eat these all day."

Seeing the big Kool-Aid smile light up his little sister's beautiful face, Jay couldn't help but to laugh to himself. No matter how irritable he could be in the morning, just one look at Nadia's little goofy self would change his whole attitude, and put him in a jovial state of mind. No longer feeling the need to pass the time by playing with his food, Jay dipped his index finger into a bowl of groggy cereal, then quickly jabbed it into Nadia's ear.

Feeling the cold milk spill out of her ear, Nadia jumped up out of her seat, cupped her hand to the spot Jay caught her off guard at, and said, "ooh, I'm a get you back good!" laughing and waiving her finger at Jay. "It's on now Joe! I ain't squashin' no beefs. The first time I catch you slippin', I'm a bust you, watch and see."

"Damn Joe, I thought me and you was partners," said Jay, throwing his hands in the air.

"Naw cuz, you just violated, so now I gots to put that work in Joe." Nadia sat back down, turning her chair at an angle where she could keep an eye on her brother. Jay just looked at her smiling, thinking to himself, 'how could such a pretty little girl be such a thugged out tomboy?' He knew he played a major role in turning her into the "baby gangsta" that she was. At a time where most seven year old girls favorite movies were The Little Mermaid and The Lion King, Nadia found more enjoyment watching movies like Scarface and Menace 2 Society.

"Don't you got to get ready for school?" asked Jay, looking at his watch. "You was late last time for class 'cause you wanted to wait all late to eat breakfast and shit."

"I'm ready now. All I gots to do is run upstairs and get my jacket. Besides, you said you was gonna take me to school anyway."

"Aight, check this out then. Hurry up and finish eating while I run down to my room and put some shit on." Jay got up from the table and dropped his bowl off in the sink. Still dressed in his tank top and boxers, Jay started laughing as he listened to Nadia telling him that he needed to pull his drawers out of his butt.

Running down the basement stairs, Jay quickly threw on some Calvin Klein blue jeans, and a plaid Armani Exchange pullover windbreaker. He reached underneath his bed and grabbed a pair of black suede Prada ankle boots, sliding them onto his feet. Looking in the mirror, Jay checked himself out, making sure he was fresh as can be while searching through his bureau for one of his gold necklaces. Personally, he didn't really care too much for jewelry, but he would buy one or two pieces here and there, just to have it.

By niggaz from D.C. having their own unique "fly gangsta" style of dress and conduct, Jay looked at niggaz who wore a lot of flashy jewelry in the city as straight bammas on some New York shit, but Bammas were taking over the world, Jay thought, as more and more young Niggaz got caught up in the MTV "commercial gangsta" generation. Grabbing his .45 Desert Eagle out of the closet, Jay tucked the gun in the front of his jeans, underneath his jacket, and sprinted up the stairs where he found Nadia standing in the foyer waiting on him.

Taking the necklace out of his pocket, Jay stepped in front of Nadia and placed the thick 14 karat gold Gucci-Link chain around her neck. It was an $1100 necklace he was giving her, but Nadia didn't know anything about how much it was worth. All she knew was that it made her look like a big girl, and for tha reason alone, she fell in love with the chain. "Oooh, thanks Jay!" said Nadia, leaping up and kissing him on the cheek.

"It ain't no thing squirt. You just better not let nobody take it from you." Jay picked up Nadia's book bag and carried it for her as they both walked out the front door. Heading to his car, he noticed a brown Taurus station wagon parked a few cars down with two people sitting in the front seat. Being in the street life, Jay had to be on point with who drove what in his neighborhood, so immediately the unrecognizable vehicle made his antennas go up. But upon closer inspection, the more he looked at the wagon, the more the person sitting in the passenger seat looked like his younger sister Rasheeda.

Escorting Nadia to his car, Jay opened the door and told her to hop in the front seat. "Stay here, I'll be right back," he said, closing the door and walking down towards the station wagon. Creeping up to the passenger window, Jay looked in and saw Rasheeda passing a blunt back to the dude in the driver's seat. Snapping at the sight of his sister trying to get her smoke on, Jay yanked the door open and snatched her up out of the car by her hair.

Infuriated by the embarrassment Jay just caused her, Rasheeda tried to fight back by scratching him in the face, but Jay quickly sidestepped the move, and threw her face-first on the wagon's hood, kicking her square in the ass with the side of his foot. Jay was about to choke her out a little bit when he saw the dude hop out of the wagon and run towards him.

Jay let Rasheeda go and spun around to face the dude, whipping out the Desert Eagle. Seeing the huge .45 in Jay's hand, the boy stopped dead in his tracks. Putting up his hands in the air as a sign of not wanting any trouble, the boy took a step back and said, "hold up cuz! I ain't trying to beef 'bout no bitch dawg — you can have the hoe."

Stepping straight into the boy's chest, Jay wanted to empty his entire clip into the young nigga's head, but not knowing who was watching, he put the gun down to his side, controlling his rage as best he could. "You bitch ass nigga!" said Jay, spitting the words into the boy's face. "This ain't about to bitch or hoe... That's my muthafuckin' sister you talkin''bout nigga."

"Oh, my bad main man, I ain't know all that."

"Who's you anyway," Jay asked, mugging the dude out viciously.

"My name's Rod, I'm from around Forest Creek," the boy said, like that was supposed to mean something to Jay.

"Aye slim, you know what... you out of bounds like a muthafucka," said Jay, slapping Rod in the face with the .45. "Bitch ass nigga, next time I see your Maryland bamma ass around here, I'ma shake yo' soul, fo' real."

"You got that big man!" said Rod, covering his hand over the open gash underneath his left eye. "Just please don't kill me slim."

"Nigga, just get your bitch ass from around here!" said Jay, watching the boy haul ass to his station wagon, and driving off at top speed, for dear life. Standing behind him with the sniffles, Rasheeda didn't know what to do with herself. Seeing how Rod had disrespected her by calling her a bitch and a hoe, she was kind of glad that Jay did what he did to him, but being a witness to Jay's violent nature, she was also introduced to a new and never before seen side of her big brother.

Jay tucked the gun back into his waist and turned around, seeing how Rasheeda looked. He walked over and placed his arm around her shoulder as she started crying against his chest. Kissing the side of her face, Jay said, "shorty, that's what I was tryn'a tell you about hoppin' yo' El' ass in these niggaz cars and shit. You don't know what type of shit these niggaz be on out here, so you can't just be joy riding with any ole body. That ain't cool at all."

"I thought Rod and I were friends," said Rasheeda, in between sobs. "We were always cool before this."

"Man, check this out," said Jay, turning her so he could look her in the face. "You ain't a little girl no more shorty. You's a pretty young thang, your lil' titties are getting bigger, your ass is starting to get phat... so you gotta start using your head. The average nigga ain't gon' try to be nice to you and let you smoke all his weed just 'cause he tryn'a be friendly. Hell naw, the average is going to be tryn'a fuck! So smarten up champ."

"I feel you Jameel, but you ain't had to embarrass me like that."

"You'll be aight," Jay said as they both started walking to his car. "But since you wanna hook school and hang wit' them Yankees, I'ma let you hang out wit' me and show you how a real nigga operate." Jay opened the back door and let Rasheeda climb into the car. He then ran over to the driver's side and hopped in, starting the car up. Looking over at Nadia, Jay couldn't help but to smile, peeping how she was up to her usual antics. Being the little shit starter that she was, Nadia couldn't help herself as she turned around, looked at Rasheeda and said, "uh huh, you got that ass beat, didn't you?"

Trying not to laugh, Jay plucked Nadia on the side of her head. "Girl, sit your little ass down," he said, not wanting to make Rasheeda feel any worse than she was already feeling. "That's why me and Rasheeda going to Georgetown today while you gon' be stuck in school."

"So!" said Nadia, pouting her little lips. Folding her arms across her chest, she looked up at Jay with her own version of a "mad dog" mug on her face. "You just better have something for me when you pick me up from school. Or else, it's gon' be some drama." On that note, Jay smashed the gas and high tailed to Nadia's school with a quickness.

Drama City

Chapter 12

Waiting in the parking lot of Lorton's Maximum Security facility, Youngblood and Preacher Man sat in the Cadillac talking, trying to catch up on the lost years as they waited for Jay to arrive. Twelve minutes into their conversation, Youngblood looked up and saw the Caprice slowly make its way over the gravel covered lot, parking in one of the few available spots that were still left.

Stepping out the Coupe Deville, Youngblood and Preacher Man walked over to Jay's car as he and Rasheeda got out, meeting them half way. Although Jay didn't show it, he was really surprised to see Youngblood and his father walking side by side like they were. It was as if they were the best of friends. Reaching out his hand, Jay gave the both of them some "dap" as he looked at the two, smiling, and said, "damn it feels good to be a gangsta."

"Shiiiid, nigga, I thought you forgot we said we was gon' visit slim and them today," said Youngblood, catching Jay with a soft blow to the body.

"Naw slim, I took Rasheeda down Georgetown this morning and bought her a few outfits, then fucked around and caught up in traffic."

"See, that's the problem right there," said Youngblood, looking over at Rasheeda. "You always spoiling them girls."

"Boy, shut up and mind your own damn business," Rasheeda shot back, rolling her eyes at him.

"You is my business, and don't forget it either chump," he said, causing her to start blushing.

Hearing the sound of tires rolling over top of gravel, they all turned around and saw a money-green Range Rover slowly driving up behind them. As the truck pulled up beside them, the driver's window came down, and Jay looked inside to see his man Eyone and Short Dog chilling, listening to "Raise Up," by Eyone's rap group P.O.W. "What's up Joe!" said Eyone, smiling, sticking his hand out of the window to give Jay some "dap."

"Aint too much wit' me champ," Jay said, giving him a nod of approval while checking out the Range. "But the word around town is you the one, jive doing the muthafucka."

"I'm doing a lil' something Joe, but check this out, you know me and my wife Aisha about to start up a book publishing company called Fast Lane Publications."

"Oh yeah, you doing it like that?!"

"Yeah slim, it ain't a game with me Joe," said Eyone, grinning. "I just got finished writing my book entitled *"Fast Lane,"* and P.O.W.'s CD is jive picking up across the East Coast. Plus my man Fat Nathan got his book coming called *"Gots 2 Love It,"* and Malik wrote a vicious joint called *"Silent Pain."* So basically, I'm tryn'a get this paper from all angles, ya dig."

"I feel you slim," said Jay, giving Eyone some more "dap" and said, "just let me know when everything's going to be coming out so I can buy a copy of them joints."

"You got that Joe, lookin' out big for the cause," he said, nodding his chin up to Jay and them as he started to pull off. "I'ma holler at y' all folks, y' all be easy."

"You know the same goes for you too champ," said Jay, as they all began walking to the visitor's registration lobby. Inside the prison's visitor waiting room, they all waited for the prison guard to come and escort them to the inmate's cafeteria, which was also used as a visiting hall. Not too long ago, being a prisoner behind "the wall" himself, Preacher Man was all too familiar with the formalities of being patted down, searched, and damn near physically molested, just to visit the people you care about, trapped behind enemy lines.

Looking around at the other visitors who were also waiting to be let into the institution, Preacher Man laughed silently to himself, seeing how most of the women in the room looked like the "hogs," who played on the offensive line for the Washington Redskins. Catching on to what it was that had Preacher Man chuckling, Jay moved over to where he was, and said, "man, ain't no way in hell I'ma let a broad that muthafuckin' big come visit me, unless she toting that 'pack'."

"Youngster, there's two things a nigga gotta learn when dealin' wit'

126

females while you in the joint," said Preacher Man, giving up some of his jail house wisdom. "The first thing is that it's kind of hard to keep one of them high-maintenance broads, unless yo' money is just as thick as her hips, ya dig? So in most cases, it's cheaper and less of a headache to just love whoever loves you. And secondly, ain't no bitch in the world gon' do a bid wit' a nigga like a fat bitch. All you gots to do is make them fat muthafucka's pay like they weigh, and you'll be set."

"I feel you and all that," said Jay, as the prison guard finally made his way into the lobby, allowing everyone to enter the prison compound. "But I just hope that I never get the opportunity to see whether your theory is on point or not."

Walking down the Lorton walkway, Rasheeda felt a little self-conscious wearing her Moschino denim wrap around skirt tightly across her curvaceous rear end. Feeling like the hungry eyes of the inmates on the other side of the fence were lusting too hard on her, she snuggled up against Youngblood, walking with him as close as possible.

Once inside the visiting hall, they all checked in with the guard who was supervising all the visits, and found an empty table over by the vending machines. Since Youngblood had a fake I.D., he and Jay were both able to call out Ernest and Dominic at the same time, while Preacher Man roamed through the visiting hall, keeping it real with all the convicts he recently left.

Seeing lil' Smooth, Roscoe, Buddy-Love, Gator, and Michael Lucas all sitting at a table accompanied by the lovely young ladies who were visiting them, Preacher Man showed everybody love, giving all the men "dap," while complimenting the women. "Eric Weaver from Valley Green," said Preacher Man, sitting in between Smooth and Roscoe. "I see you and Roc' still got y'all hoe-game down pat."

"You know shit don't stop 'cause a nigga got popped,' said Smooth, living up to his nickname.

"A nigga gotta keep a work horse in his stable, ya dig." Roscoe joined in the conversation, imitating "Goldie" from the movie the Mack. "We gorilla pimpin' down here baby."

"I can dig it shorty," Preacher Man said, laughing, while making sure there were no guards paying any attention to him. Sticking his hand inside his pants, Preacher Man reached underneath his nuts and pulled out a condom filled with four dippers of pure heroin from Afghanistan. He slid the "pack" to Smooth, and said, "that shit right there can stand a 20 or better, so you and Roscoe can split three of them joints, and give the other dipper to Nehemiah from R Street' cause I been promise to get slim when I got out."

Looking down at the "pack" in his hand, Smooth signaled for Ms. Usher, who was the C.O. supervising the visits to come over to the table. "Look here you crack head bitch," said Smooth, handing the dope to the guard. "Take this shit to my cell for me, and make sure you have my fish and cheese sub ready when you get off your lunch break." Taking and cuffing the "pack," Ms. Usher walked away, as Smooth turned his attention back to Preacher Man. "Damn slim, I see you got that glow."

"Yeah shorty, I'm getting my life together," said Preacher Man. "I don't fuck around no more, so I had to find me a new high."

"What's that?" Rosco asked, looking at him curiously.

"Robbing and killing hot niggaz," Preacher said, smiling like a lunatic. "It's the best muthafuckin' high in the world, praise the Lord."

Coming back to the table with an arm full of sodas and junk food from the vending machines, Youngblood and Rasheeda sat down beside Jay, as Riley Mercer, Lonnie Hart, Hawkeye, Larry Moe, Tre, Ernest, and Dominic all came into the visiting hall high as a muthafucka off the skunk weed. Showing their love, Jay, Youngblood and Rasheeda gave everybody a quick embrace, as Ernest and Dominic sat down at their table, watching the rest of the comrades go over to their visitors.

"What's up Joe!" said Ernest, grinning while giving Jay and Youngblood some "dap." Looking over at Rasheeda, he couldn't believe how big and pretty she had gotten since the last time he saw her. "Damn shorty, you growed up like a muthafucka. I still remember when you was a little booger eater."

"Boy, shut up!" said Rasheeda, waving him off. "I see you still look the same, except you got big muscles now."

"Well you know what I'm saying..." Ernest stuck his chest out and started making his pectoral muscles jump. "Shit like this comes from puttin' that work in, Joe."

"You see the beach bamma shit I gotta put up wit', fuckin' wit' this niggaz?" Dominic said, pointing his thumb over at Ernest. "This shit is getting out of control."

Laughing and joking on one another, they all kicked as they pigged out on the junk food scattered across the table. Ernest was live and direct as he told Jay about how Antoine from First Street and Mario from Newton Street had had a clash in the bull pen when they were in court the other day. Both of the two Lorton legends were heavy weights in tha game, and niggaz on the compound were anticipating a bloody battle between the two. While Dominic, on the other hand, was laid back, and telling Youngblood how he had crushed the nigga L.L. in the trailer after an Islamic service.

Checking his watch, Jay saw that it was almost time for him to roll out, since they had already been up there for an hour, and he had to pick Nadia up from school. Pulling out from his briefs an ounce of Purple Haze weed compressed into a concealable sized ball inside of a balloon, Jay slid the "pack" over to Ernest, while dropping five $50 bills into a small potato chip bag, passing it over to him as well.

Youngblood was leaning over taking off his brand new Timberland boots, as he swapped shoes with Dominic. The ounce of weed that Youngblood was carrying now was flattened inside the boots, so he put Dominic on point about the move. As everybody stood up and embraced one another, and prepared to leave the visiting hall, Ernest pulled Jay aside and asked him about the supposed caper some niggaz around D Street had pulled off. "I'm telling you slim, some niggaz from around the way came off like a muthafucka!" Ernest whispered, looking Jay dead in the eyes. "You mean to tell me you ain't hear nothing about no shit like that?"

"Aye slim, the only time I heard about some niggaz in the hood robbing some New York niggaz, is when Mojo and Scales went on a move together," said Jay, thinking back to what Youngblood had told him on the morning he killed Scales. "But them niggaz ain't come up on no hundred-some thousand, 27 bricks, or some heavy shit like that."

"How long ago was it when they went on that move?"

"Close to a month now."

"Oh yeeeah, that's about the same time New York Steve got smashed up W Street," Ernest said, trying to piece everything together. "and they say the nigga Scales got crushed the next morning, huh?"

"Yeah, I heard somebody broke slim off like a muthafucka," said Jay, playing the conversation by ear. "The word on the street was that the nigga was hot, working with the bodines and shit."

"Hell naw slim," said Ernest, waving his hand, "that nigga Scales may have been a vicious snake, but he wasn't no rat. I'm telling you slim, that nigga Mojo hit that lick, and then played cruddy by slobbing his partner off. Damn I wish I was out there, I'd take all that bitch ass nigga's shit, off the no bullshit!"

"I feel you champ," said Jay, with his mind now thinking heavily on the possibility of Ernest being right, "but I'm a most definitely look into that, A.S.A.P."

"Yeah slim, you do that, and be careful out there while you doing it." Ernest gave Jay some "dap" and rolled out, catching up with Dominic and the rest of the comrades behind "the wall."

Still pondering on whether there was some truth to Ernest's claim, Jay pointed out to Youngblood the concern he was now having about the move he pulled for Mojo. Even though it had been nearly a month without any signs of some snake shit, Jay was well aware that absence of evidence wasn't evidence of absence.

Out in the parking lot, Jay kicked it with Youngblood and Preacher Man for a brief moment and told them about everything Ernest had just told him in the visiting hall. They all agreed that Mojo was definitely a nigga who couldn't be trusted, but none could see how the robbery and murder of a New Yorker could affect or involve Youngblood. Personally, Jay thought that it was a bad move on Youngblood's part, getting involved with anything to do with Mojo's cruddy ass, and he definitely didn't like the fact that he killed Scales for him. But the damage had already been done, as they chose not to dwell on the past. Though if worst came to worst, and Mojo decided to pull some snake shit, Jay was going to ride with his partner until the end... Blood in, blood out.

Giving his comrades some "dap," Jay told them that he would see them around the way later on, as he and Rasheeda hopped in the car and rolled out. Driving down 1-95 North, Jay's cell phone started ringing. He grabbed it away from Rasheeda as she tried to answer it, and clicked the phone on, hearing the sound of Chico's voice saying, "What's up?"

130

"Ain't shit slim," said Jay, "what's happen wit' you though?"

"Aye dawg, I need to holler at you, with the quickness!"

"Man, what's going on?" Jay asked, hearing the urgency in his voice. Being a straight "head hitter" from the Southeast side of Benning Road, Chico was probably on his paranoid Puerto Rican shit again, and fucked around and killed some more niggaz for bullshitting, Jay thought to himself.

"Aye slim, you know I don't fuck wit' these phone and shit..." Chico said, taking a brief pause before speaking again, "but this shit is serious as a muthafucka. Just hurry up and get around here ASAP!"

"I got my liP sister in the car with me right now, plus I gotta pick up the other one from Elementary School, so soon as I drop them off at the house, I'll be straight over there."

"Aight then Joe, I'll holler at you when I see you," said Chico, emphasizing every word. "Just make sure you come straight over! And keep the hammer close to you."

Hanging up the phone, Jay quickly drove back to the city and picked Nadia up from Charles Young Elementary. Sensing that Jay was in no playing mood, his two sisters sat quietly to themselves as he dropped them off at the house. Watching them go inside, Jay reached underneath the car dash board and pulled out the Desert Eagle. He cocked the gun back locking a Hydro Shock bullet into the .45's deadly chamber, while driving off in a hurry.

Doing 90 mph down East Capitol Street, Jay turned onto Benning Road Southeast, driving over to the 24-Hour Store. Seeing Chico posted up in the "cut," dressed in a green Columbia Rain suit, Jay was about to get out until he saw Chico motioning for him to stay where he was at. Watching him dig underneath some bushes, Jay unlocked his door as Chico grabbed his Calico and ran to the car. Looking at Chico, the average nigga would probably sleep on him, thinking that he was just one of those "fly guy" types, with his curly hair and light brown eyes, but underneath his pretty-boy exterior, lurked the mind of a straight serial killer. He was loyal to his friends... but lethal to his foes.

Jay and Chico had known one another since their years at Elliot Junior High, but on one school day when some boys around Kentucky Courts tried to jump Chico, Jay had helped him rumble the little dudes, thus earning Chico's loyalty for life. "Aye dawg, you wouldn't believe what the fuck I just found out today!" Chico said, placing the Calico in his lap.

"Man, nigga what's up?!" said Jay, "you got a muthafucka all in suspense and shit."

"Eh, remember my Muslim brother, Bucky Fields, from up Barry Farms?"

"Yeah, what's up with Akhi?"

"He aight, but you know Bucky be on his SAHNA shit like a muthafucka, and..."

"Man, what the hell is SAHNA?" Jay cut him off, trying to figure out what Chico was talking about.

"Slim you know, SAHNA — Smash All Hot Niggaz Association. But anyway, me and Bucky caught this hot nigga who used to fuck with that snitch ass nigga Alpo from New York, and robbed the nigga. When slim was about to slump the nigga, the Yankee started talkin' 'bout he knew another New Yorker who was getting major paper in the city, and if we let him live, he would set it up so we could rob the dude. The hot nigga went on to say how the New Yorker was tripping lately, spending a rack of money tryn'a find out who killed his HP brother who was getting money uptown."

"Aight slim, I feel you and all that," said Jay, trying to maintain his patience, "but what do any of this have to do with me?"

"It got a lot to do with you!" said Chico, throwing up his hands. "The nigga said that word got back to the Yankee that your little man Youngblood smashed his brother, and that he put a 50 thousand dollar hit on both y'all heads."

"What?!" said Jay, wanting to go on the war path. "Who the fuck is the nigga that's suppose to be putting a hit out on me?!"

"Some nigga named C-god. You know 'em?"

"Fuck naw... but I'm trying to get to know 'em."

"Well we can get on top of that right now," Chico said, with a murderous smirk on his face. "We still got the hot nigga alive, so you can talk to him yourself, or do whatever the fuck you want to the punk."

"Yeah man, I think I need to pay cuz a little visit, ya dig?" Jay made a quick u-turn and drove to the spot where Chico and Bucky Fields had the hot nigga stashed at. Jay parked his car a few blocks down from the house where Bucky was waiting for them, which was a block and a half away from the Simple City housing projects. Both men stepped out of the car and headed over to the house. Chico was the first one to walk up on the porch, knocking on the front door three time before Tap came and let them into the house.

Standing in the doorway, Jay could see the blood stains all across Tap's white t-shirt as he walked past him. Jay had met Tap a few years ago around L Street Southwest, through Chico, and knew that he and Bucky were cousins. Not in the mood for too much conversation, Tap signaled with his hand for them to follow him, while he lead them down the basement stairs. As they all entered the gloomy room, the stench of urine was thick as fog. Jay strolled over to where Bucky Fields was standing over top of two niggaz, who were both duct taped and bleeding badly.

"What's up with you Moe-grey?" said Bucky, holding a small sledgehammer in his hands.

"Ain't shit, big Akhi," Jay said, pulling out his Desert Eagle. "I see you been having yourself a good ole time."

"Yeah moe, we finally caught these bitches," said Bucky, kicking both the niggaz in their faces. Walking over to them holding a rechargeable, hot hair curling iron, Tap kneeled down beside the two dudes lying on the basement floor. "These my codefendants Ronnie and Roland," said Tap, turning the hair curler on. "They snitched on me on a drug beef we had, and got me a life sentence. But a month after my conviction the courts had to reverse my shit 'cause of ineffective assistance of counsel. So I ended up beating the case in a retrial.

Seeing that the curler was now piping hot, Tap pushed Ronnie over on his stomach, and snatched the back of Ronnie's pants down to his thighs. Ronnie's eyes got big as headlights as Tap bent over top of him, placing his knee in Ronnie's back. "Since you like running your mouth," said Tap, looking the coward in his eyes, "tell me how these hot curlers feel in your hot ass, bitch nigga!" Tap rammed the hair curler into the rat's rectum, and even Jay had to admit that that was some diabolical shit to

133

be a witness to.

Jay heard the muffled screaming through the strip of duct tape covering Ronnie's mouth, but the pain was so intense his body couldn't take it, as Ronnie went into shock and fainted. Chico moved over to where Roland was lying in a pool of sweat, piss, and fear. Tears were rolling down Roland's face as he pleaded for his life with his eyes. Chico kneeled beside the "rat," placing the Calico to his head, and said, "This the whore right here who was telling me 'bout the nigga C-god."

Jay reached down and snatched the duct tape off of Roland's mouth. "Who the fuck is this nigga C-God and where he be at?" asked Jay, bending down to where he was at eye level with Roland.

"The nigga is a major money getter from New York" Roland started explaining, hoping the information would somehow save his miserable life. "Him and his crew be slinging heavy up Clifton Terrace, and the nigga jive fucks with me tough, so I can easily set him up for y'all if y'all let me go."

"Man, fuck all that shit you talkin' 'bout!" Jay pressed the barrel of the .45 between Roland's eyes. "I wanna hear what you know about the nigga putting a hit out on me and my partner Youngblood!"

Thinking that there still might be a chance that his life would be spared, Roland started telling Jay everything he knew about C-god, and why he had put a contract out on him and Youngblood's head. Even though Roland didn't know exactly who it was that had taken the contract, he swore to Jay that he would find out immediately if they let him go. Baffled by the whole situation, Jay's mind started working at high speed; thinking on all the details Youngblood had given him about the robbery Mojo and Scales had supposed to have pulled on some New York dudes up Northwest.

Suddenly, everything that Ernest had told Jay about how he felt that Mojo was the one who robbed and killed New York Steve seemed to be on point like a muthafucka. Yet still, for the life of him, Jay could not figure out how some shit like that would involve him and Youngblood, especially to the point where it would make another nigga want to put a hit out for his life.

Looking over at Chico, Jay motioned for him to follow as he walked off to a corner of the room. Jay quickly explained how he had to roll out and

134

find Youngblood, to put him on point about the situation at hand. Chico was reluctant to let Jay leave by himself, but seeing how he wouldn't have been able to talk him into waiting, Chico made sure he understood that if he needed any help putting some work in, to holler at him a.s.a.p.

Jay gave his man some "dap" and hurriedly made his way up the basement stairs. Right before he reached the front door of the house, Jay heard several gunshots from the Calico, as Chico shot Roland multiple times in the face. Jay knew that Chico, Bucky Fields, and Tap didn't tolerate hot niggaz, but seeing how much pleasure they took in torturing snitches made him think on the consequences of violating the strict laws of street life.

Some niggaz, especially the real ones, just took "the Game" seriously like that. Death before dishonor... Blood before betrayal.

Drama City

Chapter 13

Just getting back around the way from their visit down Lorton, Preacher Man dropped Youngblood off at the corner of 18th & D, telling him that he would be back over to his grandma's place later on, and then pulled off

Youngblood jogged over to Dumb Wayne's building. Luckily, someone had left the outside door open, so Youngblood didn't have to hit the intercom and wait for someone to buzz him in.

Stepping into the hallway, Youngblood knocked on the door and waited for someone to let him in. Dumb Wayne came to the door, looked through the peep hole and opened the door letting him into the apartment. "What's up with you dummy?" Youngblood said, giving Dumb Wayne some "dap."

"Aye slim, we 'bout to go lay them bitch niggaz down around Rosedale!" Dumb Wayne said, closing the door, revealing the shotgun he was holding at the side of his leg. "Them niggaz was fakin' like shit up Eastern after school let out Joe."

"Man, what the fuck happen? You ain't telling me shit!" Youngblood said, trying to get him to slow down, so he could better understand what was about to pop off Dumb Wayne calmed down for a moment, and briefly put Youngblood on point. Apparently, from the story he was getting, it seemed like niggaz around D Street were about to go to war because the Twinz were ego tripping again.

For some reason, all through the upper half of Northeast, damn near every neighborhood had some twins living in them. From D Street, Kentucky Court, Rosedale, 21St & Vietnam, and Trinidad, it wasn't uncommon to find a pair of identical twin brothers who were heavy in the game, representing their hoods to the fullest. Lil' Derrick and Darrel were no exception.

Hanging out in front of Eastern Senior High School, the Twinz, Fat Derrick, Dumb Wayne, K.D., and Lil' Pat were all leaning against Lil'

Pat's Cadillac STS, waiting to holler at all the pretty young ladies who were about to get out of their classes. Eastern had had a reputation for having some of the prettiest and best dressed females in high school in Northeast D.C.; so naturally, all the niggaz in the surrounding area would drive their best cars and post up in front of the joint at 3 o'clock.

On this particular Friday afternoon, the Twinz, who were lunching off the "Boat" (PCP) again, saw the Rosedale Twinz pull up, and started mugging the dudes out. Ronald

and Donald didn't really want any trouble, and had only come around to book broads like everybody else, but there was too many people outside watching how the D Street Twinz were carrying them with their disrespectful stares. Words of war were then exchanged, igniting tempers and causing Fat Derrick to punch Ronald in the mouth with an overhand right.

As Fat Derrick and the Twinz started stomping Ronald out, K.D., Lil' Pat, and Dumb Wayne all flipped out their stainless steel Hawkbill knives and began chasing Donald down Constitution Avenue. Just when Lil' Pat finally grabbed a hold of Donald and stabbed him in the lower back, a smoke gray LTD stopped in the middle of the street, and four niggaz hopped out, busting semi-automatic pistols at them.

Lil' Pat spun off between two parked cars, barely missing the barrage of bullets that were aimed at his head. K.D. and Dumb Wayne immediately crouched down and started running in a zigzag pattern, trying to dodge the "hot balls" as best they could. Fortunately for the three boys, the police were nearby, and came rushing onto the scene with their sirens blaring. Since the four dudes didn't want to get into a shootout with the bodines, they jumped back into the LTD, while pulling Donald into the backseat. As the dudes sped off, Lil' Pat caught a glimpse of the driver balling past him. It was the nigga Hallway from Rosedale.

Listening to Dumb Wayne telling him about the Eastern Situation, Youngblood knew it wasn't time to talk. Somebody had to die! Along with Jay, the Twinz and Lil' Pat were like brothers to Youngblood, and if ever there was some drama involving either one of his niggaz, he would be rolling like balls with them — off the no games. "So where everybody at?" Youngblood asked.

Dumb Wayne motioned with his head, nodding in the direction of his room. He then went over and sat on his couch, loading some deer slugs into the Mossberg 10 gage. Youngblood gave a knock on the door and walked into Dumb Wayne's bedroom. The sight of angry niggaz with automatics made it clear that murder was the order of the day. Lil' Pat had just finished loading up the Mini 14, while Fat Derrick was taping black electrical tape around two 50 round magazines. Popping one of the clips into the AR-15, Fat Derrick stood up and said, "Pops said always look a man in the eyes before you killed' em."

"Where's K.D. and the Twinz?" Youngblood asked, seeing that they were not in the room.

"They went to go steal a car," said Lil' Pat, giving him some "dap." "Where's Jay at though?"

"He had to pick up his little sister from school, but y'all 'bout to put the work in now, huh?"

"Yeah slim, I gots to! Them bitch ass niggaz tried to take my head off — no bullshit."

Youngblood walked over to Dumb Wayne's bed and pulled out the Glock 40, tucking the gun into his waist. "How y'all gon' give it to'em?"

"You rolling wit' us on this one young scrapper?" Fat Derrick asked, already knowing the answer to the question.

"In that muthafuckin' order! Y'all's beef is my beef."

"In that order," Fat Derrick repeated after Youngblood, nodding his head. He knew the young nigga meant every word he said, and that was one of the main reasons why he had major love for him. Youngblood was as real as they come.

Going over the details of the hit in Dumb Wayne's living room, they all agreed to let Youngblood go through the front way of Rosedale, while K.D. drove the rest of them around the back so they could lay in ambush and vamp down on the niggaz as they ran past. Hearing a car horn honking out front, Lil' Pat looked out the window and saw K.D. waiting for them in a stolen Honda Accord with the Twinz already in the back seat. The car only had enough room for two more passengers, so Dumb Wayne had no choice but to push his own joint, as Fat Derrick and Lil' Pat hopped inside the Accord.

Following Dumb Wayne, Youngblood got inside the Crown Victoria, as Dumb Wayne drove off, trailing behind K.D. and them. Driving down 15th Street, K.D. slowed down to let Dumb Wayne pass him so he could drop Youngblood off at the corner of Kramer Street, directly across from the Rosedale recreation center. Stepping out of the car, Youngblood started jogging down the block to 16th Street. Bending the corner of Rosedale Street, the strip was alive with all types of activity.

It was a little after 4 o'clock on the windy autumn afternoon, and the wild brave souls of inner-city children were running around all over the place. Walking past a group of little girls jumping double Dutch, Youngblood pulled the Glock out of his waist band and crossed the street to where a bunch of young niggaz were crowded in front of Candy's house, shooting a game of craps. Youngblood pulled his Black Madness ski mask up over his nose, which only covered half of his face, and crept up on the dudes rolling dice.

Candy was sitting on the steps of her front porch, braiding Lil' Meat's hair, and was the first one to see Youngblood creeping up on them. Youngblood already knew that Hallway and the Rosedale Twins probably wouldn't be out there, especially after the drama that had just ensued up at Eastern. He already had it in his mind that any and everybody from Rosedale was fair game. "Watch out y'all!" Candy screamed, leaping up on the porch, while accidently pushing Lil' Meat down the steps.

Only 14 years old, and fresh to the game, Lil' Meat never got a chance to be an official player. He felt the bone shattering slugs burn through his chest cavity.

Youngblood squeezed one more round from the Glock 40 into Lil' Meat's body, leaving him crumbled up in the fetal position at the bottom of Candy's steps. Youngblood then pivoted to the right with his gun raised, spitting several rounds at the dispersing crowd of young niggaz who were rolling dice earlier.

Just as they had planned, the Rosedale Niggaz were trying to break through the back of the rec. center to make an escape, and met a bloody fate, as they ran right into the cut where Fat Derrick and Lil' Pat were waiting with two fully loaded assault rifles. But what Youngblood didn't plan for, was for some niggaz to regroup and start busting back at him. Hallway and the same three dudes who had busted off at Lil' Pat earlier, had somehow crept back around Rosedale, and were now trying to tear a plug out of Youngblood's little ass.

Ducking behind a big green trash dumpster, Youngblood saw the two dudes step across the street while Hallway and Corey stood on the sidewalk, dumping a P12 at the slightest movement he made. Seeing that Hallway and Corey had him hemmed in, Youngblood let off two more rounds before hearing the Glock click. "Kiss my muthafuckin' ass!" Youngblood said, realizing that he just made one of the most stupid mistakes of his life.

When beefing with gun-play, Jay had taught him to never let a nigga force you up into a dead-end spot, and never to shoot all your bullets out of your gun while still in your enemy's 'hood. Yet getting lost in the excitement of making niggaz run for their lives, Youngblood fucked around and did everything he was taught not to do, and was now about to pay the ultimate price for not thinking in the heat of battle.

Hallway had figured that Youngblood had run out of bullets, as he started walking towards the trash dumpster, eagerly anticipating emptying the rest of his clip into Youngblood's head, but just when Hallway got close up to the dumpster, Youngblood heard the earth-quaking sound of the 10 gauge as Dumb Wayne came out of the cut, thumping the Mossberg pump like he was chasing the Predator.

Caught off guard and stunned by the surprise attack, Hallway found himself in a hopeless situation as the steel ball of the Deer Slug caught him in the side of the body, instantly dislocating his shoulder and collar bone. Dumb Wayne pumped the shotgun and fired a slug into Hallway's stomach, which sent him flying to the concrete. Corey and the other two dudes then turned their pistols on Dumb Wayne, forcing him to take cover behind a parked SUV. The three of them were all going to vamp down on him, desperately wanting to kill at least one nigga from the other side, but the sight of K.D. and the Twinz running out of the alley, busting their .9 mm and .45's at them was just too much, and forced them to get low and try to haul ass.

The whole situation only lasted a minute or so, but for Youngblood — it seemed like an eternity. When all was said and done, after the smoke cleared, three niggaz from Rosedale, along with Hallway, were found shot to death on that bloody Friday afternoon. Several innocent bystanders were injured, including two little 8 year old boys who were caught in the cross fire. Niggaz were going to have to lay low for a minute. The blocks were going to be too hot.

Sitting back in the passenger seat of the Crown Victoria, Youngblood was thinking on just how close he had come to getting himself killed. He never really gave any thought to his own demise before, and especially not imagining another nigga dogging him out the way he was used to dogging others. One thing was for certain; now he was a firm believer in the old saying that he'd heard many times before: "it ain't no fun when the rabbit got the gun..." and that was the God's honest truth.

Driving down C Street, Jay was so lost in thought that he didn't even pay attention to the road block that was in front of him. He didn't want to take any chances, in the event that he was pulled over and searched; Jay quickly stashed the Desert Eagle inside the dashboard. Looking up ahead through the windshield, he noticed a train of Humvees driving down 16th Street. National Guardsmen were everywhere, posting up huge spot lights on top of the Humvees, sealing off the area within a twenty block radius.

Jay drove up to the police check-point and stopped, rolling down his tinted window so the officer could look inside the car. Even though it wasn't completely dark outside, the officer still flashed his search light around the inside of the car, while asking him for some I.D. Jay reached into the glove compartment and grabbed his car registration papers, and handed it over to the officer along with his driver's license. "Damn officer, what the hell happened around here? Jay asked, genuinely curious about the surrounding presence of the National Guard.

"Four young people were killed in a shoot-out today in the 1600 block of Rosedale," the policeman said, shaking his head in a grim manner. "I don't know why these young folks choose to throw away their lives the way they do."

"I don't know either," Jay said, taking back his documents from the officer. "That's just the way it is, I guess." Jay pulled off and drove down 17th Street and parked in front of Youngblood's building. Standing out front of the apartments, Mae White was talking to her neighbor, Ms. Dorothy, when Jay walked up to her, giving her a hug and a kiss on the cheek. "What's up granny? It looks like you're about to kill somebody."

Mae sat down on the edge of the stoop, as if she were relieving her feet from a heavy burden she was carrying. She shook her head twice and looked up at Jay with tears in her eyes. "That damn hoodlum ass grandson of mines, that's what's up!"

"What happened?" Jay asked, as his heart started beating faster, hoping his partner didn't get himself caught up in some crash dummy shit.

"Dorothy was just telling me how she had seen Demetrius running down 16th Street with a damn gun in his hand," said Mae, explaining everything that Dorothy's old nosy ass had told her about the shooting. She went into details about how, even though Youngblood was wearing a ski mask half-way covering his face, after having seen him and known him for all his life, she easily recognized him by the way he moved.

Jay looked over at Ms. Dorothy, shooting daggers at her with his eyes. Watching her shuffle her way into the building, Jay couldn't be too fucked up at the old lady. He would rather have her telling Mae about the shooting than the police. With that in mind,

Jay made a mental note to make sure that he buy Ms. Dorothy a little gift for keeping her mouth closed to the fedz. Maybe a wide screen TV or something, Jay thought to himself, so next time she could keep her nosy ass in her apartment and watch soap operas and shit.

Giving Mae another reassuring hug, Jay promised her that he would find and make sure that Youngblood was okay. "I swear to God Jameel, if it wasn't for my daughter passing away, I would kick Demetrius's little ass out of my place!" Mae said, getting up and moving towards the front door. "I love that little boy more than life, but he's gon' run me to my grave having me worry about him out here running these streets. I tell you Jameel, that boy's going to be just like his no good ass father if he don't straighten up!"

"Naw granny, Youngblood's going to be straight," said Jay, kissing Mae on the cheek again. "We gon' make sure of that, ya dig." Jay left the apartment and started jogging down the two blocks, leading to 18" & D. He slowed his pace and walked past the two Humvees posted up in the parking lot. There was one guardsman standing in the back of the Humvee, gripping an M-60 that was mounted on top of it, while the other guardsman was controlling the huge spotlight on top of the Humvee next to it.

Jay stepped onto the strip, which was looking like a ghost town, and walked over to where Skip, Shank, and Lil' Gerald were leaning against an all black Suburban, showing some love to the niggaz from the hood. Jay couldn't believe how much heart they had, hustling out in the open, while the National Guardsmen were out policing the block. "Man, y'all niggaz going to jail out here bullshittin'" said Jay, as Lil' Gerald passed him a blunt he was smoking on.

"Out here bullshittin'?" Skip said, "shiiiid nigga, it's rocking like a muthafucka out here youngin'. Ain't no niggaz crowding up the strip, them krackaz ain't fuckin' wit' us... hell, this the American dream baby!"

"Man, y'all niggaz crazy, Joe." Jay stood around kicking it with his homiez for a while, smoking the blunt with Lil' Gerald. Shank was jive fucked up about how the Twinz had started all this beefing shit with them Rosedale niggaz, but since he had love for the little niggaz, he had to take the bitter with the sweet and ride it out with them. Shank told Jay about the incident up Eastern involving the Twinz, and how it lead to Youngblood going around Rosedale shooting the joint up.

After listening to Shank, Jay was convinced that it was time to have another serious talk with Youngblood. He understood that his little partner was loyal to the streets and his little buddy, but there was a big difference between loyalty and lunacy, and Youngblood was quickly becoming a gun toting, trigger happy lunatic. If it ain't one thing, it's a muthafuckin''nother, Jay thought to himself, as he gave his men some "dap," preparing to roll out. Stepping off to go back to his car, Jay stopped and turned around after he heard Lil' Gerald call his name.

"Aye slim, I forgot to tell you, that nigga Mojo was riding 'round here looking for you like shit," said Lil' Gerald, cocking his head in a questioning gesture. "What you owe that nigga some money or something?"

"Come on now shorty," said Jay, slightly insulted, "you know owing niggaz is for sucka niggaz, and I'm one of the few niggaz who's 100% sucka free."

"My bad gangsta-mack," Lil' Gerald laughed, "I just thought you was fucking with slim on the 'yayo' tip. I don't know who that nigga contact is — but Mojo jive hurting'em out here, charging niggaz $21 thousand a brick. And guess what slim? ... why the nigga bring them bitch ass niggaz Danny and bumpy face Juan back around here!"

"Danny and Juan?" Jay said, raising an eyebrow, "when did you see them niggaz?"

"They was ridin' in Mojo's 850 with'em."

"Damn Joe, I ain't think them niggaz would have the balls to show up around here again."

"Well they back," said Lil' Gerald, not hiding the disgust in his voice, "and it's only a matter of time before a nigga bust all three of they ass something terrible. But got-damn slim — what the fuck's up with you? Looking all in a daze and shit."

With Jay's mind being so preoccupied, he couldn't really disguise the confusion writing across his face. Jay wanted to ask Lil' Gerald and them if they knew or heard anything about a nigga putting a contract out for him and Youngblood's heads, but had decided it would be best not to. If they didn't know, he would only be pulling their coat to some shit he didn't need too many niggaz knowing about. And if they did know, by them not saying anything before, it meant that they were probably thinking about pulling a move against him. In his line of work, 50 grand could turn many a friend into a head-splitting foe, and Jay wasn't taking any chances.

"I'm straight lil' big man," said Jay, forcing a smile on his face, "just do me a favor, and let Youngblood know I need to holler at him a.s.a.p., if you see him before I do." Jay walked off to collect his thoughts, looking over both shoulders as he went. "Paranoia is a muthafucka," he said to himself, feeling out of pocket without his pistol.

Chapter 14

I once plucked a rose from the Garden of Eden
And the petals of the scarlet rose began to mourn
Unfamiliar with the ways of a flower
Until suddenly I was only left with thorns.
Carelessly caressing the thorns I had caused my fingers to bleed
Yet the sight of the shattered rose Was a greater tragecy indeed.
Foolish was I in my pursuit of selfishness
Unaware that the beauty of the rose would fade
And my blood beared witness to my vainful act
An ugly symbol to the mistake I had made.
Because the beauty of a rose belongs to none
I had no right to take it as my own
And as the petals became bloody tears in the grass
A painful lesson was vividly shown.

-Shaka, "Sacrilege" (The Raping of a Rose)

Parking her car on Georgia Avenue, Tameka got out and brushed some ashes off her tan leather J. Lindeberg jacket. She and Ebony had been smoking heavily all day on some skunk weed they had worked Jamaican Ta-Ta out of. Smoking, sipping, and sexing were Tameka's favorite activities, but more than anything, money was her motivation for living, and the more money she started scheming on, the more high maintenance she became.

Tameka checked her watch, seeing it was a little passed 5 o'clock. She was late again for a beauty appointment, but that meant very little in her mind, with all the money she planned on spending that evening. Ebony had been telling her about the Hair Gallery for weeks, trying to get her to check out some of the fly hairstyles the new beauty salon was becoming known for. Tameka finally gave in to the thought of trying something new, besides, she was already beautiful, and so the stylist wouldn't have too much work to do.

Walking into the Hair Gallery, Tameka and Ebony checked in with Dorey at the receptionist desk to verify their appointment. Since neither one of them had made arrangements to be seen by a specific beautician, Dorey handed them both a Hair Magazine with all the latest styles, and told them they would be seen shortly. Tameka and Ebony went and sat down in the lounge area, kicking it for a few minutes, when they both saw Pooh, Leia, and Kim walk through the front entrance.

After signing in with Dorey, the group of young ladies joined Tameka and Ebony in the waiting chairs, and started blowing the spot up, letting it be known that the Langston Terrace Honeys were up in there.

Giving Tameka the nod, Pooh pointed to her Fendi bag and walked off to find the restroom. Tameka quickly caught on the hint, and excused herself, making her way to the restroom after Pooh.

She walked inside the lavatory and found Pooh pouring a bottle of Remy VSOP into some small plastic cups. In Tameka's mind, a sip of cognac was right on time, since she was experiencing a serious case of the cotton mouth. Downing three straight cups of the alcohol, Tameka started feeling a little tipsy. "Bitch, I can't wait 'til tonight," said Tameka, leaning against the wash counter, talking loud from the truth serum, "we gonna be doing it big! Soon as them niggaz take care that business with Mojo."

Pooh, who was Tameka's partner in crime and already down with the lick, knew exactly what she was talking about. "Girl, you know June and Dink came around the 'Terrace' looking for you. Plus you said earlier you couldn't find Youngblood, so how we gon' make shit happen?" Pooh hopped up and sat on the counter, taking another swig from the Remy.

"We just going to have to improvise," said Tameka, "for real, I don't really want to see Youngblood and Jay get killed. I jive fuck with both of them niggaz, but shit, for 50 thousand we can go down Atlanta and buy us a fashion boutique or something."

"But why you just can't get June to kill Mojo? So that way you don't have to set Youngblood up to get smashed."

"Because bitch, I don't got that much time left!" Tameka said, with all the cunningness of a back stabbing vulture. "I already told you that Mojo gotta smash Youngblood and Jay by this weekend, before he can get the other 25 thousand. So soon as he handle his business tonight, he can go pick up the money tomorrow — and that's when we'll have June and Dink kill Mojo. Then we can just cuff the money and gave June and them the coke. All 27 keys of that shit, you feel me boo?" Tameka rose off the counter and got between Pooh's open legs, and started tongue kissing her in the mouth while pushing her hand between Pooh's skirt, sliding her middle finger inside Pooh's tight, hairy pussy.

Pooh let out a deep moan and bit Tameka softly on her ear. "Bitch, don't start nothing you can't finish," she said, pushing Tameka back and hopping off the counter. "Come on so we can get our shit tight, and find this nigga Youngblood."

Getting themselves together, the two women checked the mirror to make sure they were looking okay. Pooh placed the Remy bottle back into her pocket book, while Tameka held the restroom door open for her. They walked out giggling like two little school girls. What they didn't know, was that sitting on a toilet in the bathroom stall, holding in her piss, Samiko was listening and had hard every word they said...

Recognizing the sound of her voice, Samiko walked over to Tameka and said, "Hi you doing? My name's Samiko and I'll be your hair stylist this evening." Leading her over to the styling booth, Samiko started working her magic on the girl. "Ooh girl, you got such a good grain of hair," she said, massaging Tameka's scalp, "and a pretty little face which would go perfect with some African Twist."

Tameka started blushing from the compliments, sucking up the attention Samiko was showering her with. Instantly feeling comfortable from Samiko's warm display of hospitality, plus the combination of being high and slightly drunk, Tameka was easily stroked into a very talkative mood, and by the time she had finished washing Tameka's hair, Samiko had obtained all the basic information she needed to put her man on point.

Sitting in his living room holding baby Vincent, Jay was lost in thought. Never being in a position where he didn't know who or where the enemy was, Jay had it in his mind that every nigga besides Youngblood was a possible enemy. Shit was like a living nightmare, worrying about whether Youngblood was okay or not, while having concerns for his own safety. Jay looked down at his nephew, seeing the infinite potential all babies possess, and thought back to the happier years of his own childhood.

Although his 18ᵗʰ birthday was still two months away, Jay felt like he had been on this earth too long, witnessing too much hardship and misery. From his mother's past crack addiction, to his father's suicide, Jay was a street hardened soldier with a pure, yet broken heart. Since the age of 11, he had to fend for himself in the heartless streets of the inner city, and forced to be a man child trapped in the ghetto, while being the sole provider for his younger sisters.

The more Jay started thinking about his situation, the clearer it became in his mind. It all boiled down to one thing — he had fell off the top of his game by still being in the game. Becoming so sidetracked with the wants and needs of everybody else, he had almost forgotten one of the most important rules to the drug game: get in and get out! Hustling wasn't meant to be made a career, and Jay knew that all too well. Although he was far from a millionaire, he was nowhere near being poor.

With a little over 200 thousand saved up, Jay still considered himself broke, no matter how much money a nigga made and saved up; if that money wasn't working to make more money, then that nigga was broke. At least that was Jay's opinion concerning financial stability. But what really set Jay apart from the average young nigga in the game, was that by looking at him, the average nigga could never tell he was getting as much money as he was. Jay was a financial shark, letting niggaz front him bricks, and breaking the whole thing down into 50's all the way down into nickels. The only flicked up thing about that was the fact that he had to play the strip so hard, but so far the pros had outweighed the cons, and he was definitely cool with that.

Breaking his train of thought, Mink walked into the living room and sat on the armrest of the loveseat. "Jay, me and momma got to run out Maryland and check on Aunt Jean," said Mink, picking up her son, "so we gon' need you to watch Nadia 'til we come back."

"Naw, I can't do it," Jay shook his head, "you might as well take her with you." "Boy, you know we can't take her little ass up there with all them old folks. She'll mess around and give one of them people a heart attack with her crazy self!"

Jay started laughing, knowing how Nadia really was a little hell raiser. "Why's Rasheeda spending the weekend over Muffy's house and Nadia ain't?"

"Them girls too old to have her following them around. Plus, Aunt Renee won't let Nadia spend the night over her house no more ever since she super glued Muffy's toes together." Mink stood up and took the baby off to get dressed. Ten minutes later he saw her and Ray-Ray creeping out the front door, trying to sneak past him. Right before they reached Mink's car, Jay ran to the door and screamed off the front porch, "that's messed up y'all trying to stick me wit' shorty — but it's cool! Just recognize it when it comes back around."

Jay closed the door and walked to his room, finding Nadia laying on top of his bed playing Zelda on the Super Nintendo. He sat down beside his baby sister, rubbing his hand through her soft curly hair, and said, "what's happenin' squirt? You looking all down and shit."

"Man, I'm bored Joe," said Nadia, pausing the game, "momma and them supposed to took me to the carnival tonight, but they rolled out over Aunt Jean's house instead. So now I'm stuck here with nothing do!"

Looking like a sad little kitten, Nadia worked her "baby girl" act to the hub, knowing just how to soften her big brother all the way up. Propping herself up on her knees, Nadia wrapped her little arms around Jay's neck and placed her head against his chest. "Can you take me to the carnival, pleeeease Jameel?" Nadia whined.

Thinking that maybe it wasn't such a bad idea to get out of the house and get some fresh air, Jay told Nadia that he would take her, and to go get ready. He smiled as she hopped off the bed, giving him a kiss and breaking up the stairs. Jay felt a strange feeling in his guts telling him to stay home tonight, as he walked to his closet, grabbing a sweater. Staying in the house really didn't work for him at that moment either, feeling like he was going through an anxiety attack.

Basically, there was a good chance he would drive himself crazy thinking too much, because, physically, there wasn't too much he could do. After finding out through Chico that the nigga C-god had put a hit out on him and Youngblood, Jay drove straight down Clifton Terrace Apartments to find the New Yorker. Straight bloody murder was the only thing on his mind as he rode through 14th and Clifton looking for C-god.

Unable to find the dude, Jay spotted his man Tim Dog and pulled over to holler at him. After kicking it with Tim Dog for a while, Jay had found out all he needed to know about C-god and where to lay on him at. Now all he had to do was find Mojo and see what role his cruddy ass played in his bullshit, then deal with him accordingly. Jay slid the Desert Eagle into his waist, thinking back on how Youngblood had told him that Mojo had squashed the bill he had owed him for the brick of coke a while back, knowing that shit was too good to be true.

Jay walked into the foyer, putting on a black leather jacket, when all of a sudden his cell phone started ringing. He answered the phone and was filled with relief to hear the sound of Youngblood's voice. "Nigga what's up — where the fuck you at?!" Jay asked, "I been looking and calling for you all evening."

"Aye slim, I know you probably heard about that shit around the way today," said Youngblood, "me, dumb Wayne, and Lil' Pat had to go out to M.D. to lay low for a minute, but anyway, how shit looking on that end?"

"It's jive hot as a muthafucka right now. Plus Ms. Dorothy told Granny Mae that she saw you running from the spot with a joint in your hand."

"Man stop playing Joe!" Youngblood said, as if he were about to come through the cell phone, "nigga you for real? Man, I'ma slaughter that old bitch. She wrong as —"

"Shorty, calm your hyper ass down," Jay cut Youngblood off, seeing Nadia running down the stairs towards him, "we got some more important shit to address."

"Like what?"

"Niggaz got money on our heads slim!" Jay said, in a casual tone of voice.

"Got what on who?" Youngblood said, not sure he heard him correctly, "nigga, why you on joke time like that for?"

"Blood, this shit ain't no game," Jay said with a quiet seriousness that sent chills down Youngblood's spine, "and I think that bitch nigga Mojo had something to do with it." Letting Youngblood know that he was about to leave to take Nadia to the carnival, Jay told him to meet them there at 7. Jay hung up the cell phone and walked Nadia out to his car, trying not to spoil her excitement with his personal problems.

It had only taken them five minutes to get to the carnival, since it was right around the neighborhood. Every year the Midway carnival would come to D.C., and set up in the RFK Stadium parking lot. This brought out all the lovely ladies and heavy hitters in the game throughout the city to hook up and enjoy the festivities. Jay parked the car on East Capitol Street, and got out with Nadia, crossing the street on to the carnivals ground. It was so crowded, because it was Midway's last weekend in the city that Jay had to hold Nadia's hand to prevent losing her in the crowd.

Walking past a group of young ladies from Lincoln Heights, Jay saw Lil' Pug, Face, Reamo, and Chip from the Azebates projects, all spitting their game, trying to get some booty for later on that night. Jay said 'what's up,' showing the young niggaz some love, and was about to kick it with them, but Nadia wasn't going for any of that, pulling him off toward the merry-go-round.

Jay bought a hundred dollars worth of tickets and gave them all to Nadia, letting her do her little thang. Taking her to every kiddy ride they had available, Jay just laid back, enjoying the sight of Nadia enjoying herself. However, Jay was unaware of the fact that three niggaz were hiding in the crowd watching him - waiting for the right moment to make their move.

Mojo couldn't believe his luck as he stood by the arcade watching Jay. In Mojo's mind, all he had to do now was lay on him until he went to his car, run up, and put the clamps on him. Standing beside Mojo, Danny watched the crowd, keeping an eye out for the law, as they waited for Juan to come back from the portable bathroom. Both Danny and Juan were "strip hoppers," bouncing from neighborhood to neighborhood, cutting into niggaz so they could hustle around other nigga'z strips.

The last time the two of them were around 18th & D, they were suspected of robbing and killing a dude in the alley on C Street, but when the homicide detectives hit the block investigating the murder, somehow the feds locked up and charged Baby Daddy with the beef. Niggaz from the hood were about to punish Danny and Juan, since everybody felt they were the ones who got Baby Daddy arrested, but once again Mojo came to their rescue by convincing everyone that they didn't have anything to do with Baby Daddy's predicament.

Walking back from the bathroom, Juan was hollering at a group of broads from River Terrace, when all of a sudden he caught a glimpse of

Jay leaning against a hand rail, laughing with his little sister. Juan, along with Danny were both with the move Mojo had plotted against Jay. All three of them had been riding through the 'hood trying to catch him slipping earlier that day, but having no luck, they all decided to go hang out at the carnival and wait 'til 9, when Tameka would have Youngblood set up for his murder.

Not wanting to be seen, Juan tried to step in between two broads who were walking beside him, but being on some super paranoid shit, Jay was constantly checking his surroundings and spotted Juan through his peripheral vision as he tried to avoid being seen. Jay called out Juan's name, while grabbing Nadia's hand as they walked towards Juan. An eerie feeling came over Jay, remembering what Lil' Gerald told him earlier about Juan and Danny chilling with Mojo, looking for him. This nigga should know where Mojo's at, Jay thought, as he confronted Juan.

"What's up slim? You seen Mojo lately?" Jay asked, staring directly into his eyes.

"Naw slim, I ain't seen that nigga all day!" Juan lied with a straight face. Jay knew that the nigga was lying, and was about to slug him out right there, when suddenly, the sound of Tracy's voice caught his attention.

"Mojo... Mojo! C'mere boy!" Tracy yelled, waving her hand back and forth. "I want you to win this teddy bear for me." Jay spun around looking in the direction where he heard Tracy's voice, and saw Mojo and Danny standing outside the arcade room, watching him. Jay shot a quick look back at Juan, giving him a vicious Holyfield "grit," before walking over to Mojo.

Making his way through the crowd, Jay peeped Danny stepping off as he approached the arcade. Tracy saw the way Jay was looking, and knew something was up in the air. She moved in front of him and tried talking to him, but Jay simply told her to watch Nadia so he could holler at slim for a minute. He stepped to Mojo, who was looking at him smiling, "what's up champ? I been looking for you like shit slim," said Mojo, like he was really glad to see him.

"Yeah, I been looking for you too," said Jay, getting straight to the point, "man look here, I already know about the move you and Scales pulled on the bamma up W Street, but what I can't figure out... is why the nigga brother — some nigga name C-god - put a hit out on me and

154

Youngblood? Saying we the one who smashed his peoples."

In the back of Mojo's mind, he was wondering how in the hell Jay had found out about C-god and the hit, while not knowing he was the one who took the money for the hit. But being the perfect snake Mojo's face didn't reveal the thoughts he was harboring as he played dumb to the situation. "I ain't hear nothing about no shit like that slim!" Mojo said, with concern in his voice, "but we can go uptown together and find this nigga — what did you say his name was again... C-god? Or whoever, and crush'em right now!"

Mojo overplayed his hand just then, as Jay saw through the bullshit he was running. He knew Mojo was a cruddy and selfish nigga, who was only concerned with things that could benefit him, so when he so easily offered to help find and put work in on C-god, Jay automatically knew the nigga was up to something. "Naw, I'm aight," said Jay, already plotting on killing Mojo the first chance he got, "I'm just disturb how you can be the one who kill a bamma, but me and shorty get the beef for it."

"Hold up slim... what the fuck is you saying?!"

"I ain't saying nothing big boy," Jay said with a smile, keeping his cool, not wanting to cause a scene.

"Cause nigga, you got me nicked up," said Mojo, acting like he was insulted by the indirect accusation, "coming to me like I supposed to know what the fuck going on with you and your little do-boy!"

"Nigga stop faking 'fore I slaughter your bitch ass in here!" Jay said, finally losing patience with Mojo's tough guy shit.

Seeing that things were about to turn lethal, Tracy stepped in between the two of them, holding Nadia's hand. "Won't y'all cut that shit out," she said, hooking her arm around Jay's, "can you take me back around D Street? 'Cause I gotta do my little niece's hair tonight."

Jay checked his watch, seeing it was fifteen minutes to seven. "Come on, I'll take you around there now," he said to Tracy. He looked at Mojo one last time, and said, "I ain't tripping off that shit... you got that Joe."

"That's good you don't trip," said Mojo with a smirk on his face, "'cause you just might fall and hurt yourself."

Jay took the comment on the chin for the time being, and walked off with Tracy and Nadia to his car. Crossing the street to where his car was parked, Jay went to the front passenger's door and opened it, hearing the sound of the cell phone ringing. Speed balling, he had left the phone inside of the car, as he watched Nadia hop into the front seat, grabbing and turning the phone on. "Hello? Who's this calling my brother? Nadia said, as Jay unlocked the rear door so Tracy could get in, while walking over to the driver's side.

"Nadia put Jay on the phone right now... It's very important!" Samiko said in a state of panic. Nadia reached over and unlocked Jay's door, but before he even had a chance to get in, Jay turned his head and saw Danny creeping out of some hedges. Jay pulled the Desert Eagle from his waist and pointed it at him as Danny fired the 1 0mm three times aimlessly at him. Danny was caught off guard by the fact that Jay was strapped, and was forced to take a rest as Jay returned fire, pumping two Hydro Shock rounds into his chest, sending him to that eternal snake pit down below.

Hearing the terrified screaming of his little sister, Jay looked up and saw Tracy hop out of the car, trying to run, but not getting far. Mojo and Juan came out from nowhere, hidden behind t-shirt made masks, barking their pistols like there was no tomorrow. Mojo, who was working the Glock 17 with the 35 shot extended clip, fired several slugs into Tracy's back, causing her to slide under some bushes. Seeing that he was out-gunned two to one, Jay's only concern was his little sister.

With Nadia's safety on his mind, Jay ran away from his car, hoping that Mojo and Juan would follow him and overlook her balled up in the front seat, but as Nadia looked out of the rear window, seeing her brother running away, she jumped out of the car and tried to run after him as fast as her little legs would carry her. "Jay... wait for me — please...!" Nadia yelled, but her words were cut short, as Mojo's bullet caught her in the base of her neck, severing her spine and sending her face-first into the pavement, killing little Nadia instantly.

Jay's heart beats stopped. Time stood still. Hearing Nadia yelling out his name, he couldn't believe she had gotten out of the car to follow him. Turning around and seeing Nadia lying on her stomach in a pool of blood, Jay's body became numb. Police were coming from everywhere, forcing Mojo and Juan to stop shooting and make a hasty retreat. Jay chased them into an alley, letting loose every round he had left, but that did no good. Mojo and Juan seemed to disappear.

With his legs feeling like rubber, Jay spotted a storm drain and tossed the .45 into it. He walked back to the middle of the street and kneeled down in front of Nadia's broken little body. Jay picked her up and cradled her in his arms as if he were rocking her to sleep. Nadia looked so beautiful and innocent, as Jay used his sleeve to wipe away the blood dripping down her mouth. When the cops finally showed up on the scene with their guns draw on Jay, they quickly holstered their weapons. They police already knew he had to be related to the little girl, for only a relative would be crying the way he was.

But he was more than a relative... if they only knew...

Chapter 15

Sitting on the steel bench in the juvenile holding pin in R&D, Youngblood stared out of the big Plexiglas window at the adult inmates, lost in thought. The first month of his three months in D.C. Jail were the toughest to adjust to, being as it was his first time being locked up. His first day down North-one (the juvenile range) was especially difficult. The other juvies who were on Detail tried to put him on "Dick Gregory," and take his breakfast, lunch and dinner trays, not feeding him.

He quickly put an end to the way that they were carrying him, however. The next day, when the C.O. popped his cell door, Youngblood caught one of the little dudes in the TV room and stabbed him in the neck with a sharp pencil. The C.O.s rushed the range and pulled Youngblood off the young nigga, and moved him over to the Left Tier, where Baby Daddy was locked down at. Instantly, Youngblood became used to every day wars between the young niggaz on the Right and Left Tier. It was an unwritten policy on the juvenile range that the strong must prey on the weak, and only the strong survive. That's what Baby Daddy showed him, as he had the "full court press" on every sucker he came across.

However, Youngblood's stay up North-one was coming to an end. He sat in the holding pin, waiting for the U.S. Marshalls to transport him to D.C. Superior Court for his sentencing hearing. Thinking back on the longest year of his young life, Youngblood closed his eyes and opened his mind. Reliving in his thoughts the chain of life-altering events that lead to him being chained and handcuffed... trapped in the belly of the beast.

It was 7:43 p.m. as Jay sat in the interrogation room, with Nadia's blood still fresh across his clothes. For the past fifteen minutes, the investigating officer, Detective Bell had been questioning him about the murder of his sister, Tracy Brown, and Danny Harris. Perplexed and angered by the shoot-out, resulting in three young people being slain, Detective Bell was determined to find and arrest anybody he suspected to be involved in the shooting.

The Captain at the 5th District Police Precinct had made it quite clear that heads were going to roll if there wasn't a suspect in custody within a week. Downtown Washington was in an uproar about the news of the triple homicide, along with the killing of the four young men from the Rosedale earlier. Even the Mayor, Sharon Pratt Kelly, had made a personal phone call to the precinct, voicing her displeasure about the series of murders, and made it be known that jobs would be at stake if the cases were not closed.

Sitting across the table from Jay, Detective Bell told him that after the crime lab technicians did a sweep of the crime scene, numerous amounts of shell casings were collected from four different guns and wanted him to explain how that was possible. However, after seeing that Jay wasn't going to cooperate and offer any information, Bell slid him his card and told Jay to call him if he ever changed his mind and decided to help solve the case.

Bell stood up and walked Jay out of the room, when two detectives ran over to them in complete excitement, pointing at an officer who was escorting Mojo into the precinct. "We got a suspect for you, chief," said the white detective, Melborne. "Officer Pittman and Randall spotted this slime ball fleeing down Benning Road and tossing what appeared to be a handgun. After a ten minute car chase, he crashed into a lamp pole and Pittmen apprehended the punk."

Excited by the prospect of an open and shut case, Bell looked over at Jay and said, "all you gots to do is tell me that's him," Bell pointed in Mojo's direction, "and I'll personally make sure he'll never see the streets again for what he did to your sister."

"I don't know what you talking about officer," said Jay, staying true to the code of the streets. "I ain't seen that dude do nothing to my sister." Jay walked past Mojo and stared at him as he headed out of the precinct. It took every ounce of will power Jay had not to snatch the gun out of Detective Bell's side holster and empty the whole clip into Mojo's face. But Mojo wasn't tripping, as he smiled at Jay. The silence said, "you got lucky."

Walking out the front entrance, Jay saw Youngblood, Samiko, and the rest of his family waiting for him. Samiko rushed over to him and wrapped her arms around his neck, crying against his chest. Stepping over to Ray-Ray, Jay pulled his mother to him and tried to comfort her, as she was screaming and crying hysterically. He then grabbed Mink by her shoulder and told her to take Rasheeda and their mother home, while he went to handle some business.

Jay snatched his sweater off and looked at the blood stains one last time before tossing it on the sidewalk, and hopped into the back seat of Samiko's black Mazda 626. On their way back around D Street, Samiko told Jay and Youngblood how she had overheard Tameka talking in the bathroom at the Hair Gallery about setting them up so Mojo could kill them both. In full detail, she described Tameka and Pooh's conversation, from Mojo collecting 50 thousand for killing them, to June and Dink robbing and killing Mojo after the hit. Samiko was overwhelmed by grief with tears running down her face. She expressed to Jay how sorry she was for not being able to prevent Nadia's death, and how she had started calling his cell phone as soon as she found out about the plot but couldn't get through.

Youngblood was in the front seat, zoned out in a daze, feeling sick with confusion. Listening to Jay as he told him and Samiko everything he'd learned about C-god putting a hit out on them. Youngblood couldn't help but feel like he was to blame for Nadia's death. Thinking back on the time he smashed Scales for Mojo, something had told him not to get involved in that bullshit back then, but he went against his better judgment for the temporary gain of 15 thousand. Youngblood now had to wear the permanent scar of losing a loved one.

"Aye slim, we gotta find that nigga Juan and Tameka's bitch ass tonight!" Youngblood said, with his voice crackling with fury. He looked up in the rearview mirror and saw Jay's ghostly reflection looking back at him. All the years they had known and loved each other, Youngblood had never seen such hatred in his partner's eyes. For over a decade, Jay had been a brother and best friend to him, riding through whatever by his side. On that night with Nadia's blood all over his clothes, Jay gave him a look so murderous that it sent a chill down Youngblood's spine, making him question their love for one another.

"Them niggaz shattered my heart slim," said Jay in a calm and eerie voice, "and now I'm just a shell of a man."

Samiko parked the car on D Street and they all got out and walked to Dumb Wayne's building. Stepping inside the apartment, the place jam-packed with people mourning Tracy and little Nadia's death. One after another, the neighborhood broads gave Jay hugs and kisses, telling him how sorry they were about his sister. He accepted their condolences and went through the motions of being courteous, but deep inside, venom was flowing through their veins as the words murder, death, and kill flashed in the back of his mind.

Motioning all of his men into Dumb Wayne's bedroom, Jay explained everything, and made it plain and clear that he wasn't going to rest until Juan and Mojo were resting in their graves. Taking his clothes off, Jay went into Wayne's closet and changed into some all black jeans and a sweatshirt. After hollering at Fat Derrick, the Twinz, Lil' Pat, and K.D., Jay stepped in some black Nike gloves, as Dumb Wayne passed him the AP-9. Jay cocked the joint back, sending a Black Talon bullet into the gun's chamber, then popped out the clip and loaded in another bullet, giving him 33 cop-killing rounds at his disposal.

Youngblood was just finishing loading the 9 millimeter slugs into the extra clip he had for the Mac-11. After almost being killed up at Rosedale for running out of bullets, he had learned a valuable lesson, and wasn't taking any more chances. Sticking their guns into their waist, Jay and Youngblood left out the back door of Dumb Wayne's apartment. They jogged through the alley where the Bronco was parked, hopped inside, and drove off. Since there were so many fedz patrolling the block, along with the National Guard, Jay played the alleys and side streets before reaching East Capital Street.

Driving back around the Southeast side of Benning Road, Jay looked over at Youngblood and said, "aye slim, I saw how you was looking at me when we was riding back from the precinct. I already knew what you was thinking... but I want to let you know that this shit ain't your fault champ."

"I ain't gon' lie to you Joe," said Youngblood, remembering the deadly look Jay had given him back in Samiko's car, "I jive thought you wanted to bring me a move and shit."

"Come on shorty... never that! You my little brother for life."

"But slim, if I ain't never get involved with that nigga Mojo, we wouldn't even be in this bullshit! You know I loved Nadia as a baby sister too, and would've died for her, but because I called myself trying to make a come up, I got shorty killed in the process... something told me not to fuck wit' that bitch nigga!"

Jay parked the Bronco on 46th Street and killed the truck's engine. "We both losted a sister tonight, but shit happens for a reason, I guess. But one thing I do know, is that soon as we clean up this bullshit — I'm out the game. I getting back on my Deen, Inshallah, packing my bags, and buying a house out South Carolina for me, Ray-Ray, and Rasheeda."

Shocked by the news, Youngblood felt hurt and abandoned. "But what about me?" Youngblood asked, "you can't just roll out on me like that slim... you're all I got."

"Blood, you know muthafuckin' well you can come and live with me," said Jay, putting everything on the table, "but you also know you ain't gon' want to stay out in the country. Mink already got her mind made up that she ain't tryn'a move, so if you want to roll with me, cool. If not, I'll just make sure I'll leave y'all something to hold y'all down till I get everything situated."

Stepping out of the truck, Jay and Youngblood walked up the block into the Circle of Simple City housing projects. Niggaz were everywhere on this end of the Southeast side of D.C. From the woods of the Hillside, all the way up to Southern Avenue, young niggaz were strapped with gats and sling "yak" 90 going north! Since Simple City was a popular PCP strip, it was common for niggaz from all over the District to come through and cop a few sacks of Loveboat, so when niggaz saw Jay and Youngblood walking past, ain't nobody really think nothing of it, because the bar was already understood. It was only one way in and only one way out of the Circle, so if a nigga was on some bullshit, he was going to get his shit split right where he stood.

But Jay's mind was far from the "petty hustle" school of thought, as he saw June standing in an apartment doorway. Dink, Benji, and Lil' Joey stepped out of the building seeing Jay and Youngblood walking towards them, letting it be known that they were packin' heat by grabbing the handles of their pistols. June recognized Jay by his style of walk, stepping off the front steps with a smile and said, "what's up champ?! You finally come around and holler at a nigga, huh?"

"Yeah slim, I jive need a favor from you scrap," said Jay, giving June some dap. He could remember when he and June used to play football together up Benning Park as kids. Jay knew he could count on June to be

163

the real nigga that he was. "You know that bitch Tameka tried to set me and my partner up so Mojo could smash us for some money and shit?!"

"Aye Joe, get the fuck out of here... you for real slim?!"

"The nigga Mojo just tried to bring me a move at the carnival, and fucked around and killed my little sister." Jay quickly went over everything and put June on point about his situation. June wasn't surprised by Tameka's cruddiness, being as she had set more than a few niggaz up for him, but hearing how she was working Youngblood and Mojo to be killed cast a new light on her wickedness.

"Aye slim that's crazy!" June said, "That bitch had told me about a move Mojo pulled, and said she would set the nigga up for me and Dink to rob him for 27 bricks. And all she wanted out the deal was that we made sure we smashed the nigga. That's why me and slim was outside the Metro club when you put that work in in that U-Haul. But I ain't know you was the one Mojo was plotting on."

"He was really laying on Youngblood," said Jay, getting the facts straight, "but he knew he had to crush me too, to get away with all this bullshit."

"So where the nigga at now?" June asked.

"The fedz snatched him up running from the scene, but he ain't got to worry about doing no time... he already got a death sentence!"

"I feel you Joe, and you know you gots my aid and support," said June, but with a different frame of mind, June stuck his toothpick in his mouth and looked at Jay with a murderous glint in his eyes, "so what you want to do about Tameka?"

With a vicious smirk of his own, Jay said the first thing that came to his mind. "An eye for an eye."

Thirty minutes later, Tameka pulled into the parking lot of the Days Inn hotel in Largo, Maryland. Having a major attitude after not being able to catch up with Youngblood, she was definitely not in any mood to be driving around with a car trunk full of coke. She had specifically told Youngblood to pick her up from the Hair Gallery at eight, and when he didn't show up she had to drive all through D Street looking for him, and couldn't find him anywhere.

Not used to being stood up, Tameka was upset that things weren't going as planned, but what had her more confused than anything, was the fact that Mojo hadn't called or come looking for her, since it was well past 9 o'clock, and tonight was the night she was supposed to set Youngblood up so he could kill him. Everything had seemed to be falling apart until June gave her a call and put the pieces back together, coming up with a new plan that was more to her liking. June told Tameka all about how Mojo got locked up earlier for a triple homicide by the carnival, and since Mojo was out of the picture for a while, she might as well bring him all the coke and let him push it for her, breaking everything down 50/50.

Tameka knew that was a sweet ass deal, almost too good to be true, but she had to try her hand, especially since June had promised her that he and Dink would slump Mojo if he were to beat his case and come home. Tameka drove into the back area of the parking lot, and found an empty space beside June's silver Lincoln Continental. Stepping out of the car, she walked up the flight of steps leading to room 37A and knocked on the door.

Opening the door from inside, June let Tameka in with a kiss on the cheek and closed the door. The room was dark, all except the light that was coming from the television. June walked over to the nightstand and switched on his portable CD played, crankin' the smooth sounds of If This World Were Mines by Luther Vandross. Grabbing a bottle of Dom Perignon, June popped the cork and took a sip. "To 500 thousand in the bank," he said, passing the bottle over to Tameka, "ain't no lookin' back from here champ."

"Shit nigga you making my pussy get wet, talking numbers like that!" Tameka purred like the slutty feline she was.

"Let me see your car keys, so I can check everything out in the trunk."

"It's all there like I said it would be on the phone," said Tameka, sitting down and getting comfortable on the bed, "but just hurry up and see for yourself and get back up here. 'Cause tonight, not only am I going to give you some pussy... I'm a let you try this asshole out."

"Oh yeeeah, you going like that?" June said, smiling, as he walked out of the hotel room. Checking to make sure the coast was clear; June jogged over to Tameka's car and popped the trunk. Seeing the big Louis Vuitton Luggage bag, he unzipped it and found 27 kilos of crack cocaine wrapped in cellophane; just waiting to be broke down.

165

Taking the luggage back and tossing it into the front seat of Tameka's car, June hopped inside and pulled out of the parking lot. A half a minute was all it took, the sweetest caper a nigga could ever dream of. 500 G's in the bank, June thought to himself 500 muthafuckin' G's.

Stripping down to her black lace thong and bra, Tameka laid on top of the bed, massaging the swollen lips of her vagina. Taking another sip from the "Dom P.," she was getting her pussy nice and wet, anticipating having a long and sweaty night of sucking and fucking the shit out of June. Being as June was taking his time coming back to the room, Tameka decided to kick things off early, and started finger fucking herself. Right when she was just getting into the groove of things, she heard the sound of the bathroom door creaking open. Two dark figures stepped out with guns pointed at her head.

Not even getting a chance to see their face, Tameka hopped off of the bed and bolted for the door. She knew she wasn't going to make it out of the room alive, but the fear of losing her life made her try anyway. Tameka instantly lost all hope when she felt the pull of the man snatching her back to the bed by her hair. Feeling like a trapped snake, she frantically looked up into the faces of her tormentor, and nearly died before they even got a chance to kill her.

"Blood... Jay... what the fuck is y'all doing in here?!" Tameka said in shock, not believing what was going on.

"I jive was missing you," said Youngblood, picking up the bottle of Dom Perignon she had knocked over, "so I decided to pay you a little visit."

"Where the fuck is June at?" Tameka asked, looking over to Jay.

"He should be on his way around the Circle with all the coke you brought him," said Jay, dropping his gun to his side, "all twenty seven bricks."

Tameka was about to lie and tell him that she didn't know what he was talking about, but Jay cut her off, waving his hand for her to be silent. "Bitch, we already know about you and Mojo, so don't insult my intelligence."

Looking back over at Youngblood, Tameka tried pleading for her life. "Youngblood, please listen to me baby... Mojo threaten to kill me if I ain't do what he told me to do," she said with tears flooding down her face. Putting all the blame on Mojo, Tameka told them how he and Scales were the one who robbed and killed New York Steve for the 27 bricks and over a hundred thousand in cash.

Breaking down the whole scheme, Tameka explained how Mojo used Youngblood to kill Scales for 15 thousand, so he wouldn't have to split the hundred thousand and coke with him. And once Mojo had found out that Steve's brother C-god had put a hit out on whoever had done the murder, Mojo had gone and told C-god that Youngblood and Jay were the ones responsible for his brother's death, thus picking up the 50 thousand dollar contract for both of their heads.

"So you mean to tell me that day we fucked in Dumb Wayne's bathroom and you talking 'bout being my girlfriend and shit... was all because Mojo sent you at me?" Youngblood asked, pouring out the champagne on the carpet.

"Baby I swear he made me do it!" Tameka said, pulling herself up to her knees, "Mojo said he was gonna kill me and my family if I didn't do it."

"Don't worry about it boo, 'cause I ain't like Mojo, I'm not gonna kill your family and shit... just you." Youngblood cocked his arm back and smacked Tameka in the side of the head with the champagne bottle, sending her tumbling off the side of the bed, knocked out cold. Jumping on top of her chest, Youngblood brought the thick green glass of the Dom Perignon bottle down against Tameka's face; delivering blow after bone shattering blow.

Blood was splattered everywhere, as Jay had to grab Youngblood and pull him off of Tameka's broken body. Looking down at the girl, Jay saw that her eyes were swollen shut, her front teeth were missing, and her face totally disfigured. As her head immediately swelled to twice the size it normally would be, she laid unconscious after being severely beaten. Jay knew the girl wasn't quite dead yet, though. Reaching over and grabbing a pillow, he placed it over her face, pushing the barrel of the AP-9 into it, and squeezed the trigger.

Silencing Tameka's agonizing groans with a slug to the head, Jay ran and got a towel out of the bathroom and started wiping down the room, making sure they left no prints. Snatching up June's CD player, Jay turned off the TV and walked out of the room. Then they hopped into June's Lincoln, and drove out of the parking lot, heading straight for

167

Tameka's place.

Twenty minutes later, turning into the horse shoe bend of the Langston Terrace housing projects, Jay parked the car a couple of spaces up from Tameka's apartment. June and Dink were already inside the building, waiting for them, as all four men walked up the flight of stairs to Tameka's place. June slid off the backpack he was wearing, and passed it to Jay. "Here's your breakdown of the shit," he said, watching Jay go through and count the ten kilos of coke in the bag. "Me and my man gon' split the other 17 joints like you said, and lock the Circle down like a muthafucka."

"Do it like it's supposed to be done champ," said Jay, as they handed each other back their car keys. June gave him and Youngblood some dap, and told them that he had to drop Dink off, so he could drive Tameka's car to the junkyard and get rid of it. June tossed Tameka's apartment keys over to Jay, and turned around to leave, alongside his partner Dink.

Handing the backpack over to Youngblood, Jay slid the key into the door and opened it, walking inside the apartment. Youngblood stepped in behind Jay, closing the door a bit too hard, and heard what sounded like a shower running in the back of the room. "It's about time you got home, 'cause I been calling your cell phone like shit," the girl said inside the bathroom. Automatically thinking she was talking to Tameka, "so I guess you finally caught up with that nigga Youngblood, huh?"

Hearing the sound of his name, Youngblood stood still for a moment, trying to recognize the female's voice. "Bitch, I know you hear me talking to you...! Tameka?" She said, cutting off the shower. Youngblood and Jay both pulled their guns out, and stepped over towards the bathroom. "Tameka... don't make me fuck your ass up —" the girl snatched open the door and nearly pissed on herself as Youngblood grabbed her by the throat and pressed the Mac-11 against the side of her head.

"Bitch, you say one word — and I'm a leave your brains hanging on the wall," Youngblood saw it was Pooh, who was standing in the bathroom dripping wet with a towel wrapped around her. He led her into the bedroom and threw her against the bed, ripping the towel off her naked body. "Now what the fuck you mean — 'finally caught up with that nigga Youngblood?"

It seemed like all the blood had drained from Pooh's face, seeing

168

Youngblood and Jay standing in front of her with two semi-automatic pistols. She was at a loss for word, and asked what was going on, trying to play the innocent role, but instantly changed her course of thinking, as Jay came and sat down on the bed beside her, placing the AP-9 on his lap. He tossed Tameka's keys at Pooh, looking her in the eyes, and said, "Tameka told us you'd be here waiting for her to come back from setting Blood up. She told us everything Joe. I can't believe you'd go against me for Mojo... I thought we was way better than that slim."

Not even thinking on what Jay had just said, Pooh fell for his game and started telling them everything she thought would save her life. "Whatever that bitch told y'all — she's lying!" Pointing over at Tameka's walk-in closet, "I ain't have nothing to do with that bullshit. All the money she was gon' cuff from Mojo is right over there in her closet."

Youngblood went straight to the closet and yanked the doors open, pulling out the small green duffle bag. He quickly rummaged through the top layers of clothing and saw the money stuffed at the bottom of the bag. Over 100 thousand dollars in cold blooded cash. Youngblood picked up the bag, tossing it over his shoulder, and gave Jay the nod to roll out. Feeling like her life had been spared, Pooh let out a small sigh of relief, watching Youngblood walk out of the bedroom.

"I'm gon' crush Tameka's bitch ass when I find her!" Pooh said to Jay, watching him get up and make his way to leave. "That bitch just straight up and lied on me and —"

Before Pooh could even finish what she was saying, Jay turned around and pointed the gun at her, causing her to throw her arms up into a shield, as if she were somehow going to block the bullet that was going to come her way. Pooh was about to scream, but never got a chance to, because Jay squeezed the trigger and sent a clip full of slugs into the face, neck, and chest of her beautiful, wet, naked body. They left her balled up in a pool of blood beside Tameka's big comfortable bed.

Drama City

Chapter 16

Standing underneath the black tarpaulin in Harmony Cemetery, the rain drizzled down from the sky in slow motion, as if the angels were weeping in the heavens, witnessing the caretakers lowering Nadia's little casket into her grave. Jay stood in the back of the small group of family and friend, watching everyone mourn over his baby sister's death. He looked over his left shoulder, hearing the sound of a car driving up the cemetery's road, and saw Ned park his black S Class 600 Benz.

Jay walked toward the car as Ned got out, and gave him some dap. Unfolding his umbrella to shield them both from the rain, Ned glanced over at the funeral procession, and said, "I came by to pay my respects, and to let you know I got the sucka lined up for the kill."

"I can dig it slim," Jay pulled out a Newport and lit a match to it, taking in a deep drag, "but the damage is already done. I just wish I could've caught this nigga the day I found out about the move... Maybe shit would've played out differently, ya know?"

"We all experience the hurt and pain of losing a loved one during the course of our lifetime, but knowing how close you and your little sister were, I can't imagine the shit you feeling right now," Ned leaned over and gave Jay an one handed embrace. "Aye slim, I give you my muthafuckin' word," he whispered into Jay's ear, "before the ground hardens up over top of Nadia's grave — they gon' be puffin' that nigga into his."

"A favor for a favor?" Jay asked, watching Ned move around to the driver's side of the car.

"Naw, this one's on me." Ned hopped into the Benz and pulled off, leaving Jay to mourn on that rainy, dreary morning.

For five straight days, Jay and Youngblood scoured the city, searching for any trace of Juan's whereabouts. From Michigan Park Northwest, Montana Avenue Northeast, to the Streets of M.L.K. Avenue Southeast, they went from 'hood to 'hood looking for him. Being as though Juan was a serial strip hopper, there really wasn't any telling where his snake hole was, but fortunately for them, he wasn't a good thinker — the type of nigga who would shit where he'd lay his head at.

It didn't take long for word to get to Kevin Gray, who was a heavy hitter in the game on the Southside, that two niggaz from D Street were looking for Juan — who did some petty shit, and ran off with 62 grams of coke that belonged to him. Seeing an opportunity to make Juan cash in on his debt, Kevin drove through 18th & D and hollered at Jay and Youngblood, giving them Juan's mother's address. Twenty-eight minutes later, they pulled up into a parking lot behind an old abandoned building in Robertson Place southeast, dressed in black and ready to smash something.

It was a gloomy and windy Friday afternoon as they sat in the smoke-gray Buick 225, looking across the street to Juan's mother's house. It was a nice looking red brick house — a kind of place where you can tell the owner took pride in living there. Four hours into the wait, Youngblood was getting restless, cutting off the Gameboy he was using to kill time. He looked up after hearing a car pull up across from them, and saw the lady parking a small mini-van in front of the house. "That's that nigga mother right there," said Jay, watching the lady get out of the van and enter the house. "I remember seeing her come around the way looking for him one day."

"I should smash that old bitch!" Youngblood said, getting a good look at Juan's mother. "We gotta bring that nigga out of hiding somehow."

Jay looked over at Youngblood, contemplating the thought of doing just that, but knowing in his heart that he didn't have that level of viciousness — to walk up and shoot somebody's innocent mother. Jay came clean and spoke his mind, "Aye slim, as bad as I want to make this nigga suffer — I can't bring myself to kill his mother for no reason scrap."

"For no reason?" Youngblood said, not understanding where Jay was coming from. "Man, that nigga Juan had something to do with Nadia getting killed — and you talkin"bout for no reason!"

"Blood, I understand all that... but his mom's ain't have shit to do with that. Nigga — Nadia was my heart! You know I feel her death more than anybody, but I ain't with killing no innocent people that ain't even in the game and shit, ya feel me?"

172

"Naw, I really don't." It was the first time he ever doubted Jay's words before. Since they were little kids, Youngblood had always looked up to Jay, and would never second guess the advice he used to give him coming up through the ranks. Yet now, as he sat in the car pondering over Jay's behavior, his outlook on his partner's thoroughness was somewhat in question. Youngblood saw something in him that he had never expected to see: weakness.

For the remainder of the time they spent in the car laying on their victim, Jay and Youngblood didn't say too much to each other. They were both lost in their own train of thought. It had been over fifteen hours since they first pulled into the parking lot to lay on Juan, and with fatigue getting the best of the both of them, Jay said it would be wise to roll out, get some sleep, and come through there again later fresh and alert. Youngblood nodded his head in agreement, not saying a word, keeping his thoughts to himself. His mind was already made up on what it was that needed to be done — and he was more than willing to do it.

At 7:03 Sunday morning, Ms. Shirley Bush was going through her Sabbath day ritual of preparing for early morning church service while listening to the Hour of Power Christian broadcast with T.D. Jakes. Taking care of her hygiene, Ms. Bush put on her makeup while singing a gospel hymn — she loved to sing At the Cross, which was her favorite song. Finishing up her chores, Ms. Bush threw on her wool coat, walking to her front door. Before leaving the house, she picked up a small picture of Juan that was sitting on a stand in her hallway, and whispered a little prayer for her only son.

"In the name of Jesus, I pray clear Lord that you protect my son," said Ms. Bush, worrying about Juan's well-being. It wasn't unusual for her not to hear from him in a long period of time, being as he was a 26 year old grown man, but on this occasion, things were different. She was having strange feelings about his disappearance.

Leaving her house, Ms. Bush walked down her front steps, making her way to her mini-van. Thinking about Sister Price and all the other elderly sisters she had to pick up for church service that morning; Ms. Bush didn't notice the young man creeping up behind her. Stepping into the front seat, she closed the door and started up the van, allowing its engine time to warm up. Hearing someone tapping against her window, Ms. Bush looked over at Youngblood, who was smiling at her, waving his left hand.

What a handsome smile, Ms. Bush said to herself, rolling her window down to speak to the young man. She picked up her Bible and was about to read him some Scriptures — that was her way of greeting strangers, when all of a sudden she saw him raise a huge black gun and point it at her head. It was a four shot .50 caliber Colt revolver that Youngblood had bought from a crack head a day before. He had never had an opportunity to try the gun out until now, and was geeking to see the after effects of such a powerful weapon.

Using both of his thumbs, Youngblood pulled back the hammer of the .50 cal and braced himself, holding it with both hands. Ms. Bush didn't know what to think, staring down the barrel of something that looked like it was used to kill an elephant. "Lord Jesus..." was the last thing she said before Youngblood pulled the trigger. The gun's discharge was so loud it cracked the mini-van's windshield, rocking the vehicle inside out. As for Ms. Bush, she was no longer herself, lying on the floor of the passenger side of the van, damn near decapitated.

The impact of the bullet had sent Ms. Bush across the other side of the van, knocking out the whole right side of her head all the way down to her shoulder. Seeing the way her head had exploded almost made Youngblood throw up himself, as he ran to the stolen black Acura Integra, where Lil' Pat was waiting behind the wheel. Jumping into the car, Youngblood took of his black hoodie, as Lil' Pat hit the gas, making a speedy escape out of the Southside of Robertson Place.

Sitting in a little 500 dollar bucket he had recently bought, Ned secured the Velcro straps of the bulletproof vest around his chest, and slid on his Hugo Boss sweater over top of it. It was 9:50 p.m. on that dark and chilly Wednesday night — he was ten minutes early for his meeting with C-god. For two days in a row before this night, Ned and C-god would meet up at different locations to negotiate the price for a package deal for 15 bricks of coke. C-god had a ten brick policy, that meant he never fronted over ten kilos to niggaz he had never dealt with before, but being pressed to start some kind of business relationship with Ned, he had made an exception to his rule, and even lowered the price of each individual brick to 15 thousand.

Since his infiltration into the D.C. drug circuit, C-god had heard a lot about Ned and his reputation as a money getter/head hitter, and for the past few years had been trying to cut into him to form a sort of partnership between the two. Up until now, Ned had battled down all of C-god's advances, telling him that he was too busy dealing with the "connect" he already had. While in truth, the real reason was that Ned couldn't stand his Yankee-ass, and was looking for any reason to rob and smash him.

Ned wasn't the hating type of nigga who wasted his time being upset about other niggaz who were getting money in the city. Even with "out of towners," he respected everybody's hustle, but ever since that hot nigga Alpoe came to D.C. from New York, and had a rack of good men killing their own homies over crumbs, Ned couldn't stand New Yorkers, and had no problems with killing their asses off of the block.

Seeing the blue MPV stop at a traffic light on Georgia Avenue, Ned grabbed his cell phone and called his men Donell and Karim, letting them know that everything was ready to go down. He parked on a side street behind the W.U.S.T. radio station and got out of the car, putting on his thick suede leather jacket. Hiding the two Browning .44 automatic pistols he had tucked in the shoulder holsters he was wearing underneath. Ned walked across 8th Street, over to the old abandoned Roy Roger's lot, where C-god and his four cronies pulled up with their guns in hand — checking the scene for any signs of some funny shit.

Donnell was just starting the car up when he'd gotten the call from Ned. Donnell was another one of those wild and crazy young niggaz, from 7th & 0 Street Northwest, who was quickly making a name for himself around the city. Being on all moves and big money schemes, he didn't have to think twice about a lick like the one he was on now. For 5 "keys" he didn't have a problem putting in a little bit of work — it all came with the territory. Putting the taxi cab into gear, Donnell drove down 9th Street and turned on to Florida Avenue, making his way to the homicide waiting to happen.

Ned had put Donnell on point about the caper over a week ago, so he already knew what was expected of him. Earlier that day he had caught the Metro subway train, and went around Wheeler Road Southeast, hailing a taxi cab like he needed a ride to get home. When one cab driver finally decided to pull over for him, Donnell hopped in the back seat, letting the Nigerian cab driver drive off down the street.

Before the Nigerian could even ask him where he wanted to go, Donnell whipped out the plastic-looking Glock, and placed it behind the man's right ear. Being from the Southeast himself, the Nigerian was all too familiar with the familiarities of getting robbed, so he drove into the nearest alley he could find, and started collecting all the little chump change he had made all day. His money was the farthest thing from Donnell's mind, as he made the Nigerian get into the back of the cab's trunk.

Not knowing what to expect next, the man just did what he was told, and turned around, facing the back of the trunk. The Nigerian's body jerked twice, but he didn't feel anything as Donnell fired two rounds into the back of his head. Closing the trunk, Donnell made his way back uptown, and picked up Karim from up First & Kennedy Street.

Karim, who was also down with the caper, was now in the back seat of the cab, popping the 50 round magazine into the AK-47. Ned had put him down with the lick because he knew that slim was in need of some quick cash. Ever since Karim's partner Benny Lee Lawson ran up in the police headquarters and shot three cops, he and his twin brother Koby had been on the run for conspiracy and a rack of other trumped up charged. Being as though his twin was over in Africa hiding out, the niggaz around Kennedy Street were getting locked up like crazy. Karim jumped at the idea of a come up of 5 free bricks.

Ned was standing in the middle of the lot, when C-god stepped out of the MPV, holding a brown shopping bag with the 15 kilos inside. Walking over to Ned, C-god's flunkies moved out of the side door of the van, watching the two men conduct the business they had come to do. Letting it be known that they were strapped and ready for any bullshit. "Peace god," said C-god, seeing how Ned was looking at his flunkies. "You know I come in peace son — it's just a nigga's on some super paranoid shit right now. You feel what I'm saying yo?"

"I feel you slim," said Ned in a casual tone of voice, motioning with his head, he pointed to the bag C-god was carrying. "Is everything straight on your end of the table?"

"It's all right here son," C-god smiled, tossing his dreadlocks away from his face. They started talking about the arrangements for dropping off the money, when Ned saw the yellow cab bend the corner off Florida Avenue, steady making its way over to the lot. Even though C-god's flunkies were wide alert, checking out the area for any signs of a possible robbery, no one paid any attention to the innocent looking cab pulling up beside them.

C-god had just handed over the shopping bag to Ned, when he heard the rapid explosion of multiple gunshots. Turning around to see what was going on, C-god felt sick seeing the way Donnell and Karim were chopping down the last two remaining flunkies of his crew. C-god looked back at Ned, wondering what this was all about, and saw him aiming the .44 at his head. "Yo money! It don't have to be like that..." C-god tried to say, before Ned silenced him dead with three soul shattering slugs to the face.

Running passed Donnel and Twin, who were already back inside the cab balling out, Ned hopped into his bucket and pulled off, heading back over First Street. Looking through the shopping bag, Ned saw the 15 kilos and smiled to himself. That meant five bricks a piece between him and his men, which either way he looked at it, it was alright with him.

Juan stepped out of Pope's Funeral Home with tears still running down his acne scarred face. Attending his mother's wake service, he had had to leave early, not being able to take the sight of her big glossy photograph sitting on her closed casket. The mortician and funeral director both informed him that, due to his mother's missing skull fragments, the funeral proceedings had to be closed casket. It would have been impossible for them to make her face presentable to viewing. Juan, overwhelmed by grief, just sat silently in the front row, accepting the condolences of his mother's church family and friends, wondering why this had to happen.

Walking to his car, all kinds of thoughts were running through Juan's mind. The detectives had told him that there were currently no suspects, nor motive, to his mother's murder. Knowing all the cruddy shit he was into, he had a feeling that it was something he had done that finally came back to haunt him. Only this time, making his mother pay the price for his sins. Getting inside the Q45, Juan started the car and slid his Sade CD into the disk player. He needed to be by himself for a while to mourn such a great loss. Juan fired up a blunt of skunk weed, driving off into the intersection of Pennsylvania Avenue, as he headed back towards his snake hole out in Culpepper Virginia. He didn't notice the smoke-gray deuce and a quarter two cars down from him slowly following his every move.

Allowing Juan to stay a good distance away, Jay kept a close watch, determined not to let him slip through the cracks again. Even though Jay didn't approve of the killing of Juan's mother, he had to admit that the murder had now served its purpose — bringing the snake out of its hole. Because of the major media coverage, it wasn't hard to find out where they were holding Ms. Bush's wake. So after checking with some members of her church, Jay got all the information he needed, and drove to the funeral home, waiting for the dead man to join his mother.

When he first spotted Juan pulling up in his Q45, Jay had had an urge to go and smash him right on the spot, but there were so many news reporters, camera men, police detectives, and family members outside only a fool would have tried their hand against odds like that. Suddenly, Jay was kind of glad that Youngblood's simple ass wasn't with him on this move.

Jay sent Youngblood and Lil' Pat out to Boston on the Amtrak due to the public outcry caused by Ms. Bush's death. They were to stay in Boston for six months with his Aunt Jasmine. Even though, for the moment, it looked as if they had gotten away clean with all the murders they were involved in, Jay wasn't leaving anything to chance. The way niggaz were snitching nowadays, along with the fedz hitting dudes with bogus beefs, he knew it was only a matter of time before they got locked up for a couple of bodies if they stayed around the 'hood.

Bringing his attention back to the present matter at hand, Jay turned off Pennsylvania Avenue as he remained a steady distance away from Juan. He saw Samiko drive past him in the little hooptie he had bought her for this occasion. Just like they had planned, Samiko drove up behind Juan's car, and tailed him till he came to a traffic light on Minnesota Avenue. Watching Juan come to a complete stop at the red light, Samiko waited until the last minute to hit her breaks, causing her to smash into the rear-end of Juan's Q45.

Being already hip to the "bumping the back of the car" move, Juan grabbed the 9mm from underneath his seat, and hopped out of the car, pointing the pistol at the car behind him. He was about to start dumpin' on the car, until he saw the broad inside looked scared to death. Juan took a quick look around him, checking out the scene, before putting the gun into his waist band. He walked over to the woman to see if she was alright, while surveying the damages to his car.

"I'm sorry for running into your car... please don't hurt me," said Samiko, stepping out of her car. "I got insurance to cover the damages. They'll take care of everything, I promise."

"Naw, I ain't gon' do nothing to you sweetheart," said Juan, looking her up and down. He saw that she was dressed in a light green cat suit, and he could tell that she wasn't wearing any underwear. "I just had to be on point, ya dig. You know go hard niggaz like me can't afford to be slippin'."

"Ooh, you be going hard, huh?" Samiko smiled, showing her pearl-white teeth.

"Naw boo, I'm just flicking with you. I just wanted to say something to make you laugh, so I could see your pretty smile." Juan started running his game, telling her that he was just coming from his mother's wake service, trying to play the sympathy card, hoping to stumble up on some pussy. He was getting all the signs that she might be willing to go for something, as Samiko flirted and teased him with her body.

Getting so caught up in his own rap game, Juan didn't even peep Jay driving past them, and parking on the next block over. Creeping back up towards the accident site, Jay crouched between two parked cars, holding the Mac-11 tightly in his hands. He was so close to Juan, he could hear him telling Samiko to move on to the side way, so they could get out of the way of oncoming traffic.

Watching Juan get inside his car, Jay knew he finally caught his man with his pants down. He rose up, squeezing the trigger of the Mac-11. He let off round after round, as Jay ran down on Juan, sending the 9 millimeter slugs into his body and face. Standing beside the Q45, Jay emptied the remaining thirteen bullets he had in his clip into Juan's face and head, leaving him beyond human recognition.

Another closed casket funeral was now in the making... just like his mother.

Chapter 17

"Jones — Marice Jones!" the C.O. shouted, stepping out of the control bubble. Mojo looked up from the TV room after hearing his name being called and saw the C.O. standing in the sally port, waving a hall movement pass. "You got a legal visit," the C.O. pointed to the little white strip of paper in his hand, "so hurry up and get ready."

Mojo walked to his cell, taking his time while putting on his blue jail jumpsuit. Sitting on his bunk, he lit up a Newport. He could already feel the oncoming headache, as he went through his legal paperwork that he kept in a brown commissary bag. Mojo anticipated more bad news from this unexpected visit. Stressing out was an understatement for Mojo, who had spent the last three months locked up at the D.C. jail. Along with worrying about a possible life sentence, he had to deal with the fact that he was now broke, without a dollar to his name, and time was just getting harder with each passing day.

At first thought, Mojo didn't trip about the bodies that he was facing. Like so many times before, he knew that money had the power to get cases thrown out of court, but when he showed up at his arraignment hearing, after his first night in custody, he knew something wasn't right. He stood beside some geeked out court appointed attorney — who looked like a straight up sell-out artist.

As soon as he made it over to the jail's intake unit, Mojo played the telephones hard, trying to get in contact with Tameka. He had called up everyone he knew, sending the word for her to get on top of his lawyer situation. Knowing that attorneys Bernard Grim and Michelle Roberts were going to want 35 to 60 thousand for his case, he had needed her to drop off the 20 thousand dollar retainer fee to them, but not being able to catch Tameka for a whole week straight, Mojo's cruddy mind immediately started thinking that she had ran off with his drugs and his money. Until someone anonymously mailed him a copy of Tameka's obituary, that is.

Within a matter of days, Mojo's entire appearance went through a complete change — looking ten years older than what he really was. He wasn't eating, sleeping, taking shower, or anything anymore. He was so busy stressing about his money, wondering if somebody had robbed and killed Tameka for his stolen stash. Throughout the week following the news of Tameka's death, Mojo had desperately tried to get a hold of Juan, who was still out there in the free world, yet was unable to get in contact with him either. Mojo's mind was really starting to crack.

Mojo and Juan had been tight with one another in years past, sharing an honor amongst thieves type of bond, but knowing no matter how cool they appeared to be, he could never play him too close, as it was in their snake nature to bite one another the first chance they got. The only reason Mojo didn't suspect Juan as the one that smashed Tameka is because he knew that Juan didn't know her, and he was smart enough not to let him know that she was the one who was holding his stash. Yet still, Mojo couldn't figure out why he was having such a hard time getting in contact with Juan. That is, until a week later when someone anonymously mailed him another copy of an obituary. This time it belonged to D'Juan Cartledge, AKA Juan.

Walking down the prison corridor, Mojo stopped in front of the visiting hall entrance, where a C.O. shook him down before letting him enter the room. He looked through the Plexiglas window of the sliding steel door, shaking his head at the sight of the befuddled looking white man who was supposed to be his lawyer. Mojo moved into the back of the visiting hall, which was designed specifically for legal visits, and sat down at the briefing table directly across from his attorney.

"Good morning, Mr. Jones," his attorney, Matthew Bear, said, shaking Mojo's hand. "Now remember, whatever you tell me is protected under attorney/client privilege, so you can be straight up with me buddy." Bear went through his manila folder, and slid a sheet of paper with the words United States v. Maurice Jones, printed at the top in bold black letters, over to Mojo. "Here's your indictment for three counts of First-Degree murder. Right at this moment, the government doesn't have any solid circumstantial evidence against you, but the fact that a little seven year old girl was killed is not a plus in your favor."

"So what are my chances of beating the case if I go to trial?" Mojo asked, weighing his options in his mind.

"Well, taking advantage of our right to a speedy trial would be a good tactical move in my opinion. Since you made it clear that you were not taking any plea offers. As I mentioned earlier, the government doesn't have any physical evidence. They just have some police reports stating that an officer Pittman and Randall apprehended you, after spotting you running from the direction of the crime scene. No eye witnesses have been produced against you as of yet, but speaking of eye witnesses..." Bear went through his folder again, and handed Mojo a notarized affidavit. "Do you know a Jameel Hinton?"

Mojo's eyes got big as headlights, hearing Jay's name. He turned his head while raising his eyebrows, pretending like he was searching his mind for some type of recognition. "Naw, I can't say I've heard that name before... 'cause it don't ring a bell," Mojo lied, wondering what Jay's name had to do with his case. "Why you ask me that?"

"Because this Mr. Hinton fellow..." said Bear, looking at Mojo suspiciously, "who was the brother of the little seven year old girl — uh let's see, right here — oh yes, the brother of decedent Nadia Hinton stated that he was present at the time of the shooting, and claims that Maurice Jones was not the person he had seen the night of his sister's death." Bear leaned back in his chair, folding his arms across his chest. He had a knowing little smirk on his weasel-like face. "So that means we have a key eye witness on our behalf to clear you of these charges."

Reading over the affidavit, Mojo didn't say a word. All types of thoughts were going through his head. One thing was for certain, Jay was definitely keeping shit all the way gangsta, for there was no doubt in Mojo's mind what Jay was planning. Most niggaz in his position would just sit back — and maybe even assist the courts in handling a street beef, by getting a nigga a life sentence, but Mojo knew that Jay wasn't thinking on that type of time... He was planning on holing court in the streets!

Stepping out of the taxi cab, Youngblood paid his fare and grabbed his luggage bags out of the cab's trunk. It had been over three and a half months since he'd been away in Boston. Taking in the sight of D.C.'s unique urban flavor, Youngblood walked up the steps of Jay's front porch, and rang the doorbell. He thought to himself how good it felt to be back home, while he waited for someone to let him into the house. He looked up and down the snow-covered street, checking out the climate change on that cold wintery January month.

"Boy, what you're doing over here?" Rasheeda said, after opening the door and seeing Youngblood standing on her porch. She ran over towards him, giving him a big hug and a kiss on the cheek, and asked, "why you ain't up Aunt Jasmine's house?"

"Gotdamn Joe..." Youngblood stepped back getting a good look at Rasheeda's well stacked body, dressed in a t-shirt and nylon stretch pants. "You act like you ain't happy to see a nigga and shit."

"Nigga stop playing with me!" Rasheeda said, punching him in the arm. "You know I miss your crazy self... but I don't want you to be getting into no trouble."

"Who me?" Youngblood said, giving her his innocent look, while walking into the house. Rasheeda just smiled as she followed behind him. She was very happy to have the boy that she had a crush on back in the city.

Walking down the basement stairs, Youngblood didn't knock on Jay's door before entering the room. Seeing Jay and Samiko cuddled up in the bed together watching a movie on a cable network. Youngblood spread his arms into a group hug gesture, and said, "Aye y'all — what's up with a ménage a trois?" They both turned their heads in Youngblood's direction, catching the sight of him leaping in the bed between them. Surprised to see his young partner back so soon, Jay busted out laughing, as he and Samiko jumped on top of Youngblood's back.

"Aye man — what's up Joe?!" Jay said, kissing Youngblood on the side of his head. "Why the hell you leave from Aunt Jasmine's joint?"

"Man does it matter why I left?" Youngblood said, trying to throw Jay off his back. After a few seconds of wrestling with him, and not being able to break loose from his hold, Youngblood looked over at Samiko for help. "Can you please get your gay-ass boyfriend up off me?"

"Shiid, you got my nigga fucked up," Samiko laughed, rubbing her hand over the slight bulge in her belly. Youngblood stopped moving as the realization that Samiko was pregnant kicked in, and looked over at her as if seeing her for the first time. "Stop playing Joe!" Youngblood said, raising up, after Jay finally decided to let him go.

"It's not a game champ," said Jay, slouching back into his bed smiling. "I'm 'bout to be a father for real."

"Aye slim, that's big as a muthafucka," Youngblood gave Jay some dap, while stepping towards Samiko and giving her a hug. "Aye 'miko, I'll give you some money if y'all have a son and name him after me and shit," he said to her laughing.

"Boy, you always on joke time."

"Naw Joe, I'm dead serious."

Samiko cocked her head at Youngblood, giving him a funny look like he was tripping. "Blood, you always be tryn'a get somebody to name a baby after you and shit," she said, pondering the veracity of her words. "Why you just don't find a nice girl to settle down with, and make your own gotdamn baby. That way you can name him or her whatever you want!"

"Man, first of all, I can't find no nice girl... 'cause these bitches 'round here be bad for nigga's health! And secondly..." Youngblood paused, shaking his head with all the theatrics he could muster, "I think my joint broke or something — 'cause my sperm ain't working right."

"Nigga you really is crazy!" Samiko walked over to Jay, giving him a quick kiss on the lips. "Well, I'ma leave you two handsome young men down here for a while, and let y'all talk or whatever," she said, as she slowly sauntered to the door, giving them both an eye full of her big, voluptuous, high yellow ass, encased in a pair of Donna Karen stretch pants. "Besides, I gotta help Ray-Ray and Mink cook dinner anyway.

As soon as he saw Samiko leave out of the room, Youngblood turned around to Jay, and said, "Aye slim, 'miko fat as a muthafucka Joe!"

"Yeah, I jive think she wife material slim — plus she a straight soldier," Jay said, giving Youngblood the spill on how Samiko was willing to go on the move to smash Juan, and actually playing a part in his murder. Jay also gave him the run down on how the cold case squad had been doing an operation "clean sweep" in the 'hood, locking niggaz up on all types of conspiracies and murder charges. Jay went silent for a moment, thinking of the reason why he had sent Youngblood up to Boston to lay low, and asked, "but what's up with Lil' Pat, he come back down with you?"

Youngblood threw up his hands in mock disbelief, acting like it was the end of the world. "Aye slim — you won't believe this shit here!" Youngblood said, exaggerating the story. "Why this nigga done met some baked bean eating-ass bitch out Boston, and fucked around and fell in love and shit."

185

"Oh yeah... so that nigga still out there, huh?"

"Man, that nigga lunching — talking 'bout staying out there forever!"

"It might do shorty some good to stay gone for a minute!" Jay said, walking to the nightstand beside his bed. "It ain't shit out here in these streets for us anyway, for real-for real." Jay pulled out a small compartment in the nightstand, and grabbed a set of keys, tossing them over to Youngblood. "I know your birthday already passed, but happy sweet sixteenth birthday champ."

Checking out the keys, Youngblood smiled until he caught on to Jay's slick remark. "Hold up nigga — ain't sweet sixteen is for broads?"

Stepping into the driveway behind Jay's house, Youngblood pulled the blue plastic covering off of the car, and went crazy, seeing the bubble shape of the all black twin turbo 300Z. Jay standing behind him like a big brother, was tripping off Youngblood's excitement, as he watched him hop inside the Z. "Nigga, I know you ain't gonna try to drive that joint out here in this snow," he said, stepping back, hearing the roar of the Z's powerful engine come to life. "You gon' fuck around and kill yourself!"

"Nigga I'ma ride till the wheels fall off!" Youngblood yelled out the window, working the clutch, causing the Z to fishtail out of the driveway. Heading straight for 18th & D, Youngblood couldn't help but to feel glad to be back home in the 'hood, because home is where the heart is... and Youngblood's heart was forever in the 'hood.

Four months later, escorted by two U.S. Marshals, Mojo stepped into the courtroom dressed in a dark blue Ralph Lauren suit. It was the third and final week of his trial, as today was the day that his attorney was presenting his last witness to the testimony stand. The past weeks had been long and agonizing for Mojo — being forced to sit through the tedious testimony of numerous government witnesses, all presenting nothing more than speculative theories that he was the one responsible for the homicide.

Except for the two police officers testifying that they had apprehended Mojo after spotting him tossing away a pistol, while running away from the murder scene, the government really didn't have a strong case against him. Since Danny and Juan were both dead now, Mojo had decided to put the beef on Juan, claiming in his defense that he was chilling at the carnival with Juan, when all of a sudden Juan and Danny got to shooting

186

at each other. That was the reason why he was running away from the scene. The fact that the homicide detectives were never able to retrieve the murder weapon had really helped put Mojo in a position to beat the case. As a slight smile crept across his face, thinking about the possible not guilty verdict, Mojo adjusted his gold framed Versace personality eyeglasses, and leaned back in his chair, waiting for the jurors to file into the jury box. Out of curiosity, Mojo looked out into the small crowd of people who had come to witness the outcome of his trial. and saw Youngblood sitting in the back of the courtroom, looking at him with a blank stare.

"All rise for the honorable Judge Stolker," announced the court's clerk, bringing Mojo's attention back to his trial. Seeing Youngblood in the courtroom had thrown him off for a second, but Mojo didn't trip too much. He knew that whenever opportunity presents itself, he was going to make Youngblood a few pounds heavier, by filling him up with a hundred round clip of hot lead.

After standing up and going through the formalities of showing respect to the judge, Mojo sat back down and watched the jurors take their seats in the jury box. His attorney, Mr. Bear was going through some papers that were on top of their table, when he looked up at the judge, and said, "your honor, we would like to call our final witness to the stand... Mr. Jameel Hinton." A few seconds later, Mojo watched as Jay entered the courtroom, and got on the witness stand. He showed no emotion in what he was about to do.

Mr. Bear listened to Jay take the solemn oath to tell the whole truth, before walking over to him in his favorite Perry Mason style of walk. "Can you please identify yourself and your relationship to the decedents, Nadia Hinton and Ms. Tracy Brown, for the court please?"

"Yes I can sir," said Jay, in a casual tone of voice. "My name is Jameel Hinton. I am the brother of Nadia Hinton... and Tracy Brown was a personal friend of mines."

"Thank you Mr. Hinton," said Mr. Bear, leaning against the witness stand. "Now, were you present at the time of your sister and Tracy Brown's murder?"

"Yes I was."

"Can you please explain in detail the events that occurred at the time of the murders?"

"Yes sir, I can." Jay looked at the jurors with a sincere look of honesty, and began telling them the made up story that Mr. Bear had told him to say before Mojo's trial.

"Nadia, Tracy, and myself were walking to my car, coming from the carnival when we saw two men arguing out loud. The next thing I know, the two men started shooting at each other... and that's when Tracy and my sister were both shot and killed trying to run for cover."

Jay let a few tears run down his face, so the jury could see, while Mr. Bear walked to his table and retrieved two blown-up mug shot photos of Danny and Juan. "Are these the two men you saw doing the shooting?"

"Yes — that's them!" Jay said, pointing an accusing finger at the photos of the two niggaz he had personally shot and killed. "Those are the men who murdered my sister and friend Tracy!"

"And have you seen this man before?" Mr. Bear pointed over to Mojo, sitting at the table.

"Yeah, I've seen his face before around the neighborhood."

"Do you know that man sitting in this courtroom?"

"No, I don't actually know him..."

"Well, can you please tell me this," Mr. Bear turned to the jury, while pointing over at Mojo again. "Did you see this man anywhere near the scene, when the shooting took place?"

"No I did not," said Jay, in a convincing tone of voice. "The people responsible for my sister and Tracy's death are those two men in those photos you showed me."

"Let the record show that Mr. Hinton identified the photographs of Danny Harris and D'Juan Cartledge as being the culprits in the case... not my client Mr. Maurice Jones." Mr. Bear said to the judge with a triumphant smirk on his face. Turning back to face Jay, Mr. Bear said, "thank you Mr. Hinton, that'll be all. The defense now rests its case."

Sitting at the table beside Mr. Bear, watching the prosecutor trying her best to trip Jay up on cross examination, Mojo studied the jury's reaction to Jay's testimony, and knew in his mind that he was a free man. After several minutes of the prosecutor trying to get Jay to contradict himself in his statements, and getting nowhere, Judge Stolker had become so angry at her incompetence to effectively pursue the case, that he stopped the prosecutions cross examination, and dismissed Jay off the stand himself.

As he stepped down from the witness stand, Jay walked past Mojo and gave him a quick sideways glance. No words were needed to be said — both of them already knew that one of them was going to die. Mojo's silent poise displayed none of the thoughts running through his mind, while he watched Jay and Youngblood leave out of the courtroom. He had a lot of respect suddenly for the two young niggaz, with the way that they were carrying their beef with him. It was almost to the point where Mojo was starting to feel bad, being that he was going to murder them both, but killing them was never personal in the first place, he thought to himself. So there was no reason to feel bad anyway.

Three and a half hours after the jury went through the ritual of listening to the prosecution and the defense's closing arguments, Mojo was pacing back and forward in the holding cage, that was built behind the judge's courtroom, waiting for the outcome of his trial. It seemed like an eternity before the marshals came and informed him that the jury had finally reached a verdict. Throwing back on his suit jacket, Mojo checked himself out, making sure that he was looking presentable, as the marshal escorted him back into the courtroom.

Judge Stolker was already sitting in his seat, Mojo noticed as he walked over towards his attorney. After a brief moment of discussing their case, they both stood up as the jury started to reenter the courtroom. Trying to read the juror's facial expressions, Mojo had gotten conflicting signals — until the judge ordered the jury to render their verdict. Some skinny hippy looking white guy, who was the jury's designated spokesman, stood up and said, "we the people find the defendant, Maurice Jones, not guilty on all counts of first degree murder for the murder of Nadia Hinton, Tracy Brown, and Danny Harris."

Mojo couldn't help himself from smiling, as the judge polled the jury's decision, making their verdict unanimous. After relieving the jurors of their duty, Judge Stolker started going through his paperwork, signing the various documents that required his signature. "Mr. Jones, I am releasing you out of the immediate custody of the D.O.C., seeing as though you do not have any outstanding warrants or anything of the like," the judge said. Taking off his glasses, the old wrinkled up white man looked Mojo straight in the eyes, and said, "Mr. Jones — for your sake, I hope I never see you in my courtroom again."

"Oh you ain't gotta worry about that your honor," Mojo said, feeling like he was a Teflon Don. "'Cause y'all muthafuckas will never take me alive again." It was the first time Mojo had told the truth, as he and Mr. Bear walked out the courtroom together. Mojo was definitely correct when he said, "they will never take him alive..." because he was already a dead man — he just didn't know it yet.

* * * * *

Leaving out of the D.C. Superior Court building, Mojo walked to a hotdog stand and bought a chili & cheese half smoke and some chips. He saw a yellow taxi slowly driving up towards him, and Mojo hailed the cab with one hand, while waiting for the vender to give him back his change. The cab pulled up beside two parked police squad cars, and waited for him to finish his business at the hotdog stand, ignoring the honking horns of the angry drivers who were behind the cab, who were mad because he was holding up traffic.

Hearing the commotion and not wanting to cause a scene, Mojo jogged over to the cab, and saw the slim figure of a dark skinned old man, with long black dreadlocks, in the driver's seat of the cab. Stepping inside the back of the car, Mojo closed the door as the cab driver pulled off, hitting the master lock switch, locking all of the car doors. Hearing the clicking sound of the locking mechanism, Mojo looked at the door panel, and saw that the silver knobs for the locks had been taken out. That wasn't uncommon to see, as he thought about how niggaz were famous for hopping out of cabs to avoid paying their fare.

"Aye mon, way you wun go to?" the cab driver said in a heavy Jamaican accent. Looking through the clear, thick, bulletproof glass that separated the rear passengers from the driver, Mojo laughed to himself, seeing the man dressed in a bright red rudeboy t-shirt, with a big red, black, and green Rasta' hat overtop of his dredz. The hat was so big and funny looking that it partially hid the man's face, making him look like something out of a Caribbean circus.

"Take me out Oxen Hill, Maryland," said Mojo, reclining back in the cab's comfortable leather seats. "You know how to get there, right?"

"Oh yeeeah, mon!" the cab driver laughed out loud. "Me be drivin' this bloodclot cab for fee-teen years don't yah know. I and I know 'tis city like the back of me hand, star."

"Yeah aight," Mojo mumbled under his breath, "you black-ass, banana boat riding-ass nigga." Sitting through the thirty minute ride, Mojo looked at the digital clock in the cab's dashboard, and noticed that it was 6:17 p.m. Turning off of Suitland Parkway, the cab driver made a quick right onto a small dirt road. Thinking that maybe it was some shortcut to where he wanted to go, Mojo didn't think too much of the cab driver's change of direction until he noticed that the dirt road they were on was leading them straight to some wooded area.

"Aye man, where the fuck you going?!" Mojo snapped in a rage, wondering if the cab driver had lost his mind. He was about to start cussing the man out, but his words got caught in his throat, seeing the all black twin turbo 300Z driving right up behind the cab's bumper. The Z had dark tinted windows, so Mojo couldn't see who was driving the car, but it didn't take a genius to know that this was definitely not a good position to be in on his first day coming home.

"Man, I tell you... God is good all the time, praise the Lord!" said the cab driver, but this time the heavy Jamaican accent was gone from his voice. Mojo stared in total disbelief as he sat in the back of the cab, watching the man take off the big Rasta hat, and the long dreadlock wig he was wearing underneath. "It's about time I can take this hot ass shit off my head, ya dig?" Preacher Man said, turning around and smiling at him. That was all it took for Mojo to realize... this was his last day on Earth.

Knowing that the doors were locked, Mojo tried to open them anyway, but seeing that he was stuck that way, he did the next best thing he could, and started kicking at the rear side window. It had taken Mojo three attempts before the glass finally shattered, but by that time, Preacher Man had already stopped the cab and was at the back door, pulling him out onto the dirt covered ground. Fearing for his life, Mojo was going to fight to the death, as he tried to grab a hold of Preacher Man's leg to pull him down to the ground, but Preacher Man swiftly pulled out a handheld stun gun, sending 1,000 volts of electricity into Mojo's body.

Stepping out of the Z, Jay and Youngblood walked over to the folded up figure of Mojo lying on the ground. He was in a daze, but still aware of his surroundings, knowing that the inevitable had already come. Jay kicked Mojo hard in the face as he tried to beg for his life. "Bitch nigga don't say shit!" Jay said through clenched teeth. Pulling out a small steel mallet and hitting him in the side of the face, he shattered the entire left side of Mojo's jaw.

Jay continued to beat Mojo unmercifully, until the only way they knew he was still living — was through the tiny blood bubbles that were gurgling out of his mouth and nose. Jay slammed the mallet one more time against Mojo's head, causing his eyes to roll upward. Youngblood stepped around with the Mac-11 in hand, and squeezed a quick barrage of 9 millimeter rounds into Mojo's head, spitting in his unrecognizable face for what he had done to Nadia.

"Aight y'all, we did what we came here to do," Preacher Man said, pushing them both towards the Z. "Y'all two niggaz rolled out... I'll take care of the body. Soon as I'm done here, I'm a meet y'all around the way."

Jay and Youngblood hopped into the Z and turned around, balling on the small dirt road until they reached the parkway. Doing 90 mph on the expressway, Jay weaved in and out of traffic until finally crossing back over into D.C. The boys had seemed to be all in the clear, as Jay cruised out of the 9th Street tunnel, when suddenly out of nowhere, police squad cars came rushing behind them from all directions.

Watching Jay maneuver the twin turbo, Youngblood knew that it was only a matter of time before the fedz would block them off. There was just too many of them. Speeding down I Street Southwest, Youngblood had made up his mind as he saw two squad cars turning off Delaware Avenue towards them. Thinking about how Jay was about to be a father to Samiko's baby and how they had planned on moving out to South Carolina this coming summer, Youngblood pulled up the emergency brakes, causing the car to come to a screeching halt.

"I love you slim," was all Youngblood said, before hopping out of the car.

"Man, what the fuck you doing slim?!" Jay yelled, but it was too late. Youngblood ran towards the two squad cars, firing the Mac-11 in their direction, forcing them to stop and take cover. Just as he had planned, the cops started to pursue him in a chase on foot, while taking their attention off of Jay, giving him a few extra seconds to find a new escape route.

Running through the back streets and alleys, Youngblood tossed the gun into the backyard of a beige brick house, and slowed down to a trot. Just when the coast was starting to look clear, Youngblood calmed down to catch his breath and began walking down South Capitol Street. Seeing a good area to go and lay low, in Randall Park, Youngblood crossed the intersection and saw the police woman hop out of her car with her Glock pointed at him. "Freeze muthafucka — you better not move " the cop screamed, moving towards him.

"Bitch, picture that!" Youngblood said, as he broke up the street running again. Anticipating the bullets flying his way, Youngblood knew that that was the only way the cops were going to get him. Though he still couldn't figure out why the police had jumped out on them in the first place. However, Youngblood sensed that he would soon find out all he wanted to know, as he felt himself being lifted off his feet and slammed to the pavement.

Looking up in a daze, Youngblood saw the two big kracka-ass cops who had just slammed him were now standing over top of him while the police broad had her knees in his back, placing the handcuffs on him. As the white cops picked him up, Youngblood looked around and saw what looked like a whole battalion of cops. "Damn, what the fuck I do now?" Youngblood said to himself as the cops lead him to the back of the patrol car. No matter what he was facing, or whatever he must suffer, Youngblood knew that he would accept his fate like a man.

He just prayed that Jay had benefited from his sacrifice... as Youngblood's love for his comrade wouldn't allow him anything but the thought of Jay's get away.

Drama City

Epilogue

And they ask me if I changed much
I told them yeah — even though I'm still the same nut
Then they offered me a furlough
But what they don't know
When I get free
I'm killing five mo'...

- Tupac
When I get free

Four Years Later...

(August of 1999)

Stepping into the gymnasium of the Occoquan Correctional Facility in Lorton, Virginia, Youngblood waited to sign in with the C.O. before moving over to where his visitors were. For four years straight, since Youngblood's incarceration, Jay would drive down from South Carolina, and pay him a three day visit every month. But on this particular month, Jay had brought he whole family down to see him, as Youngblood stared into the smiling faces of Samiko, Ray-Ray, Lil' V, Mink, Rasheeda, and Lil' Demetrius, who was Jay and Samiko's four year old son.

Throughout Youngblood's prison bid, Jay had fulfilled all of his obligations as a brother and comrade in the struggle, and Youngblood truly appreciated the monthly visits, but more than anything in the world, he looked forward to the completion of his 3 to 9 year sentence. Youngblood briefly pondered the circumstances that lead to his arrest.

On the day they had murdered Mojo out in Maryland, the cops in D.C. had been giving an A.P.B. on a stolen black '91 twin turbo Nissan 300Z. The same color and model that they were riding in, so when the cops spotted Jay and Youngblood driving into the city, they had automatically started pursuing them as if they were out joy riding in an U.U.V. Not even bothering to check their license plates.

Not knowing why the police were trying to pull them over, Jay sped off, being as he was covered in Mojo's blood, and Youngblood himself was strapped with a Mac-11 that had more than a few bodies on it. As worse came to worse, the cops finally cornered them off. That was the moment when Jay witnessed the power of loyalty, and saw Youngblood stop the car and hop out, blasting the Mac at the fedz, giving Jay time to get away.

Initially, after his arrest, Youngblood was charged with three counts of attempted murder for shooting at the police officers who were chasing them in the two squad cars. That is, until Jay paid the 45 thousand for the legal expert from Georgetown University to take Youngblood's case. The old Jewish female attorney, Cynthia "The Sharp Shooter" Stern, went straight to work, shooting holes into the prosecution's case against him.

After three weeks on the case, Cynthia had found so many legal technicalities where the government had violated Youngblood's Fifth Amendment right to Due Process that the prosecution immediately offered him a plea agreement that would drop all three attempted murder charges, if he would plead guilty to first degree assault. Youngblood reluctantly took Cynthia's advice, and "copped out" to the assault charge, receiving a 3 to 9 year sentence. At first he was fucked up with the time that the judge had given him, but thinking on the 60 to life he would have been facing if he had gone to trial, Youngblood charged his loss to the game — knowing that he was just going to have to roll with the punches.

"That's a fluke ass way to get laid down," Youngblood said to himself silently, sitting down at the visiting table with Jay and the rest of the family, but what Youngblood had yet to realize, is that sometimes the curveballs life throws our way are, a lot of the time, meant to put us on the straight path. Yet in due time, Youngblood would get an opportunity to enter the folds of enlightenment... because it was all a matter of time, and within time, all things are possible.

"Aye Shaka... Shaka... aye man, I know you hear me slim!" Youngblood said, yelling my name through the window of my dormitory. I got out my bunk and let him inside 6 Dorm, which was nicknamed the "Animal House," and walked back to my bunk, listening to him tell me all about his comrade Jay visiting him with his family. I wasn't ignoring Youngblood — just kind of half hearing him, as I was somewhat lost in my own thoughtes; a prisoner to my own self-righteous philosophy.

"Aye Blood, let me ask you a question," I said, snapping out of my daze, and looking over at him.

"Aaaw shit..." said Youngblood, shaking his head."Here you go on your Fu Man Chu shit."

"Naw, seriously Blood... I want to know, do white people commit crimes in D.C.?"

"What?!" Youngblood asked, looking at me like I was crazy.

"I'm saying — everyone in this dormitory is black and Hispanic." I said, explaining the reason behind my question. "Everywhere I look on this compound, I can't find a single white person wearing a blue institution outfit. Just our black asses."

"You know what... you got a point!" Youngblood snapped his fingers, and pointed at me. "Every time I read the paper 'bout a kracka getting locked up, them muthafuckas always get diplomatic immunity and shit."

"Man you always on joke time," I said, shaking my head. "You young brothers need to wake up and realize what you are doing to y'all selves."

"Man fuck that... I need to wake up and really get out of jail." Sitting down on the edge of my bunk, Youngblood looked over at me, and asked, "So did you finish writing Your book yet?"

"Yeah, I'm finish."

"So what you named the joint?"

"Drama City."

"I hope you got me up in that joint Joe," said Youngblood, smiling, looking like the 15 year old child he once was.

"The whole book is about you slim," I said, matter of factly.

"Oh yeah... well make sure you let me read the joint, so I can see if it's on some official gangsta shit."

"What's officially gangsta to you, Blood?" I asked.

"You know what I mean slim," Youngblood stood up, balling his hands into a pistol holding gesture, "make sure I'm in that joint punishing all types of niggaz!"

197

"That's all it is that stimulates your little mind, huh?" I said, feeling somewhat disgusted at his excitement. "All that ignorant ass beefing shit."

"What can I say, Shaka," Youngblood said, walking away, smiling. "Ignorance is bliss!"

I rose up from my bunk and watched him walk down the dormitory. I wondered if he really knew the magnitude of the statement he'd just made. Since the first day I'd met Youngblood, I knew he had the potential to be a good soldier in the re-creation of the black community, and over the past few years, had even grown a brotherly type of love for him. But sitting here, pondering Youngblood's destructive mentality, I came to the inescapable truth of the matter within myself, and knew that I hated the possibility that Youngblood represented the future of our young Black Nation.

THE END

Acknowledgements

Man may easily sever the ties of kinship, for the bond of Blood is an ephemeral convenience at best. Yet the solidarity of the kindred spirit...it's virtually impossible to compromise the integrity of such a union.

I thank Allah for giving me the insight to perceive the bounty that has been placed before me.

To my beautiful wife, Khadijah Alima Long; I love you for being "you" and thank you for blessing me with the years out of your life.

To my cousin, Muffy – you are my "Booga-Butt" and thank you for your love and realness, even though you are soooo disrespectful.

Also, thank you Ms. Sydney Hoffman for helping me see the light at the end of the tunnel; you are one hell of an attorney.

Throughout the seventeen years of my incarceration, there have been numerous good men to enter my life and help shape the character of the man I am today. To Davin Hart-Bey, Ernest Smith, Ned McAllister, Antione White, Julian "Hawkeye" Riley, Dale "Smiley" Given, Terry Steadman, Terry Trice, Tyrone Nobles-Bey, Darryl Diggs, Carol "Buddy Love" Montgomery, Reginald Gaither, Butch West and many more.

To my brother, Eyone Williams, I'm proud of you slim and know that my love for you is Bullet Proof.

And to my dead homies from 18th – N – D St, Lil Gerald, Fat Gerald, Lil Freddy, Lil Shelton, Shank, Ugly, Dumb Wayne, Lamont, Jughead, Joyce and all the rest … you live forever in my childhood memories.

R.I.P.

And, for those who are still incarcerated, remember this:

"Verily, with every difficulty there is relief." Surah 94:5

Sincerely,

Colie Levar Long

-Shaka- 2013

My Wife Khadijah & my baby Amira

My Lil'man Jamir, Khadijah & Amira

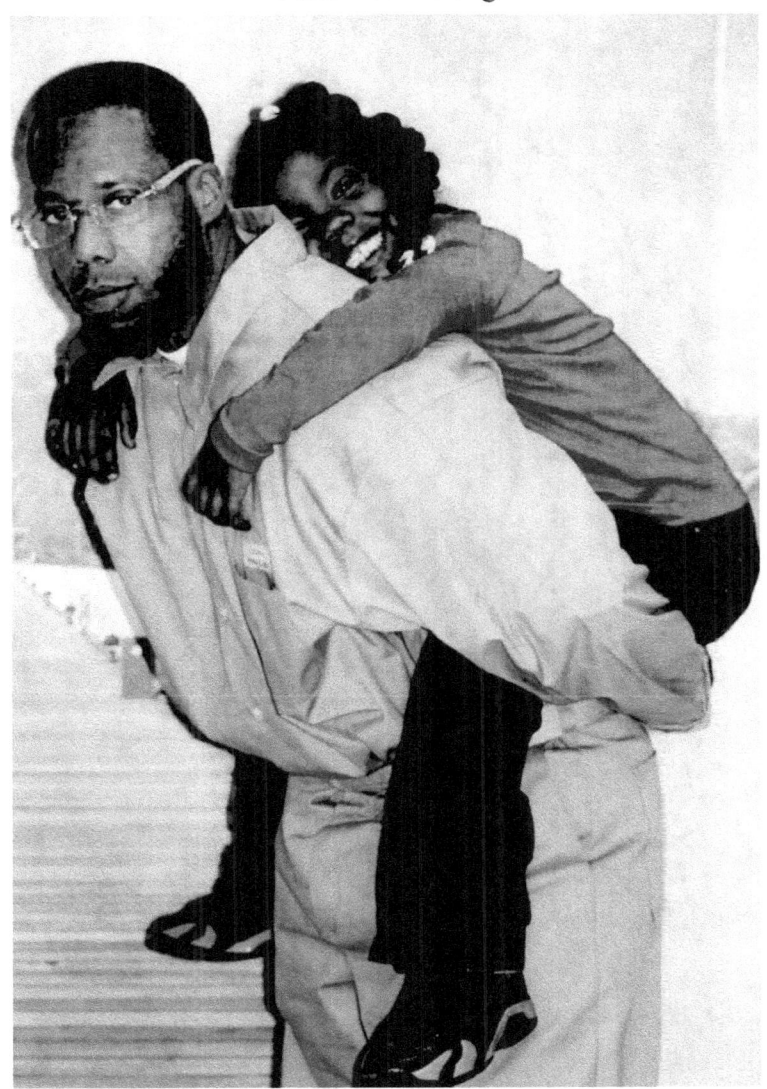

My future

My future

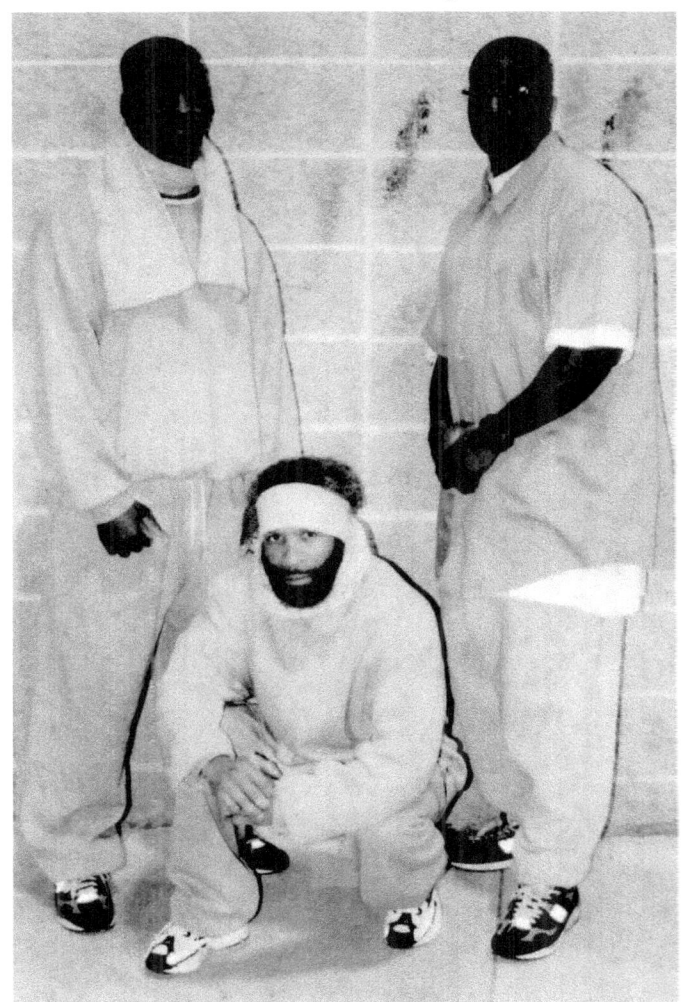

My partner in crime, Ned
FCI Cumberland

My Big Homie, Tone

Anthony "Bucky" Fields

My Brother, Eyone

Luis "Tun-Tun" Figueroa & Partner, Robert Aguon

My A.C. Bone

My business Partner, Michael Blackson

Kenneth "Supreme" McGriff

USP Lee

Colie Levar Long

The struggle continues

www.ingramcontent.com/pod-product-compliance
Lightning Source LLC
Chambersburg PA
CBHW070107260626
47160CB00004B/1363